Sandhurst Library
The Broadway
Sandhurst
GU47 9BL
01252 870161

11/19

To avoid overdue charges this book should be returned on or before the last date stamped above. If not required by another reader it may be renewed in person, by telephone, post or on-line at www.bracknell-forest.gov.uk/libraries

Library & Information Service

A Selection of Recent Titles by Matt Hilton

Tess Grey Series

BLOOD TRACKS *
PAINTED SKINS *
RAW WOUNDS *
WORST FEAR *
FALSE MOVE *

Joe Hunter Series

RULES OF HONOUR
RED STRIPES
THE LAWLESS KIND
THE DEVIL'S ANVIL
NO SAFE PLACE
MARKED FOR DEATH

* *available from Severn House*

FALSE MOVE

Matt Hilton

This first world edition published 2019
in Great Britain and the USA by
SEVERN HOUSE PUBLISHERS LTD of
Eardley House, 4 Uxbridge Street, London W8 7SY
Trade paperback edition first published
in Great Britain and the USA 2019 by
SEVERN HOUSE PUBLISHERS LTD

British Library Cataloguing in Publication Data
A CIP catalogue record for this title is available from the British Library.

ISBN-13: 978-0-7278-8865-5 (cased)
ISBN-13: 978-1-84751-988-7 (trade paper)
ISBN-13: 978-1-4483-0200-0 (e-book)

Typeset by Palimpsest Book Production Ltd.,
Falkirk, Stirlingshire, Scotland.

ONE

When he was a cop, Aaron Lacey regularly joked that if he knew where he was going to die, he'd damn well steer clear of the place. It was one of those throwaway remarks you made when engaged in a job where death was a possibility at any time, and usually earned him a snort of cynicism from folk who shared a similar outlook on their career choice. Alas, Lacey didn't possess the power of precognition, no more than any of his colleagues did. Besides, most of the time they didn't get a say on where their latest call took them, and sometimes the destination turned out to be their last. Mikey, Lacey's best buddy despite their twenty-year age difference, and senior patrol partner for over seven years, sure as hell wouldn't have chosen to die in the aisle of a convenience store, lying in a pool of spilled coffee and blood. If Lacey had his way, he sure as shit wasn't about to perish lying among the weeds and trash of a vacant lot on the Boston side of the Neponset River either. Sadly, the odds for a quiet death in a comfortable bed, surrounded by his loved ones, were severely stacked against him.

He lay on his side, partly concealed by overhanging foliage, surrounded by darkness, and wanted to groan in misery. But he daren't. His left palm was clapped tightly over the wound in his side, but he couldn't staunch all the blood one-handed. The wound was a through and through, and bled profusely from both sides directly above his hip: his shirt and trousers were sopping. His right hand clutched a revolver, but it was of little use to him being empty of ammunition. At most it could be used as a blunt instrument, but that wouldn't save him from those stalking him. They could stand off at a safe distance and riddle him with more bullets.

His best hope for survival was to sit tight and pray that his pursuers moved on: the brief but noisy gunfight would have been reported by now and the cops should be en route. His hunters would clear out. Not that his past service with the NYPD would earn him any special dispensation from prosecution; he'd be deemed as complicit as the others in the gun battle, whether his part was in self-defense or not, and he'd be whisked to lock-up by way – hopefully – of an ER. But better a cell than a grave. At fifty-eight years old, he'd had decent innings, but he wasn't ready to go yet.

There were three of them. Two men and a woman. It had started with four, but during a frantic exchange of rounds one of his bullets had hit its mark, and while Lacey had staggered away clutching his side, his would-be slayer had fallen, and his silence was damning of his fate. He trusted that one of the living trio was engaged in dragging away their friend's corpse, but that left two trailing him and it would only take one of them to kill him.

The river whispered to him from nearby, and a breeze rustled the trees along its bank, set the vacant lot's chain-link fence rattling. The noise masked the sound of those chasing him but hopefully his rasping breaths and subdued groans were equally obscured to them. He was, however, positive he could hear his life ebbing from the holes in his sides. The wound burned like a bitch, as if a hot poker had been rammed through him.

You're used to pain, he reminded himself. His knees gave him hell most of the time, and his arthritic shoulder made rising from bed difficult and excruciating most mornings. But this pain was something else. It stole his strength. No, fatalism was the thief. And he wasn't going to give in. He crabbed up his aching knees, and rolled so he was on his butt. The branches hung over him. He peered towards the entrance of the lot, the direction his pursuers would most likely come, and could discern no movement in the darkness. Despite his resolve to stay where he'd crawled to, he couldn't. Wouldn't. He rose up, shuddering at the fresh blast of agony through his side. If nothing else, the flaring pain took his mind off his complaining knees. He stole away, keeping close to the bushes so he wouldn't present an identifiable silhouette, and approached the fence at the lot's rear. Kids had used the lot as a hangout – evidenced by the proliferation of flattened beer cans and broken bottles – and a shortcut, or escape route, onto the Neponset

Trail, a hiking path that followed the contours of the river. During the daytime dog walkers and joggers used it, but in the dead of night the trail was the domain of ex-cops being hounded to death by merciless killers. He slipped through a beaten-down portion of chain link and onto a shallow incline of rock-strewn earth onto the track. His feet belonged to somebody else. At a crouch, he moved onto the asphalt path, one ear on the lot behind him. He heard distant sirens.

Fuck fatalism! Now he was on the move again, he preferred to trade freedom for the jail cell he'd wished for only minutes ago. He staggered along, feet slapping earth. Behind him he dripped a trail anyone could follow. He looked at his gun. Earlier he'd considered it only as a blunt instrument, but even empty it could be used to threaten: they could have no way of knowing he was out of ammo. He held onto the revolver as tightly as he did his side.

The river curved. On the land that jutted out into the water the trees retained their summer foliage. Under the boughs it was intensely dark. If not for the fact he could be easily tracked, he would have holed up there, tried to staunch his wounds with his shirt, and waited for his pursuers to leave. He continued on the trail, to where the river grew broader and was dotted with a number of low but shrub-crowned islands. Distantly he saw a road bridge spanning the river, delineated against the night by the wash of streetlights. A responding patrol car shot along it and for a moment Lacey experienced a pang of nostalgia for the lights and siren. But he also ducked, averted his face, made his silhouette small. If he hadn't done so, he might have missed the figure stealing along the path behind him.

Surprisingly spritely when his life was threatened, he bounded up, extending the revolver. 'Not another fuckin' step, buddy!'

His bark was as loud as a gunshot in the night and it had the desired response. His stalker drew up short, and opened his arms wide. He didn't drop the knife. 'You killed Mathers, Lace.'

'Yeah, and I'll kill you too, motherfucker.' For emphasis, Lacey thumbed back the hammer on his gun.

The man was younger than Lacey, with the stocky build of

a wrestler, all neck and arms. In a stand-up brawl, he'd be the bookies' favourite. But the young man had brought a knife to a gunfight.

'Drop it, Ethan, or by fuck I'll put one between your eyes.'

Ethan judged the threat calmly. Weighing his options. Even in the dark he'd make out Lacey's pained stance, his desperation. A desperate man was more inclined to shoot first and make demands later. 'You're outta ammo, Lace.'

'Wanna try me?'

'Things didn't have to come to this, Lace.' Ethan's use of Lacey's nickname was purposeful. To humanize him in Lacey's eyes, reminding him of their previous comradeship. He'd be less inclined to slay his old pal in cold blood, right? 'We don't have to fight. Just gimme what you stole and I'll let you walk away. You have my word on it.'

'Your word means shit. If I hadn't turned just now, you were gonna stick that knife in my back, you punk.'

Ethan graced him with a world-weary smile. 'Not gonna lie to you, Lace. I'd'a split you open, but it wouldn't'a given me any pleasure. This ain't personal, buddy.'

'So *you* walk away. If it ain't personal, what does it matter if you get the memory stick back?'

'Lace, gettin' it back's my job.' He nodded at a ring prominent on the hand Lacey pressed to his side: it was a gold NYPD shield ring, now smeared with blood. 'Your job was important to you too, right? You were prepared to lay down your life for it. You prepared to do that now you've retired?'

'Sure I am. But I'll take your life first.'

Ethan smiled again, this time in remorse. 'You'd better do it then, Lace, cause I'm comin' for ya.'

'Not another fuckin' step, Ethan! I'm warning you, man!'

Ethan took a step.

'You want me to kill you?' Lacey thrust the gun an inch forward, but they both knew it was an empty threat.

Ethan stepped again, building momentum. Then he hurtled forward.

'Son of a bitch!' Lacey yanked the gun back over his shoulder, then hammered down as Ethan's knife speared at his throat.

The butt of the gun landed an instant before the blade found flesh. In the next instant they crashed together, and tumbled off the trail, down the leaf-littered decline to the river. Their brief death struggle thrashed the water to bloody froth.

TWO

N icolas 'Po' Villere gunned the engine of his Mustang, and then let it idle.

'Sweet,' he said, satisfied with the throaty grumble. Recently the car had been in the shop for repair after it had been employed as a battering ram, and he'd taken the excuse to modify and upgrade the engine. He gave the muscle car more gas, and the restrained power surged through it making the car rise and dip on its suspension.

Seated in the passenger seat, Tess Grey cast him a sidelong glance, her lips tightening. He returned the glimpse.

'Hoodlum,' she said. 'You going to peel away from the curb next?'

'Tempted to.' A smile touched his turquoise eyes. 'Truth, Tess? You like it when I peel away, don'tcha?'

'Must I remind you we're on a stake out? There's a time and place for juvenile antics, Po. Say, twenty years ago in your case?'

'F'sure, except twenty years ago I didn't get much opportunity to satisfy my need for speed.'

His comment shamed her. Twenty years ago he'd been incarcerated, only partway through a fourteen-year term behind bars. He'd spent most of his early adulthood in the Louisiana State Penitentiary, known to its inmates as Angola, so didn't get to do the things other youths did. Who was she to deny him the small pleasures he'd missed out on? But she couldn't resist taunting him. 'I'm sure you're having a mid-life crisis,' she said. 'What's next, Po? You going to buy a motorcycle and take a pilgrimage down Route Sixty-Six?'

'I'll reserve that trip for when I'm old and grey.'

Tess laughed. 'That's the epitome of irony, right there.'

'OK, so I meant older and greyer.'

She reached across and teased the short hairs on the back of his head. 'Don't worry; the silver makes you more distinguished. Plus, they match your wrinkles.'

'These ain't wrinkles, they're experience lines. Seem to have gained quite a few since we met.'

'Stick around, Po, you're about to get another.'

Immediately their good-natured bickering dissolved, and Po's attention was hawk-like as he checked out the three men leaving the bar across the street. The trio had been drinking, but it was only early evening so not to excess. They nudged and shoved shoulders, sharing jokes as they stepped out into the cool Maine evening.

'That's him, the guy on the right,' said Tess needlessly.

Po had already noted Thomas 'Moondog' Becker's appearance in the photos she'd shown him earlier. Becker was a big, rangy guy, carrying off the double-denim look, with a hairdo, moustache and sideburns as retro as Po's taste in cars. His 1970s styling fit his role as a lead guitarist in a country rock band. His friends were also members of the band, but didn't dress for the stage during their afternoons off.

As the trio crossed the street, Po set the Mustang rolling in reverse. Its back bumper came to rest barely a finger's breadth from the front end of a large silver SUV he'd purposely blocked in. Thinking he was manoeuvring to gain space to pull out, his driving didn't immediately attract attention until Po turned off the engine and stepped out of the car. On the sidewalk he lit a cigarette, and stood smoking, nonchalant, with all the time in the world to enjoy the nicotine hit.

'Hey, buddy, how's about making a bit of space there? We need to get going.' It was one of Becker's band mates who'd spoken, his tone amiable enough.

'Just finishing up my smoke,' said Po.

'We're on the clock, buddy,' the guy said, offering a friendly shrug. He barely topped Becker's shoulder, a small bulldog of a man.

'What's the rush?' Po nodded over at the bar they'd left.

'Seemed no hurry when y'all were havin' a beer. I know, 'cause I've been out here waitin' all this time.'

'Whaddaya mean, waitin'?' The third man was the youngest, so fair his eyelashes were almost white, and his pink cheeks so smooth he probably only shaved once every other week.

'What does waitin' imply to you?' Po drew on his cigarette.

'You've been waiting for *us*?' the kid asked dumbly.

Po aimed a finger at Becker. 'Been waitin' on Moondog, and it ain't for his autograph.'

The trio exchanged glances. Becker rolled his neck as Tess got out of the Mustang: he'd guessed her purpose for being there. His next glance was at the proximity of the Mustang to their ride. He rose up on his toes.

Po flicked ash. 'Don't try movin' your car, Moondog. Put a scratch on my ride and you'll have to extract my boot from your ass, and trust me it'll be a tight fit.'

Becker chewed his moustache, and for a second he almost exacerbated his flight-risk status by making a single lunge away. Tess barred his escape. She barely stood as tall as his shoulder, and was half as wide, but she wasn't moving. Becker swayed in place, but his attention was on Po. Po said nothing, he had no need because there was enough warning in his baleful gaze.

'Aww, c'mon, you guys . . .' Becker groaned. 'I've a gig to play tonight.'

'Sorry, Moondog, but your comeback tour's cancelled.' Tess laid an officious hand on his sleeve. 'You broke the terms of your surety, so you're coming with us.'

'Y'all are what?' It was the kid again: his face glowed red and it wasn't from the beer he'd imbibed. 'Some kinda bounty hunters? Don't y'all need to show us licenses or somethin'?'

'We don't need to show you squat,' Po said, and moved to put himself between Becker and his two pals. There was no legal requirement for a bounty hunter to hold a license in the state of Maine, only that they be affiliated to a licensed bail bonds agency, from which Tess had procured the authorization to arrest on their behalf.

'Thomas Becker,' said Tess, doing the legal bit, 'I'm arresting you to ensure your attendance at court in Augusta tomorrow morning.' She also narrated the name and location of the bail bondsman who'd hired her as a skip tracer, so that everything was above board and official. She took out a set of handcuffs and without further complaint Becker extended his wrists: he knew he was done. Tess snapped the cuffs home.

'C'mon, guys, can't you give us a break?' the bulldog-shaped guy groaned. 'What if Moondog promises to come quietly once we've played our set?'

'I did give you a break,' Tess said. 'My associate here wanted to come in and drag you out of that bar an hour ago, but I let you finish your beers first. Besides, Moondog might find playing a guitar difficult in handcuffs. These aren't coming off till we're back at the bondsman's office.'

'So what are we meant to do now?' The youth's translucent lashes flapped wildly. 'I mean, we can't rock up as the Moondog Trio missing the main man.'

'See this as your opportunity to step from behind the drums and into the limelight?' Po suggested. The guy shook his head morosely, and Po shrugged, tossed aside his cigarette. 'I'm outta ideas.'

'Come on, Becker,' Tess said, and led her oversized charge towards the Mustang. 'Let's get this over and done with without any fuss, shall we?'

Po opened the back door for him. Gave him a look. 'There ain't a mark on that upholstery, see that it stays that way.'

Becker's band mates stood round-shouldered and defeated. Momentarily, Tess felt sorry for them: their evening was ruined, and quite possibly their employment prospects for the foreseeable future. Becker was, in his young friend's words, the main man, and without him the Moondog Trio was a nonentity. Well, she thought sourly, it's them or me, and I won't get paid either if I don't take Becker in. She aimed a nod of finality at Po, and her partner directed their captive to sit.

'Tip for you, buddy,' Po said, leaning close to conspire with Becker. 'Next time you think about skipping bail, don't go advertising your tour dates on the damn social networks.'

'You're telling me,' Becker grumbled from the back seat. 'It was a stupid idea in hindsight.'

'F'sure. You took all the fun outta the hunt for us.'

THREE

'I prefer it when the bad guys put up a fight,' Po said as Tess slid in the car alongside him. He was parked outside the bail bondsman's office in Augusta, having earlier delivered Becker to lock-up pending tomorrow's court appearance. 'That way I don't feel so guilty about handing 'em over to the law.'

'That's a residual effect of your outlaw days,' Tess observed with a wry smile. She sniffed, shrugged her shoulders. 'Becker was a decent enough guy. I felt like a heel turning him in. But that's the job, Po; we can't be choosy if we want to earn the bounty.'

Po pursed his thin lips. He had money; the ten percent of the full bail amount earned by Tess was hers. Since medically retiring from the Cumberland County Sheriff's department, she'd tried to make ends meet first as a genealogist, and then as a freelance private investigator on the payroll of a specialist inquiry firm, headed by Emma Clancy – her future sister-in-law, if her brother Alex ever agreed a wedding date. For a private eye the downside of living and working in Maine was that the state had one of the lowest crime rates in the USA, so regular work wasn't exactly rolling in. Taking on skip tracing jobs went somewhat against his grain, but not to a point that'd exclude his involvement. They were partners in every sense, and he'd walk barefoot across hot coals for her.

'I know you're uncomfortable with this, Po, but . . . well, I've bills to pay and a house to keep.' As soon as she said it she knew she'd hit a nerve. Po had suggested she move into his sprawling home near Presumpscot Falls, but to date she'd turned down his offer. Her refusal had nothing to do with her commitment to their relationship and everything with her need to retain a sense of independence denied her during her previous serious relationship. Which, she understood, was contradictory, when Po gave his time, money and physical assistance selflessly to allow her to do so. 'I promise it's only a stop-gap, only till something better comes in.'

'Hey, you have to diversify if you want to succeed. Who can say: we might grow to enjoy this new venture.' Po owned a thriving bar–diner and an auto repair shop among other businesses, but was rarely hands-on at those venues anymore: he enjoyed the variety of being Tess's sidekick when it came to chasing down the bad guys: maybe it was in recompense for his past behaviour or in rebellion against people's perceptions of ex-cons. For Tess, slapping on handcuffs was a nice nostalgia trip back to the days when she was a sheriff's deputy; for Po, getting to smack civility and acquiescence into an obstreperous criminal was a bonus. He peeled out from the curb, resisted shooting her a grin. Getting to drive like a street outlaw was a bonus to his job too. He'd have them back in Portland in no time.

As he negotiated Augusta's streets, Tess frowned at her cell phone. She'd missed a call from her mother. Also, there were three text messages stacked up from her. Checking them she found the messages curt and ambiguous. All three said: *WHERE ARE YOU WHEN I NEED YOU?*

She endured a prickly relationship with her mom. If not for the fact she was often brusque and downright snarky with Tess, the messages would have been cause for concern. She was tempted to ignore them, wait until she was back home and ring back then, but it was unusual that her mom had made the effort four times to contact her. Usually one summons from Barbara Grey was all she'd allow, and if it was not answered then woe betide her daughter next time they met.

'Trouble?' Po ventured.

'My face says it all?'

'And then some.'

'It's my mom,' Tess said, again reading one of the texts.

She tried not to apportion a sarcastic tone to the words, though it was difficult. Read in another context, the damn thing sounded like a plea. She might not get on with her mom, and dislike her constant sniping and disapproval, but dammit, she still loved and cared for the old harridan! Immediately, she returned the call. Po cast sidelong glances at her, but said nothing: he knew something was wrong, simply because Tess normally grumbled under her breath before calling Barbara.

'Mom? It's me, Tess,' she announced the instant her call was picked up.

'Where are you?' Barbara was as brusque as ever.

'I'm on my way back from Augusta. I've been on a—'

'You need to be more specific, Teresa. When you say "on your way back" that tells me nothing about how soon I can expect you here.'

'What's wrong, Mom?'

'I prefer to wait until I see you in person, rather than speak on the phone. Where are you?'

'Just leaving Augusta.'

Barbara snorted in disappointment. 'I suppose you're with Nicolas? No need to answer. That's a given these days. For once, I'd say that's a good thing. He can drive you here much faster than you can.'

'Mom? What is it? What's wrong?'

'I'll tell you when you arrive. It's already getting late, don't keep me waiting all night.' With her demand made Barbara ended the call.

Tess stared at her phone, as if she could convey her outrage to her mother by the power of thought alone. Po said nothing.

'She is infuriating . . .'

'She give you the royal summons, huh?'

'Sometimes she treats me like I'm still thirteen years old.'

'That's parents for ya,' Po said. 'Don't matter how old you get, you're still a baby to them.'

Now Tess said nothing. Po wasn't exactly the ideal person to offer advice, considering he'd no experience of an over-bearing parent. His dad died before Po grew to adulthood, and his mother was out of the picture. She supposed he could be speaking from observation.

'She didn't say what she wanted?'

'It's enough that when she barks she expects me to come to heel.' Tess exhaled, expelling the bitterness. 'There's something wrong, Po. She was even sharper-tongued than usual.'

'I overheard her askin' about me . . .'

'Yeah. That's why I know something's wrong, she was actually happy to hear I'm with you.'

'Yep.' Po grinned. 'Totally out of character for her.'

Tess laughed without humour. Barbara didn't dislike Po. She only disliked that he was with Tess. In her mom's opinion, she'd have been better staying with her ex-fiancé, the ultra-safe and self-conceited Jim Neely, popping out grandchildren and changing dirty diapers, than chasing after criminals. Then again, none of Tess's life choices suited her mom.

'Wonder what I've done wrong now?' She was fairly confident that there wasn't anything major to worry about. Barbara would have reached out to her brothers, Michael Jnr and Alex, before asking for Tess, and if she had she was also confident that her brothers would have tried to make contact before now.

'Only one way to find out,' said Po, as they reached the highway south and he stamped the gas pedal.

FOUR

Barbara Grey's house was set in woodland on the shore of Capisic Pond, a tributary of the Fore River in western Portland. Po steered his Mustang down the short tree-lined driveway towards the house less than fifty minutes after speeding past the outskirts of Augusta. It was fifty minutes too long a wait for Barbara: she stood at her front door, arms crossed, and her mouth set in disapproval. All that was missing was the tapping of a toe.

The car's headlights leached her features of all colour. She had the same pale complexion as her daughter, and her blond hair had prematurely gone to ash. Her cardigan and trousers were the shade of roof slates. She literally was Mrs Grey, in name and in appearance. Before Tess was out of the car, Barbara approached, arms still tightly crossed over her chest. She glanced once at Po, gave an unsubtle shake of her head, and he got the message.

'Looks as if I'm minding the car,' he said.

'That's unfair,' said Tess.

'I'd let you do it, but it's you she wants to speak with,' Po countered.

'I meant it's unfair you feel so unwelcome you have to sit out here.'

Po laughed. 'I know, Tess. I was only tryin' to lighten the mood. Besides, I want a smoke, and you know how your mom frowns on my "dirty little habit".'

Barbara was tired of waiting. She rapped her knuckles on Tess's window, beckoned for her to follow, and immediately headed for the house.

'I'll try to keep things short and sweet,' Tess promised.

'Good luck with the latter.' Po delved in his shirt pocket for his pack of cigarettes. Tess eyed the cigarette he fed to his lips with envy. She gave up smoking years ago, but was severely tempted to start again and thumb her nose at her mom's displeasure. She followed Barbara before the temptation grew too strong.

Her mom disappeared inside, but Tess knew where to find her. She went directly to the kitchen and Barbara was at the breakfast bar, pouring them coffee from a jug she'd kept warm. Tess's heart sank: the presence of drinks was a sign that their discussion could prove lengthy.

'Sit, sit.' Barbara indicated a stool, and Tess sat like a well-behaved puppy. For a moment the woman turned her back, and Tess was positive she was trembling, and trying to gather herself.

'Mom . . . what's wrong?'

Barbara sat before answering, turning her upper body so she could regard her daughter. Her eyes were red, and for once it wasn't through restrained anger. Tess reached towards her, but her fingers fell short of offering any comfort.

'Mom?' she said again.

Barbara hitched her eyebrows, and her shoulders, a couple of times apiece, before she cleared her throat. 'I was always against you having a law enforcement career,' she began. Nothing new there, Tess had heard it all before. Expect this time, she couldn't miss the unspoken "but" in Barbara's tone. 'This latest venture you're involved in, this private detective nonsense, I've never been comfortable with it either. I think it's a waste of your talents.'

Tess had majored in history and cultural anthropology at Husson University. Her mom had never made it a secret that she felt Tess could put her education to better use than as a down-at-heel gumshoe: her daughter chasing after criminals and straying spouses was not the kind of return she'd hoped for against the investment she'd made in university fees. It was a bone of contention often cast during their arguments, except now there was the 'but' still went unsaid. Tess sipped coffee, waiting for the denouement.

'The thing is, I don't know another private detective, and well . . .' Barbara was rarely lost for words. The difference here was she wasn't delivering orders or scathing criticism, and the alternative proved difficult. She got up and walked across the kitchen, tipped some coffee from her cup into the sink. It was a diversion while she ordered her mind. She added more cream.

'Mom, are you asking for my help?'

'I'm asking for *nothing*.' Barbara's gaze was diamond-hard. She visibly trembled again, and it helped release some of the tension she'd built. Even her eyes softened. 'I'm . . . well, I'm asking on behalf of . . . well, let's say an old friend, shall we?'

'And *they* need a private eye?'

Again Barbara was lost for words. She reclaimed her seat, and again faced Tess, but her gaze was lowered. 'I'm not really sure.'

'Mom,' said Tess. 'I know this is difficult for you, asking me to do something you're normally against, but I don't know if I can help if you won't tell me what the problem is. To start with, who is this old friend?'

'Do you remember Estelle Lacey?'

Tess dug through her memory, dredging up a youthful face she hadn't thought about in decades. 'Do you mean Stella? My friend from elementary school?'

Barbara found the idea of shortened names loathsome, hence Estelle, and also why she'd never term her daughter other than with her full given name. She once slapped a man who'd had the temerity to call her 'Barbie'. 'Yes, Teresa, I mean your friend Estelle.'

'You've kept in touch with Estelle Lacey all these years?'

'Why the hell would I?' Why she'd respond with such denial Tess couldn't say, but apparently her mom felt she had to rebut the notion. 'She contacted *me*! Why she didn't just get in touch with you directly, well, I don't know . . .'

Whichever of them Stella had approached for help didn't really matter to Tess, but it did matter the way Barbara saw things. Perhaps she disliked being made an intermediary in a business she was fundamentally opposed to. Tess decided to cut to the chase. 'What does she want?'

Barbara stared at the floor. 'Do you remember her father?'

'Vaguely.' She recalled he'd been her grandfather's long-time friend and patrol partner with the NYPD, though he'd never been around much when she attended school alongside Stella. She was young when her grandfather was shot dead when he walked in on a convenience store robbery, and could only conjure a fuzzy image of his buddy Aaron Lacey, a dark-haired broad-shouldered young man in NYPD uniform. Fleetingly, she pictured him at her grandfather's funeral, but was unsure if she was ordering her memories to fit the sad scene, when Lacey had picked her up in his arms and held her while Barbara and her dad, Michael, dropped rose petals into the grave.

'Lace,' she said, his nickname coming back to her, and it immediately earned her a curl of Barbara's lip.

'*Aaron* is missing,' her mother stated.

'He still lives in New York?' After her grandfather's death, her parents had brought her and her two older brothers to Maine, and Tess knew it was her mom's idea so her dad wouldn't end up murdered on duty the way his had been before him. Ironically it wasn't a drugged-up robber that killed Michael Grey, but bowel cancer: sometimes Tess had entertained the notion that – given a choice – her dad would've preferred going down in a hail of bullets rather than endure the horrible, lingering death he'd suffered.

'How would I know where he lives after all these years?' Barbara flapped a hand. 'You'll have to check with Estelle. Supposing you agree to look for him, that is. Personally, I'd prefer it if you left well and good alone.'

Tess shrugged. 'It'd be best if Estelle hires a detective local to her, rather than me traveling to New York.'

'Aaron was last seen in Boston,' Barbara said, and immediately regretted the admission. Even it were in another state, Boston was only a couple hours' drive from Portland. 'But, no good can come from stirring up the past. I promised Estelle I'd inform you about her dad's missing person status, but not that you'd take on his case. I've done my bit, now I suggest you make contact and let her down softly. Suggest she finds a private eye in Boston, I'm sure they're a dime a dozen down there.' She plucked a handwritten note from her cardigan pocket and placed it on the breakfast counter. Tess reached for it, and Barbara placed her hand over hers. 'Teresa,' she warned ominously, 'I don't want you taking this case, but, well, the final decision is yours.'

It was just like her mom to place the onus of disappointment back on Tess. Hell, if she didn't want her taking the job, she could have kept quiet about Stella's call, and allowed things to slide. She eyed her mom, wondering if she was playing a double bluff, while also saving face after her previous attitude towards Tess's career path. As Barbara released her, Tess drew the note into her palm and slipped it into her jeans pocket. 'I'm making no promises either,' she said, and left things at that.

FIVE

The following morning found Tess and Po seated at a table outside a hotel on Huntington Avenue in Boston's Back Bay area. Tess nursed a sixteen-ounce concoction of coffee, froth and flavoured syrups that made Po retch at the thought of drinking it. He'd stuck to a straight-up black Americano, but was yet to touch it; he preferred feeding his nicotine habit first. He was oblivious of the sneers of disgust from passers-by who deemed his habit filthy, and his smoke poison that'd shrivel their lungs if they got too close. One woman wafting a sheaf of papers at him raised an eyebrow, and he chuckled at her expense. 'Boston tough, my ass,' he grinned at Tess, 'when they're afraid of a little second-hand smoke.'

'Hey! Try not to upset the locals,' she suggested.

'It's a bit late for that.' It wasn't long ago that Po had kicked a would-be extortionist out of Portland, not to mention doled out some heavy-handed punishment to the hitters the guy had brought in to deal with Po, and they all hailed from Boston. Hopefully they could leave town before their enemies learned Po had made an incursion of their home territory. Despite trying to keep a low profile, they had chosen the location on the wide thoroughfare opposite the Central Boston Public Library for the purpose of visibility. It wasn't to advertise their presence to the local hoodlums, but so that Estelle Lacey couldn't miss them.

Last night, before she'd arrived home on Cumberland Avenue, Tess had rung the number given to her by her mom on the slip of paper. A brief conversation ensued, and while Po pulled his Mustang onto the ramp outside Tess's home above an antiques and curios shop, she'd assured Stella that they would meet her in Boston. Speaking to Stella had been like conversing with a stranger, unsurprisingly, seeing as approaching three decades separated them from the little girls who used to play together during recess. As she waited, seated in the morning sunshine, Tess tried to mentally age the small, round-faced, buck-toothed and bespectacled child she once knew, casting her eye on any woman that approached to see if there was a match. When Stella arrived, Tess saw she was way off the mark.

Stella Lacey – correction Stella Dewildt, as she had married and taken her husband's name – was wholly unlike the picture Tess had formed in her mind's eye: she was beautiful. She was tall and slim, and her blond hair cascaded down her back. She wore a bolero jacket over a form fitting dress, and high-heels accentuated her height without affecting her bold gait. Po watched her approach with a hint of appreciation he hadn't given any other passer-by, but perhaps Tess was projecting her envy on her partner. She sniffed loudly, and Po's turquoise gaze slid to her. 'You think this could be your friend?'

Tess shrugged. But she knew the attractive woman was Stella, even before she received a wave and the woman's mouth twitched a nervous smile. Stella picked up pace. Tess stood, feeling underdressed in jeans and a sweater, and black leather bomber jacket, returning her old friend's smile of greeting, and suspecting she looked equally as nervous. 'Hi,' she said, extending a hand.

Stella surprised her by stepping directly into a hug, and air-kissing her. Next she stepped back, appraising her at arm's length. 'Oh, wow, Tess! How long has it been?'

'Too long,' Tess said, but there was no sincerity in her words. She had expected to lay eyes on Stella and immediately slip back into a comfort mode with her childhood playmate, but this woman remained a stranger. She recognized nothing of the socially awkward Stella Lacey she'd once known.

'You haven't changed one little bit!' Stella went on.

'Thanks,' said Tess, secretly fuming. 'I have to admit, Stella, I wouldn't have recognized you . . . you're . . .'

Stella chuckled. Ran her hands down her front, wiggling her hips. 'This isn't the chubby girl you remembered.' There wasn't a jot of pride or egotism in her as she waved off her image. 'Trust me, if it were my choice I'd be wearing jeans and sneakers too. They're far more practical, right?'

Po grinned unabashedly at Tess's flat expression. Stella was oblivious of slighting her. She checked for a spare chair.

'We don't have to sit out here,' Tess offered, 'if you prefer we can speak in private?'

'No, no, here's just perfect. In fact, I'm just about to bum a cigarette from your friend?' She'd posed her words as an invitation to an introduction.

'This is Nicolas Villere,' Tess said. 'He's my partner.'

Stella wagged a finger between them, one eyebrow cocked in question.

'Yes,' Tess said. 'In business and in our private lives.'

Po offered his hand: his knuckles were permanently ingrained with traces of engine oil. Stella didn't balk at the idea of accepting his hand and shaking. 'Stella,' she said.

'Most folks call me Po. Pleased to meetcha.'

'That isn't a Maine accent.'

'I hail from Louisiana.'

'As I thought; I had you pegged as a southern gentleman.' She winked conspiratorially. 'How's about that cigarette, Po?'

'F'sure.' Po offered his pack, and once Stella had fed a cigarette to her lips, she cupped her palms around the lighter he held for her. Tess was tight-lipped. She sat: Stella could drag a chair over for herself. Except Po – the *southern gentleman* – stood and offered his seat. Tess glanced sharply at him, and he winked at her. 'I think I should leave you girls to get reacquainted,' he said, and the line of Tess's mouth softened. He sauntered away, pluming blue smoke, while Stella set down her purse and got comfortable in his vacated chair. Po didn't wander far. He stood at a respectful distance, one thumb hooked in his belt, seemingly still but alert to his surroundings.

'You've done well for yourself, Tess,' Stella commented with a nod at Po.

'That depends on who you're talking to,' Tess replied. 'My mom said your dad is missing and you want help to trace him.'

'Directly to the point? You don't want to catch up a little first?'

'I thought we could do both at the same time.'

Stella's face grew thoughtful. Their purpose for meeting wasn't to swap anecdotes or memories. Tess wasn't interested in how Stella had arrived at this point in her life unless it had any bearing on why Aaron Lacey had disappeared. She certainly had no intention of relating her story: she wouldn't with any other client, so why start now with a girl she only shared a tenuous historical link to?

Stella took a few puffs on the cigarette, before she dabbed it out in the ashtray Po had earlier commandeered from a nearby table. She blinked a few times, and exhaled loudly. The cigarette had been her first in a while, or she was mentally preparing to get started on a troubling issue. She looked at Tess, starry eyed. 'Do you remember my dad?'

'Vaguely. He was my grandfather's patrol partner, and I saw him a few times, but I don't have any specific memories.' She didn't think her recollection from her granddad's graveside was genuine; it could have been any of his colleagues that had picked her up while her parents paid their last respects.

'He was a dyed-in-the-wool cop. He retired from the NYPD after twenty-five years, but that wasn't of his choosing. He'd some medical issues that threatened to sideline him from active duty, and he wasn't the kind of man to work from behind a desk.'

'What kind of medical issues?'

'None that'd explain his disappearance if that's what you're thinking? Trouble with his knees, an arthritic shoulder . . . age-related problems that were beginning to pile up. He immediately took another job with a security outfit, apparently he'd made contacts in the private industry during his law enforcement career and it was one of those who recruited him.'

'He still works for the same company?'

'Yes. At least he did until a week ago. If not for them, I wouldn't have been aware my dad had gone missing.'

'They told you?'

'I haven't been close with my dad in some years. Not since my mom divorced him. A representative of the security company contacted me when he failed to show up for work.

I was listed as his next of kin, and they hoped I could tell them where he was.'

'I'll need the details of this company,' said Tess.

'I thought you might want to start with them.' Stella lifted her purse off the table, and pulled out various sheets of paper. 'I've also collated other details I thought you might find helpful: his home address, cell phone numbers, credit card records . . .'

Tess accepted the slim stack of papers, but didn't study them. She folded her hands on top of them on the table. 'You said your parents divorced?'

'Yes. It's possible that Dad has taken off with another woman. He never was a loyal husband to my mom, and now there's nobody holding him back, well . . .'

'You don't believe that.'

'That he'd disappear with a woman for a few days?' Stella snorted at the inevitability. 'No I don't. Not this time. When he disappeared in the past, he was never fully out of contact. He didn't switch off his phone, and he never let down his employers, and always showed up for work. This time's different, Tess. It's almost as if he has deliberately cut all ties.'

'It sometimes happens with men of a certain age.'

'You think he's having a mid-life crisis?'

'It's not unknown,' said Tess, with a glimpse at Po. 'I only mean that, well, maybe this time he's more serious about things, and needs more thinking space. He's been out of contact for a week?'

'More like nine or ten days. According to his employers he failed to show for work last Monday, but they hadn't been in contact with him since two days beforehand. He once gave me a key to his apartment in Manhattan, so I went there. As far as I could tell he hadn't been home since at least the Friday before last.' She indicated the stack of notes she'd made for Tess. 'That's how I managed to get hold of his credit card statements; they were unopened in his mailbox. Judging by the date stamp they'd been delivered after he disappeared on the Friday.'

The thought had crossed Tess's mind how his daughter had gotten access to Lacey's bank statements. It was a question she needn't ask now. 'So your dad's apartment's in Manhattan, but he was employed here in Boston?'

'The security company's based here, but my dad usually worked wherever contracts took him. But, yeah, they told me that prior to disappearing he was on a private security detail for a local client.'

'They wouldn't say who?'

'No, they gave me some BS line about client confidentiality.'

'Figures,' said Tess, unconscious of the fact she had picked up some of her partner's speech pattern in the couple of years they'd been together. She was confident she'd easily find out whom Aaron Lacey had been working for, not that it would necessarily tell where he'd gotten to since. 'It's only a guess that he went missing from here, rather than home, then?'

'Or anywhere in between,' Stella suggested.

'You've thought of checking hospitals, right? I know it isn't something you want to think about, but he could have gotten in an accident . . .'

'I had no idea how to do that apart from going through the phonebook and checking with all the hospitals between here and Manhattan . . . It seemed like an endless task. Besides, I assumed that if he'd been involved in a serious accident somebody would've contacted me by now on his behalf. Right?'

Tess mentally shrugged. Stella was probably correct.

'I did however do an online search,' Stella went on, 'and found this.' She reached for the papers under Tess's hand, and Tess allowed her to flick through them and tease out a folded sheet of paper. Tess opened it out and placed it flat between them. It was a print-out from a local news webpage, dated from the previous Sunday. Tess absorbed the headlines before glancing at Stella for clarification. The news article concerned a body found washed up on the strip of beach at Squantum Point where the Neponset River emptied into Massachusetts Bay, and identified as Ethan Brandon Prescott, a twenty-six-year-old male. 'I find it worrying,' said Stella.

'Why?' Tess again scoured the article for a clue. There was

some conjecture that the discovery of the dead man could be related to reports of a gunfight two nights earlier, upstream near to Mattapan Station. The details were sketchy and the only injuries cited in the article were from blunt force trauma to the dead man's skull. 'This has no bearing on your dad's disappearance as far as I can tell.'

'Except for one thing,' Stella pointed out. 'Last time I spoke with him, my dad mentioned working with a younger guy called Ethan Prescott. What are the odds of this being a different man?'

Slim, Tess would bet.

SIX

'So who's the other blond?'

'Beats me,' said Hayden James with a brief glance at his partner, 'but I guess we'll find out soon enough.'

Seated alongside him in a nondescript van, Megan Stein studied the young woman sitting across the table from Stella Dewildt with an envious eye. The 'blond' was dressed down, her fair hair unruly having been subject to the breeze gusting down the open plaza, but she was as equally pretty as the immaculately presented Stella; Megan immediately despised her, the way in which she despised most attractive people. She turned to briefly check out Hayden's opinion of the woman, and despised the slow smile he showed her. Unconsciously she raised a hand to her cheek, concealing the twisted scar tissue that marred her from chin to left eye socket. Under her palm the flesh felt cold and dead, each lump and furrow a reason to hate those with flawless complexions. 'She looks like trouble to me,' she muttered.

Hayden shifted incrementally, and his gaze drifted from the two women to where a tall guy leaned nonchalantly against a nearby storefront, smoking a cigarette. The man was wiry and long-limbed, almost gangly, but there was nothing uncoordinated about his movements whenever he shifted his stance.

Even from a distance, the guy appeared alert, though the only hint was in his sharp gaze as he observed passers-by. *He* looked like trouble, to Hayden; he appeared to be a man who expected danger at any moment and was prepared to meet it. 'See that guy over there?'

'Who?' Megan spotted the guy even as she asked the question. 'The red neck?'

'I get the impression he's with Dewildt's girlfriend.'

'He hasn't looked at them once,' Megan said, even as the target of interest watched the passing traffic.

'Yeah,' Hayden agreed. 'That's my point exactly. Two good-looking women like those, and he ain't as much as raised an eyebrow in their direction.'

'Maybe he's gay. Or he isn't into dumb blonds.' Megan sucked air between her teeth.

Hayden again offered her a smile. Megan was short, solidly built, and dark haired, her complexion café au lait: Dewildt and her friend were her negatives. 'You ask me, he's purpose-fully not looking at them, so nobody puts them together. Pity we didn't get here a minute earlier, we could've settled the question . . .'

They had tailed Stella from her hotel in the van, wrong-footed momentarily when she elected to walk rather than hail a cab, and they had to complete the one-way circuit of the street adjacent to the library whereas she'd cut across both streets to the plaza. By the time they were in position, parked so they could observe her from a safe distance, Stella had already been seated at the table, and smoking a cigarette. The tall guy dressed in denims, plaid shirt, and high-topped boots was already a fixture against the wall ten yards distant.

Discreetly, Megan aimed her phone at the guy, zooming the image on screen so that his upper torso and features were fully displayed, and took a series of photographs. With that done, she switched emphasis to the women conversing at the table and repeated the process, concentrating on the stranger. Done, she composed a quick message and sent the images as attachments back to their office. 'If they're in the system, we should get an ID on them in a New York minute,' she told Hayden needlessly.

'Yeah,' said Hayden. Not everyone that Stella had met with in the past couple of days had earned similar attention, but they'd be fools to disregard the importance of this meeting. He'd already gained the impression that Stella had reached out for assistance in finding her father, and any extra set of eyes was a bonus to him, and ultimately to their employer. 'While you're on with control, see about getting another team out here. I want them on Stella, I don't want to miss any opportunity with the new girl.'

'We should stay tight to the daughter,' Megan countered.

'Lacey hasn't reached out to her yet, and I don't think he will any time soon. He's no fool, he'll know we are watching her, and won't make direct contact. He cares too much about his kid to put her in danger. But he won't feel the same for this new woman though; she could lead us directly to him.'

'Or get in our damn way.'

'Well . . .'

'If she does, we move her?'

'Lace killed Ethan and Mathers. He doesn't get to walk away from this, even once we get the USB stick back. And we will get it back, and God help anyone who gets in our way.'

'Is that your call, Hayden?'

'Is anybody gonna object?' Hayden turned and stared directly at Megan. Lace used to be a member of their team, as had been Ethan Prescott and Jacob Mathers. He'd killed both men in self-defense, when they had been trying to kill him. In retrospect, could they blame him for saving his own life? Yeah, Hayden thought, because he'd stepped over a line when he stole from their employer, and Ethan and Mathers had only been doing their damn jobs when he shot Mathers and later stove in Ethan's skull with the butt of his pistol. Those actions had condemned him in Hayden's judgment, and he was certain Megan had a similar strong opinion on Lacey's just desserts: particularly when she'd been screwing Ethan. Megan rarely formed attachments with other people, she was a loner, but she had felt something for Ethan even if for the simple fact her ugly mug hadn't put him off. If only she knew that Ethan had boasted to his male pals about using her: You don't look at what's on the mantle when you're poking the fire, Ethan had grinned.

'Object? Not me,' Megan said. 'You can kill him dead for all I care, but only after I cut off his fucking balls.'

'See, I knew we were on the same page.'

As Megan punched in the number for their office, Hayden concentrated on what was going on at the table. Stella had stood and slowly her friend got up, just as Stella moved in for a hug. The shorter blond returned the embrace stiffly. Hayden shifted his attention to the tall guy. He had disappeared.

'Shit . . .'

Megan glanced across at him, her hand cupped over her phone.

'Did you see where the red neck went?' Hayden asked.

He earned a grimace in response, and a curl of Megan's eyebrow. OK, so she'd been otherwise engaged, and he was the one supposedly watching. He'd only taken his eyes off him for a moment and the guy had practically dissolved in the puff of blue cigarette smoke he'd left behind. Hayden pursed his lips in thought, returned Megan's quizzical stare, and said, 'Maybe you should ask for more than one team to back us up.'

SEVEN

A man with enemies didn't get to survive a fourteen-year stretch in one of the most violent penitentiaries in the country by trudging around in a neutral gear. If he was anything less than switched on, then he'd be the recipient of a shiv to the gut, or a gang beating, and it would be solely his fault. Po had survived The Farm, although he still bore the scars of his incarceration on his forearms where one determined attacker had tried to rip out his eyes with a piece of sharpened metal. His vision had been spared but at the expense of deep gouges in his arms where he'd first fended off the stabs, then took the improvised blade off him and returned it – fatally

– to its wielder. Po valued his eyesight, but equally he prized the sixth sense he'd cultivated that had served him well over the years and saved him from other sneak attacks. When his inner trigger flipped he knew he'd be a fool to ignore the warning. He'd spotted the pair of watchers in the van, knew without seeming to return their perusal that he was under scrutiny. They were also interested in Tess. Keeping them in his peripheral vision he smoked and showed a feigned interest in passers-by, but all the while waiting for the right moment to move. He glanced only occasionally their way, allowing his gaze to slip over their van as if it brought him no concern, and evaluated. He couldn't make out their features, but from their shapes a man was in the driving position, a woman alongside him. She was the one who brought up a phone and took snapshots of him, then of Tess and Stella. They conversed, and their body language was enough to tell they both ached from subdued frustration. The woman turned back to her phone, and this time began speaking into it, her head tilted down to it; the driver's gaze was fully on Tess. As a clot of tourists passed between him and his observers, Po dropped his cigarette, exhaled smoke, and slipped away, hidden from view by his escorts. Within a few yards he backed into the entrance of a store and allowed the doors to slide shut on him. Through tinted glass he watched as the driver jolted to attention, his head darting back and forward as he sought Po's location. He urgently conversed with the woman, who again spoke into her phone.

Who are you? The question required an answer, but all he could say for certain was that those in the van weren't who he'd been on the lookout for. He'd barely been in Boston more than an hour, and as connected as his enemies were, he doubted they had the resources to locate and set a team on him as soon as this. It was an easy enough conclusion then: Stella Dewildt had picked up a tail. The real questions were whether Stella was aware of or even party to the stakeout, or if she was oblivious to it. He'd lay a stake on the latter. The other important question was whether her watchers meant her harm, or if she was simply a lead to a more pointed target, her father, Aaron Lacey. If Lacey was important enough to attract a search

party, then the man hadn't just upped and disappeared, he'd
ran away, and to Po that meant one thing . . . trouble.

He smiled grimly. He never shied from trouble; in fact,
if he had one glaring fault, he was drawn to it. Working with
Tess he'd experienced some periods of high adrenalin, but of
late their jobs had proven mundane, boring, and he yearned
for more. Suddenly, what had begun as yet another drab and
procedural missing person case looked as if it could morph
into something far more rewarding. If it were down to him,
he'd move on the van, challenge those watching him, and
demand answers. But this was Tess's gig. However much he
ached for action, he wouldn't allow his rash nature to
jeopardize his partner's business. Instead he noted the van's
description and license plate number, and waited.

The passenger door slid open and the woman stepped out
on the sidewalk, pulling on a baseball cap and using its large
bill to shadow her features. She was short, built like a gym-
bunny with solid thighs and tight shoulders: ex-military, Po
surmised, from her gait as she moved adjacent to whomever
she followed. Within seconds Stella Dewildt strode past the
shop front, head held high and regal. Her shadow kept one
eye on her, while moving through the knots of pedestrians
on the opposite sidewalk. Her right hand was tucked inside
the front of her jacket. Hopefully Po was right and Stella
wasn't under immediate threat, otherwise he might assume
the woman was hiding a gun. The van hadn't moved, the
driver a shadowy figure beyond the tinted glass. They'd been
forced to split their resources, which was good and bad. Again,
Po was tempted to head on over and haul the guy out of the
van and get things over with. Instead, he backed further into
the shop, turned and exited through a door into the hotel
lobby. It took him less than twenty seconds to reach the main
atrium, and had a view out of the front doors to where the
van was. In that short period of time, things hadn't changed:
the guy still sat in the driver's position and, judging by the
direction his attention was centred on, he was all eyes for
Tess. Po took out his cell phone.

'Hey,' he said the instant Tess answered, 'it's me.'

'I was wondering where you'd got to.'

He didn't waste words. 'You've got a tail.'

'The blue van on the opposite side?'

Po smiled at her astuteness. 'You see the woman get out and follow Stella?'

'Yes. I didn't make Stella aware, though. I'll tell you why I kept her in the dark when I see you.'

'After you hang up, sit awhile, then make things look all natural like and come meet me. I'm inside the lobby of the hotel behind you.'

'See you in a minute,' she said, and then laughed uproariously.

He paid no heed to her odd outburst: she was playing a part, as if ending a call with a friend. He moved so he was hidden in shadow to one side of the doorway, watching the van. A short time later Tess entered through the door, but paid him no attention as she continued inside. Only once she'd made her approach to the check-in desk look natural did she turn aside, keep out of line of sight and return to Po's side. 'Is he following me inside?'

'He looks tempted. But no. Still sitting in the van.'

'So he's no amateur,' Tess supposed.

'Or he hasn't the confidence to come inside alone.' Po shook his head at the suggestion. 'No, we can't assume anything about him yet.'

'Did he make you?'

'F'sure. The woman shot photos of me . . . and of you. I think it's safe to assume they made us as a couple and want to know what we're doing here.'

'You don't believe they've anything to do with Jimmy Hawkes?' Hawkes was the criminal who thought he could stroll into Portland and extort money from – among others – Po's businesses, and who'd rapidly been shown the error of his ways. Po wasn't concerned by the thought of retribution from Hawkes, but he couldn't discount the hired muscle he'd brought in: Po had physically injured the men, but worse, he'd injured their reputations and their only way of reasserting themselves in the criminal underworld would be to come back at him, harder next time.

'It's too soon for that,' he said.

'Unless someone from Portland's tipped them off we're in town.'

'Who? Your mom? Nobody else's aware we've come to Boston.'

'I never mentioned to her we were coming here. But I'd bet she already realized it was a sure thing the second she handed me Stella's number.' Tess pursed her mouth. 'Actually, I did tell Alex and Emma we'd be out of town for a few days, not exactly where to, but I'm also betting my mom has been on to Alex by now bemoaning my rebellious streak.'

'Alex and Emma can be trusted to stay quiet,' Po said. He wasn't so certain about Barbara: except, the grapevine would've had to have been set ablaze for word to reach the wrong ears before now. He was confident this had nothing to do with local criminals. 'Plus, one or the other could prove helpful. You think you can get 'em to check who that van's registered to?'

Tess took out her cell. 'I can do that myself,' she said – she could access Emma Clancy's law enforcement databases via an app on her phone. He relayed the license number, and she punched it into the system. 'Interesting,' she said when the result was returned.

'How's that?'

'This,' she said, wagging the phone in her hand, 'confirms my initial idea. We need to go and speak with Lacey's employers.'

'The dude in the van works for the same company?'

'The van's registered to them, it's safe to assume the driver's on their payroll.'

'So let's take things direct to the man and see what he's got to say for himself.'

Tess clucked her tongue in thought. 'Ordinarily I'd agree, but I think *this* time we should show more caution.'

Po squinted briefly. *Ordinarily* Tess wouldn't be in agreement of a frontal approach, but he let it go. She glimpsed up at him, clucked her tongue once more.

'They alerted Stella her dad was missing,' she added for clarity. 'They're taking a lot more interest in the disappearance

of a wayward employee than seems normal to me. I'd like to
know why.'

'So let me go over and squeeze an answer outta that dude,'
said Po with a slow smile.

'Chances are he's only a working Joe, just like you and me.
Let's draw back a little first, Po, and go speak to his boss and
find out if anyone's throat is in actual need of squeezing.'

'Party pooper,' he drawled.

EIGHT

To his patient the doctor looked in need of medical
assistance more than he did. His skin was parchment
thin, tinged yellow and hung from the bones of his
skull in folds. His head was perched atop a scrawny neck
that struggled to bear the weight. His hands were bony, the
backs knotty with thick blue veins and purple blotches,
the fingertips tinged yellow by nicotine, visible through his
nitrile gloves. A white coat – a misnomer as it was actually
a dull grey, stained at the collar and cuffs with grease – hung
on a hook, and it was unlikely it had been worn in years.
Instead the doctor was dressed in plaid shirt and jeans, both
baggy enough to fit him twice over. He'd suffered extreme
weight loss over a short period of time. He hacked and
coughed between his administrations, dribbling phlegm into
a kidney dish. Despite his apparent ill health, the retired
physician maintained a steady hand, and his gaze was sharp
and intelligent. If he'd the option, Aaron Lacey would have
sought help from a doctor who wasn't mere weeks from his
grave, but Doc Grover was his lot. Besides, Grover had
nothing to gain from betraying Lacey.

The gauze pad Grover removed from the wound on his
back above Lacey's hip went into the kidney dish, along with
another trickle of thick phlegm. Lacey had seen the worst of
humanity and all its depraved ways throughout his years as
a cop, but he still hadn't the stomach for this. He turned his

face away, fighting down a surge of revulsion. 'Jesus, Doc?'
he wheezed. 'Do you have to do that?'

Grover was oblivious to the reason behind the complaint.
'Hold still, Lacey, or you're going to open the wound again.'

'How are those sutures holding?' Lacey said, and expelled
a sour breath.

'Fine, but not if you keep writhing around.'

The entry wound on his side had closed, but there was some
seepage from the larger exit hole on his back. Thankfully –
and despite his penchant for hacking filthy phlegm all over
the place – Doc Grover's early intervention had negated the
threat of infection. The through-and-through wound pained
him, and his entire side and hip were stiff and lacked manoeuvrability, but Lacey was on the mend. Opening the wound
would be a setback he could do without. He lay still, idly
touching the stitches over his collarbone, while Grover worked.
The sutures were iron hard, stiffened with dried blood, and
regularly caught on the material of his shirt or jacket. Already
the flesh there had knitted and was healing, and only the
itchiness of the stitches reminded him how close he'd come
to death: another inch higher and to the left and Ethan Prescott's
blade would have found his carotid artery and that would have
been it for Lacey.

Momentary guilt assailed Lacey, as it had on numerous
occasions since he'd fought with his ex-colleague in the
shallow waters of the Neponset River. He hadn't wished to
kill Ethan, far from it, but the alternative would have been
his own death. He'd put every ounce of desperate strength
into clubbing the younger man senseless with the butt of
his empty revolver. After the first blow, and their tumble
down the embankment, Ethan had lost his knife, but his
strength never slowed. The older man had thrashed wildly
as Ethan forced him under the frothing water. Lacey struck,
and struck again, and almost sensed the crushing blow that
caved in the side of his opponent's skull a moment before
Ethan's body went lax, and Lacey surged up from the river,
spitting and coughing and hacking phlegm as thick and
sticky as any Grover now purged from his lungs. Shivering
with adrenalin, and also shock, Lacey could do nothing for

Ethan. Blood spread from his submerged head, tainting the water, obscuring the wide-eyed look of accusation Ethan aimed at him.

'I'm sorry, kid,' Lacey told him, and he'd meant it. But then he used his feet and knees to shove Ethan's corpse out into the deeper water, until he was caught by a swifter current and borne away, to come to a final rest on a sandbar, Lacey heard later, downstream at Squantum Point.

He remained maudlin about Ethan's death. He had personally liked the guy, and the trouble that arose between them was of course by Lacey's making. And yet he was also conflicted. Ethan had tried to kill him, and Lacey would never apologize for defending his own life first. Ethan came at him with a knife, and he wasn't aiming to miss his throat, so smashing his head in was just desserts.

Yeah, keep on telling yourself that, Lace, he thought cynically. He hadn't given Jacob Mathers's death much thought beyond the fact he was lucky his bullet had found a fatal target, and not the other way around. It was said you shouldn't speak ill of the dead, but Mathers was an insufferable asshole when he was alive, and Lacey's opinion hadn't changed after the man's demise. Recalling their brief gun battle brought him back to the present, and he hissed in pain as Doc Grover reapplied a sterile gauze pad to the exit wound and stuck it down with tape.

'You've taken the meds I gave you?' the retired doctor asked.

Lacey had chugged down the antibiotics and painkillers prescribed to him, and more besides. 'I'm out, Doc. Could do with something a bit stronger for the pain.'

Without comment, Grover opened a drawer in his desk and dug out an unopened pack of controlled painkillers. 'On the house,' he said, and slapped them down.

Lacey sat tentatively, experiencing a pulling sensation in his side. He checked out the pack of morphine-based meds. Another doctor had prescribed them to Herbert George Grover. 'These are yours, Doc.'

'They don't touch my pain anymore, Lace; you may as well get the benefit of them.'

Lacey pulled into his undershirt, buttoned his shirt over it. He delved for his wallet and counted out two hundred dollars. Grover coughed and spluttered, and this time, swallowed what he'd hacked up, while waving off Lacey's offer of cash. 'Like I said, they're on the house. I didn't agree to help you out because of payment: remember, I owe you. Take them with my gratitude and best wishes.'

'The cash ain't for the meds, Doc.'

Grover nodded. Lacey was buying his silence: he picked up the bills and made a cursory count of them. They disappeared in his jeans pocket. 'I don't think you need come here again, Lace,' he said, and it wasn't a rhetorical statement. He was hinting that two hundred bucks only bought so much silence. 'If you're careful and take things easy you should have no complications with your wounds.'

Any number of complications could come from showing his face at the doc's house again. Neither man was stupid. Lace hadn't said he was on the run, but it was apparent to both. His wounds should have been treated by a genuine surgeon, not one who'd retired years ago to escape a scandal and possibly criminal charges. Whoever had caused Lacey's wounds might wish to cause more and could still be seeking him, and Grover had no desire of his enemy turning up on his doorstep. And they would, sooner or later, because a man with gunshot wounds could not go untreated, and his hunters would guess he'd reached out to an old contact. Grover would stay quiet under normal circumstances, but not under threat: two hundred bucks didn't guarantee silence if the stakes were raised against him.

'If I'd more I'd give it to you, Doc,' said Lacey, conscious of the pitiful amount of ready cash he had available.

'We're quits, Lace. I don't want your money.'

Just my continued silence, Lacey thought. Yeah, they both knew things about the other that were best kept under wraps.

The nitrile gloves came off, and Grover dumped them in the kidney dish with the soiled dressings and the purging from his lungs. Lacey shuddered internally: he didn't want to shake the doc's hand, as if his ailments would be transmitted through his spidery touch. Lacey clapped him once on his shoulder, and stepped away quickly. He grabbed his jacket and exited the makeshift surgery into an Upper Manhattan street.

NINE

Tess and Po knew they were being followed, and their pursuer knew that they knew it but followed anyway. At a base level it felt incredibly immature to Tess, but all involved were in a similar position where a certain amount of professional pride was at stake. The guy in the van made no pretence at subtlety, staying always in their rear-view mirror, and Po showed none of his usual verve when driving, so there was little chance of inadvertently losing their pursuer in the heavy traffic. Once, when a red light was against their tail, Po pulled in to the side of the road and waited until the van was moving again. Unerringly they led the van across Boston towards his company's office. Tess wondered if the guy had figured out where they were going yet, and if he was pissed that he'd been made so easily, or if he was more sanguine about it. A quick check of Po found his mouth turned up at one corner and his eyes twinkling in humour. He was enjoying himself, even if she weren't: being the prey in a cat-and-mouse game was never her preferred role. Before returning to the Mustang, Po had again suggested dragging the man from his van and forcing answers from him, and it was enough for Tess to frown and mutter about having to work with a barbarian for him to drop the idea with a nod and grunt of mirth. He had only partly been joking. In truth, Po's headlong style had proven its worth in the past; he'd forced answers where her investigative skills had come to a roadblock, but under these unusual circumstances she felt they should err on the side of caution. There was more to Aaron Lacey's disappearance than it seemed, and who knew who was in the wrong. As she'd cautioned earlier, their pursuer could be one of the good guys, and beating him up would do nothing for her sense of being on the side of the angels.

While Po led the van across the city, Tess keyed up some programs on her tablet and set them running, based on the information received from Stella. She'd also brought up a GPS application on her phone, and it directed Po towards a tower block overlooking wharfs where the Charles and Mystic Rivers spilled into Boston Harbor. It was prime real estate, and the expensive vehicles parked in its private lot reflected the cost of hiring Elite Custodian Services' services. Po pulled the Mustang into a reserved parking spot, with no regard for the rules. He looked at Tess. 'I ain't minding the car this time,' he said.

'I don't expect you to,' she replied, as she unsnapped her seatbelt, 'but let me do the talking.'

'Never was my intention to talk.'

Tess exhaled through her nostrils. 'Please behave yourself.'

He aimed a grin at her. 'There's no need to fret. This is still your gig, Tess; I'll be the model of integrity.'

'Do you even know the meaning of the term?'

'Sure I do. You've rubbed off on me these last coupla years; was a time when I might not have restrained myself back there.' He thumbed over at where the van had come to a halt on the street. The driver remained inside, obscured behind the tinted windscreen.

Po had a point. During their first case together they'd picked up a tail in Baton Rouge, and his instinct was to leap on the hood of their pursuers' car and try to punch through the windscreen. He'd advanced a long way towards being civilized since then. She reached over and gently gripped his wrist. 'Don't go losing all your brutish charm,' she told him, and he returned her smile.

As she strode for the entrance, Po made it his business to backpedal a few steps, aiming a jaunty salute at their observer. He sensed the fuming response of the guy behind the tinted glass, and grinned. He turned his attention back on Tess. 'Betcha he's on with his bosses right this instant warning them we're coming.'

'Good. It means we won't get the run around for having no appointment.'

Her words proved prophetic. As they pushed inside the foyer, a young man glanced up at them from behind a podium. He wore a navy blue blazer over a pristine white shirt and maroon tie. His black hair was neat to the point of severe, combed from a razor sharp parting to one side. His eyebrows had been sculpted and his flawless complexion might have been enhanced with cosmetics. He was a non-aggressive first point of contact for potential clients, but he was still a security guard. He opened his mouth to greet them, but halted when a phone rang. He made a polite apology with a flash of his pearly-white teeth, and answered the phone. His conversation was brief, coupled with glimpses at Tess and Po, before he set down the phone. 'Nicolas Villere?' he asked pointedly of Po.

'Yup, that'd be me,' said Po, giving no hint he was surprised how quickly he'd been identified. Tess wasn't the only one who could run plates through a system: that their tail had run a similar search on his Mustang stood to reason. It was all part of the game of one-upmanship they'd been involved in.

Nevertheless Tess sniffed in annoyance, and made a point of approaching the podium ahead of Po. 'I'm Teresa Grey, a private investigator. Mr Villere is my associate. I'd like a word with somebody in charge.'

The guard glanced at Po, who gave a flash of his teeth in response and hooked his thumbs in his belt. The young man transferred his attention to Tess. She stood close enough to rest her elbows on the podium to return his perusal, but kept her arms by her sides. 'Umm, Mr Holbrook is expecting you,' said the young man. 'If you'd like to come this way.'

As he stepped out from behind the podium, his gait was stiff, and his tailored black trousers hitched below one knee. He was an amputee, an ex-service man perhaps who'd lost a limb but been given a second chance by the bosses of Elite Custodian Services. He led them towards a door, through which he swiped them with an electronic key card. Beyond the doors was a set of two elevators. Even as they were let through, one elevator door swished open, and disgorged an older man and a middle-aged woman.

'Thank you, Harris, we'll take things from here,' said the older man to the guard. He was short and stocky, his shoulders straining his tailored suit. He wore his steel-grey hair high and tight, as many veterans did even after retiring from the theatre of war. His perusal was quick and astute, spending the briefest of times on Po – weighing and judging him – before he switched to Tess and offered her his outstretched palm. Tess ignored it. 'I'm Ben Holbrook,' he announced, 'it seems we might be working to a similar end, but have started off on the wrong foot.'

'You mean you have one of your investigators following us, under some illusion we can lead you to Aaron Lacey?'

'Yes. Exactly that.' Holbrook squeezed out an apologetic grimace. Alongside him, the woman remained silent, staring at Tess over the bridge of a large hawkish nose. In a plain black dress and her hair pulled back under an Alice band, the woman was as ascetic as a nun, and radiated similar assuredness in her faith: in her case it was that Tess was below her contempt. Tess raised her brows in question. The woman misread her meaning.

'Seeing as Ben has been remiss in introducing me, I'm Clarissa Glenn, a business partner with Elite.' She disdained to offer her hand, only inclined her chin to indicate she'd said enough. Clarissa's upper-class British accent rang false to Tess.

As they rode the elevator to Holbrook's office Tess made the introductions, adding that they worked for a specialist inquiry firm engaged by the District Attorney in Portland, Maine.

'You're not here in Boston at the DA's behest, though,' Holbrook stated as they alighted the elevator and crossed a corridor.

'You know we're not. We are here at the request of a private client—'

'Estelle Dewildt,' Holbrook finished for her, as he ushered them into his office. It was surprisingly utilitarian, but commanded a prime corner position that overlooked the harbour. 'She has engaged you to find her father?'

'I think we've already established that,' Tess said.

Holbrook opened his hands wide. 'Then we shouldn't be at odds with each other. We all want the same thing.'

'Do we though?'

'I'm sorry? Aaron Lacey was a valued employee.'

'The point is, your reason for wanting him found might not be the same for Stella. She's only concerned with his welfare.'

Holbrook and Glenn exchanged glances, and something guarded passed between them. Holbrook seated himself behind his desk, unbuttoning his suit jacket for comfort. Glenn moved away and rested her backside on the edge of a second desk. Tess and Po waited. The atmosphere was thick enough to chew on. Finally Holbrook broke the silence. 'We are also concerned for his welfare. As I said, Aaron Lacey was valued . . . is valued . . . and we'd be a poor example as employers if we didn't care about his welfare.'

Tess laughed.

'You don't believe me?' Holbrook appeared genuinely affronted.

Po still stood just within the open door, one ear on the elevators behind him. Tess wanted to do the talking but he was his own man. 'Buddy, do you believe we are cabbage coloured?'

Holbrook frowned at the unfamiliar term.

'What my associate means is we aren't gullible,' Tess explained. 'You know as well as we do your interest in Lacey's whereabouts has nothing to do with his welfare. You don't put a surveillance team on his daughter except for one reason: you hope she'll lead you to her dad. It's why you informed her he was missing in the first place, expecting her to have some way to reach out to him. Well, here's the rub: Stella's as much in the dark as you are. She has no idea where he is, so there's no point following her. In all likelihood she'd have informed you the minute she heard he was OK, but not now. I'm going to ask that she cuts all communication with you, and also demand that you pull your team off her immediately.'

'A fair response, but not necessarily the best one,' Holbrook said.

'Not the best for you,' Tess corrected.

'We're all looking for the same man. If we were to share information, help each other out, it could prove mutually beneficial . . .'

Before he was done speaking, Tess shook her head at the suggestion. 'Why do you really want to find him?'

Holbrook again exchanged a glance with Glenn. Without rising from her perch, the woman said, 'We are not at liberty to say.'

'I thought that might be the case. It also confirms that an interest in his welfare's the last thing you have in mind.'

'And what do you think gives you the right to march into our office and start making absurd accusations?' Glenn snapped.

Tess ignored the question, answering with one of her own. 'Why has Lacey run away?'

Holbrook raised a palm. 'It's as Clarissa says, we can't say. We have a responsibility to protect the confidentiality of our clients. Let's just say that – with one such client – Aaron Lacey's disappearance has caused us some embarrassment. We'd like to find him so that this matter can be resolved without injury to our reputation.'

'What did he do?'

'You are persistent,' Glenn snarled.

'I'm a detective.' Tess aimed a snarky smile at the woman.

'Then detect,' said Holbrook, and again he raised a palm to forestall an angry response. 'Elite specialize in close protection work, our agents are skilled, but not in an investigatory capacity. I said earlier that we could work in a mutually beneficial manner. Find Aaron Lacey for me and I'll double your usual fee.'

'No,' said Tess. 'A conflict of interests would exist. You said this was about protecting your reputation; what would going behind our client's back do for ours?'

Holbrook smiled to himself. Testing her loyalty, her moral centre and her professional ethics? 'I didn't expect you to accept,' he said, 'but I'd like to think that we can work separately without impeding each other.'

'Tell the bozo in the van to stand down,' Po drawled, 'and

the girl who followed Stella. If I come across either of them again, *impeding* them will be the least of it.'

Glenn snorted. 'First it was unreasonable demands, then accusations, and now threats?' She eyed Po sternly, her lip curled at what she found. 'You are very confident. You don't look like a military man; in fact, I'm unsure what *exactly* you look like. But ask anyone that has served and they will warn you that overconfidence can prove fatal.'

Tess exhaled sharply. 'Now who's making threats?'

Glenn's nose wrinkled in distaste. 'Just call it a word of caution.'

Before either woman could continue, Holbrook stood, raising both palms in a sign of surrender. 'I think we should all take a deep breath before we continue. None of us wants things to turn ugly, do we?'

Po squinted at Clarissa Glenn's twisted face. 'Bit too late for that, bra.'

Holbrook's lips twitched in humour, but he carefully avoided looking at his business partner. If anything her hawkish face had grown more severe, her dark eyes resembling glistening marbles. Holbrook came out from behind his desk, and made no secret of urging Tess and Po towards the exit. He kept an amiable tone, but it was apparent he would brook no further animosity from either of them, and their briefest of meetings was over. Tess was happy enough to leave, as she was of the opinion she'd learned more from what Elite Custodian Services refused to disclose than anything they'd said. However she stood her ground a moment longer. 'We don't have to be at odds,' she reassured him, 'but only if you allow us to get on with our job without being spied on. You leave us, and Stella, be, and you won't get any trouble from us.'

Holbrook nodded, but refrained from a verbal agreement. He aimed a hand at the elevators. 'Harris will see you out.'

Tess and Po entered the elevator. Before the doors closed on them, Tess eyed Holbrook as he stood in his office doorway, Glenn behind him. 'One last question?' she said. 'You said you care about the welfare of your employees: would that also extend to Ethan Prescott?'

A shadow passed behind Holbrook's features, but he managed to hold his poise. 'I'm sorry? Who?'

The doors slid shut, but Tess had no intention of continuing that line of questioning anyway. His reaction had told her everything. She looked up at Po. 'Well, I think we've established that Ben Holbrook and Clarissa Glenn are liars.'

'Yup.'

'And Lacey's disappearance is down to them.'

'Uh-huh.'

'And Elite Custodian Services are desperate enough to hide something that they'll also cover up their connection to the death of another of their employees.'

'You only have Stella's word that Lacey worked with a guy with the same name as turned up dead.' Po gave a brief shrug. 'OK, so it's more than a coincidence. The thing is, did they put Prescott down, or d'you think Lacey smashed his skull?'

'Both scenarios are concerning.'

'If it's the latter, you still set on helping find him?'

'I'm not going to judge until I learn the truth.'

'And what then?'

'I couldn't say. Let's just concentrate on finding him first.'

'Sure thing.'

'The problem is, he could be anywhere . . .'

TEN

Lacey was over two hundred miles from where he had first run for his life from his colleagues, but was no safer for the distance. The daytime population of the island edged towards four million, but even hidden among so many, Lacey felt as if he stood out like a beacon in darkness. He pulled on a beanie hat, despite the warmth, and turned up his collar, shoved his hands in his pockets and walked gamely for the nearby 145 St Metro station. No one was watching him, but it sure as hell felt like it. But hey! If the paranoia didn't get you the real bad guys would. He limped on, keeping his face averted and made it into the station. He'd no intention of riding a train. He waited until a group of passengers alighted at their stop, and moved among them as they left the exit again, having changed his woolly cap for a baseball cap and carrying his jacket bundled over an arm. He moved determinedly for the waiting taxis, ignoring his myriad discomforts, and slipped inside a cab, giving a random destination in Midtown to the driver. It was a straight shoot down Malcolm X Boulevard before the driver would have to negotiate around Central Park to pick up the route to Midtown, but before they ever got there Lacey slapped a hand on the divider and told the driver to stop. He chucked the bewildered guy a handful of small denomination bills, and was out and walking fast for Seventh Avenue, all the while checking he had lost any potential tail. He hailed another cab, told the driver to take him north, and once the trip was underway, had him cut through Harlem, then pick up Broadway through the Upper West Side. The driver, a young Armenian with a poor grasp of English, glimpsed at him a few times in the rear-view mirror, but he was used to demanding passengers so didn't quibble when Lacey eschewed his original destination for Hell's Kitchen.

As his counter-surveillance tactics went, Lacey understood they wouldn't fool a determined team, but if his tail was solo then they'd have trouble following. Not that he truly believed he had a tail, but he'd be a fool to negate caution. The taxi rides cost precious dollars he couldn't spare, but they were necessary if he hoped to live long enough to cash in on the large payday he planned for.

He disembarked short of his actual destination. Cut across side streets, went two blocks south and then returned to Eleventh Avenue, where he took another cross street, all the while checking for anyone taking the slightest bit of interest in him. By now he'd put on his beanie and jacket once more. By the time he reached his secret accommodation he felt the trip to Doc Grover's had been wasted, as his wounds were screaming in pain and his damn gimpy knees had all but seized up on him. He felt for the morphine-based pain-killers in his jacket pocket and decided to get some of them down quick-style. He entered a general store at the end of his block and purchased a bottle of Mountain Dew with some of the last few bucks left in his wallet. He downed four pills with a long gulp of the sugary drink before he'd made it to his door. As he'd allowed his attention to slip, he didn't immediately enter his home, but continued on to the next intersection and checked for anyone out of place. Nobody concerned him, so he headed on inside, and made his way to the third floor apartment he'd kept under false details for a number of years. When you were a philanderer, and Lacey knew it had always been a glaring fault in his character, it paid to have somewhere to go off radar with his latest conquest. In all his married years, not even his wife had discovered his hideaway, and he was confident she was at least as astute as his hunters.

Inside, he moved through the dimness of closed shutters, intent only on reaching the kitchen. He dumped the soft drink bottle on a counter, then dug in a cupboard under the sink. The cupboard was a repository of cleaning fluids, various plumbing tools, and a small plastic box that rattled softly as he drew it out. With his own wounds seen to, he now returned to playing doctor himself, and checked on his patient. He peeled off the lid, and set the box on the counter, dug in the tips of his fingers until he located the small flash drive.

His tumble, and subsequent fight with Ethan Prescott in the river could have ruined everything. Before he ever arranged for his personal injuries to be fixed he'd ensured the flash drive received first aid. At first he was fearful the device was ruined, but a quick Internet search showed him that flash drives were more resilient than he'd thought. Dried out, the flash drive should still work perfectly well, with no loss of data, but its life might have been shortened. Corrosion was its greatest threat. Following the best advice for protecting its integrity, he'd smothered the flash drive in dried rice, a technique almost guaranteed to draw any moisture from its innards.

He held up the device, inspecting it. Gave it a cursory shake, listening for the disappointing sound of sloshing from within, but heard nothing. He gently tapped the device on a square of kitchen towel, and studied the absorbent paper for any wet marks. All was well, but his knowledge of technical stuff was limited. Those Internet masters advised that a backup of the device's data be made at first opportunity, the longer he left it the data could become corrupted. Lacey had taken a huge risk going to Doc Grover with his physical problems, now he was going to have to seek the assistance of another specialist who could salvage the data from his dying memory stick.

There were any amount of reputable tech wizards offering their services throughout his neighbourhood, but Lacey didn't want reputable. He needed somebody who wouldn't leave a paper trail that would lead back to them, and therefore to Lacey. Thankfully, during his time as a cop, he'd met plenty technically savvy ne'er-do-wells who could be compelled to keep schtum in return for reward or his continued silence. He'd not long arrived home, but he was on the clock with this. He changed out of his shirt, pulling on a plain blue sweater, and switched out his beanie for branded baseball cap, and headed on out. He limped past the general store, where earlier, as he handed over his cash for the soda, noting all that remained in his wallet was a solitary ten-dollar bill, he'd been reminded of its ATM. He needed available cash. He fully expected that his hunters had the technical resources to monitor his banking activities, so using his card to withdraw cash so close to home would be stupid, but he had to replenish his wallet. Jeez, since swiping the data stick all he seemed to do was hand out cash, but that was unavoidable, he must speculate to accumulate. He felt for the flash drive, now deep in his pocket, and seriously wondered if the final reward was worth the expense he'd already gone to. Man . . . the expense? Two men had already paid with their lives, and there existed the genuine fear that they wouldn't be the last. Was he prepared to risk his life further for the sake of riches beyond his wildest dreams? Hell yeah, he was.

ELEVEN

Harris, the security guard, was waiting as Tess and Po exited the elevator, holding open the door to the foyer so there was no illusion about where they should go next. He'd dropped the pleasant expression, his features now set, mouth pinched. His flawless complexion had grown waxy. Perhaps he anticipated trouble, so Tess aimed a smile at him to show there was no rancour. Beside her, Po was loose and relaxed. The young guard breathed a little easier as they approached him.

'Thank you,' said Tess as he stood aside to let her through. Po followed with a nod to him. Behind them, Harris ensured that the doors were closed securely, using the moment to allow them to progress towards the exit. When he noticed them waiting for him he grimaced. They hadn't been in the elevator long enough for his bosses to relay a message that they were unwelcome visitors, but he'd guessed that much due to the narrow space of time since they'd been upstairs. His prosthetic leg gave him more trouble as he walked towards them, purposefully angling towards the exit doors so they got the message. Neither of them moved. Tess smiled at the young man again, and it was obvious he was wondering if he'd misread the situation.

'Worked here long?' Tess asked amiably.

He answered with a shrug. 'Only a few weeks.'

His answer meant: 'Don't ask me anything, I'm the new guy and know nothing'.

'Good company to work for?' Tess went on.

He shrugged disarmingly. 'I guess.' Then he smiled conspiratorially. 'It's a job at any rate. Beats patrolling a shopping mall.'

'Did you serve?'

'Military? No. I was law enforcement.' He gave a dismissive glance down at his leg. 'An off-duty motorcycling accident finished that off.'

Tess could sympathize with him; her law enforcement career had come to a screeching halt after almost losing a hand to a drugged up robber with a knife. 'I was law enforcement too,' she said, hoping to form a bond due to their shared histories. 'Sheriff's deputy up in Portland, Maine.'

The guard glanced at Po.

'Uh-uh, not me, bra,' said Po.

'I read that Elite primarily sources its employees from veterans; military and law enforcement?' said Tess. The guard didn't answer, her question being rhetorical. He aimed for the exit once more, expecting them to fall into step. He looked back at Tess, and was torn between demanding they leave and relaxing into a longer chat. Tess motivated him toward the latter. 'How does that work out? I bet there's some friendly rivalry between the vets and ex-cops? Do you guys tend to mix more with your own kind?'

'I'm a glorified receptionist,' Harris said, his tone dry. 'You think I have much to do with the guys in the field?'

'Oh, I just wondered if maybe you spoke with the ex-cops whenever they were here, you know, like sharing funny stories and stuff?'

Harris shook his head. He was young, and his law enforcement career must have been short-lived. It was unlikely he had many tales to share with older, more experienced cops.

'Did you ever speak with Aaron Lacey?' Tess pushed. 'He was former NYPD, did his full twenty-five and more . . .'

A flicker of uncertainty danced across his features, but he took hold of it, set his shoulders squarely. 'Like I said, I've only been here a few weeks; can't say as the name means anything to me.'

Tess didn't believe him. He *was* the new guy and probably wasn't privy to the goings on beyond the entrance to the elevator bank, but she'd bet she'd overheard his name spoken rather a lot lately.

'I guess not. Lacey's much older than you, probably not someone you'd have much in common with,' Tess said, as if brushing off the question. Her next was more pointed. 'What about Ethan Prescott?'

Harris looked as if he'd swallowed something sour. His

headshake came far too quickly to be believed. 'No, no, I haven't heard of him either.'

'I'm surprised,' said Tess. 'His name has been in the news lately. He's the guy found murdered a few days ago at Squantum Point. He worked for Elite, right? Surely everyone round here've been talking about him?'

'No,' he said, again far too quickly to be sincere. 'If they have, I haven't been in on the conversation.'

Tess exhaled in disbelief, but he made no further denial, only gestured at the exit, anxious now to see the back of them. He'd definitely heard about Prescott's death, Tess decided, but was likely instructed not to talk about him with anyone. The young guy was fearful, and she understood why: if he spoke out of turn his job was on the line, and there probably weren't many openings in the local security industry for a guy with his disability. She pitied him, but he was also an asset to push for more. Before she could continue she sensed Po shift alongside her. His attention was directed on the entrance. Beyond Harris the doors opened, and a large man stepped into the foyer. He was easily as tall as Po, and much heavier built, none of it excess fat. He didn't proceed further, only stood before the open door, holding them under a stern frown.

'Aah,' said Po for Tess's ears, 'I'd assume this is our friend from the van.'

Harris followed Tess's gaze, and whatever the sour thing was he'd swallowed moments ago he was on the verge of throwing it back up. The newcomer had shifted his attention on the guard.

'Are you bein' paid to stand there like a lame ass?' the big guy demanded. Harris fluttered a hand, but was lost for words. Flustered, he looked from the guy to Tess and then back again.

'I'm, I'm just showing out these visitors . . .' Harris motioned them for the door.

'Yeah, they're unwelcome here.'

Po strode forward, meeting the big guy eye to eye. The guy pushed out his chest and stood square on, except his bulk failed to intimidate Po. He stood an arm's length before him, his arms loose at his sides.

'You need to get gone, pal,' said the big man. 'Orders from the boss upstairs.'

'If Holbrook wants us to leave, you're goin' to have to stand aside,' said Po.

The man didn't appear ready to clear their path, more as if he was prepared to throw punches. Tess stood a yard behind her partner, hoping things didn't turn ugly but ready to back Po up if things went sideways.

Po held the stare off. 'What's it to be? You look conflicted to me. You want us gone, or you want to stand there blocking the door?'

'I want you gone.' The guy leaned into his words, jaw thrust out. It was an awfully tempting target, or a ploy to draw in the unwary.

'So move,' said Po.

The man jabbed a finger in Po's chest. 'I've just been told by my bosses to throw you out. Don't make me look an idiot in front of them, pal.'

'You didn't need much help from me before. Surveillance ain't your strong point, is it?'

'Surveillance? Fuck all that creeping around shit, I'm not the type to hide from any man.' The finger jabbed at Po's pectoral muscle a second time. 'Least of all a skinny-assed hick like you.'

Behind Po, Tess momentarily squeezed her eyes tight and emitted a curse under her breath, even as she took a subtle step backwards. Po had been radiating frustration ever since they'd quietly brought in Moondog Becker, he was literally itching for a fight, and even a stern warning from her would do little to restrain him now. In a blur, his left hand clamped over the big guy's and the edge of it jammed against the knuckles as his thumb curled under the extended finger, trapping both against his chest. Immediately Po slid back, levering up the man's index finger against his own knuckle. The guy hollered in unexpected agony and surprise, folding at the waist and lunging out with his right foot to avoid having his finger dislocated. Instantly, Po's left foot swept the man's right foot an inch or two more to the front, over-extending him and throwing him off balance. Po loosed the trapped hand, but only so he could step back in, butting his shoulder against the big guy and sending him crashing over sideways.

While the big man sprawled, Po waved Tess through the gap he'd made. She side-skipped past, one eye on the fallen man, one on the guard. If Harris even considered intervening, his body didn't obey him: he stood gawping. Tess got to the open doorway, held it open for Po who stood within kicking range of his fallen opponent, who by now had spun onto his back, staring – enraged – up at him. Po wouldn't kick the downed man, not unless he continued the fight, as he fought under a different set of rules. Apparently the big guy guessed so, as he didn't rise, only cupped his tortured finger to his chest with his other hand. He did, however, pull in his heels to guard his groin from a sneaky jab of Po's boot.

'This isn't finished with,' the man snarled up at Po. 'Next time I see you your stupid tricks won't work . . . I'll rip your damn head off and crap down your neck.'

Po offered him a curl of his lip. 'Y'know, a wise woman recently said: "overconfidence can prove fatal". Don't make threats you can't back up, *pal*, and in future don't go sticking your fingers where they're goin' to get hurt.'

Tess tugged at Po's elbow. 'Come on, for Christ's sake,' she cautioned him.

Po mocked the fallen man with another salute, then backed out of the door. Harris, still agog, stood peering at him. Po winked, then turned to follow Tess towards where they'd left the Mustang.

'Happy now?' Tess asked the second he drove them out of the private parking lot.

'He started it,' said Po.

'But you had to finish it, right?'

'You know me,' he said, and grunted in mirth. 'Besides, if you poke a hornet's nest you're gonna get stung. That big idiot back there just learned a valuable lesson.'

'So . . . have you got your appetite for violence out of your system, or are you hungry for more?'

'Nah. That was just a canapé before the main course. You heard that bozo, he promised next time he saw me he was gonna rip off my head. Think I'm gonna stand around an' let him do that?'

'You promised me you'd behave. What was it you said, you'd be the model of integrity?'

'I did behave. And I did show integrity: the old me would've broken off his damn finger and shoved it so far up his ass he coulda tickled his tonsils.'

Despite herself Tess chuckled at the image. 'You are incorrigible, Nicolas Villere.'

He winked. 'You did say I wasn't to lose my brutish charm, right?'

She shook her head, and dug under her seat for where she'd left her tablet running while they'd been inside the tower block. She made a rapid check of the results, which took no time at all as there was nothing to see. She switched to a web browser and brought up Elite Custodian Services' website. Unfortunately, or probably more sensibly due to the nature of their industry, personal details about the company directors was sketchy. Moreover, stock photographs had been used in the web design, so that the identities of their employees, and more importantly their clients, were protected. Expecting to find a useful list of employees was asking too much, she supposed. She shut it down and switched to a more general search, firstly typing in Ben Holbrook's name alongside the keyword 'security'. She was rewarded with a long list of links, but not all were applicable to the person they'd recently met.

'Holbrook's a retired Army Ranger; he made Major. He's a veteran of both Afghanistan and Iraq. Says here that he worked for various PMCs before setting up Elite Custodian Services.' She explained that PMC were private military companies and Po nodded in understanding.

'What about the Limey?' he asked.

She searched again, this time for Clarissa Glenn.

'Royal Air Force. She was a group captain before retiring. That's a high-level rank, by all accounts, equivalent to a colonel in the army. In other words she outranked Holbrook.'

'Explains why she has a stick up her butt.'

'Yeah. She probably feels she should be in charge at Elite, but we both know who was calling the shots back there.'

'Holbrook tried playing at diplomacy,' Po said. 'At least Glenn made no bones about disliking us. What did you make of him offering you a job?'

'It lacked sincerity, and then some. He was just testing me to see if I could be bought. He knows now that I can't.' Tess clucked her tongue. 'Maybe speaking with them in person was a bad idea. We've learned little about why they're after Lacey, and possibly caused ourselves unnecessary trouble from them.'

'What was it Holbrook said: Lacey's disappearance has caused them some embarrassment and they'd like to resolve the matter without injury to their reputation?'

'Yeah,' Tess agreed, 'and that client confidentiality is very important to them. Do you think Lacey was involved in some kind of corporate espionage; that he's been stealing info about their clients and Elite are worried he'll hand it over to a competitor? It'd explain why they're so intent on finding him.'

'Would that information be sensitive enough they're prepared to kill to get it back?' Po grew more sombre as he contemplated the dire possibilities. 'What if we jumped to the wrong conclusion before and Lacey had nothing to do with Ethan Prescott's death? Could they have been working together and Elite caught up to Prescott first, and that's why Lacey has run away? Would explain why they denied knowing who Prescott was.'

'I'd be interested in hearing if the cops made the connection between Prescott and Elite,' Tess said, 'and how Holbrook dug them out of that hole.' She brought up the recent news reports about the discovery of Prescott's body. 'There's nothing here about him working for Elite Custodian Services.'

'So maybe Stella got it wrong, and the name she heard her dad mention had nothing to do with this Ethan Prescott.'

'You asked earlier if I still wanted to find Lacey; and I've wondered about it since. What if he is the bad guy in this, Po? If we locate him before Elite do, is it right to protect a criminal from them?'

His only answer was a rising of his eyebrows. To him, and by association her, the line between criminal and lawful was blurred. Their best friend, Pinky Leclerc, was the definition of a criminal, but also one of the most loyal and wonderful people either of them could wish for in their corner. 'Yeah,' she said softly, having answered her own question. Lacey's criminality would have to be measured and as long as he hadn't progressed too far along the spectrum then it should not be an issue to her. Besides, she'd been hired to find Lacey for her old school friend, and despite the many years separating their friendship she wasn't about to renege on the agreement she'd made with Stella. And then there was her mom. She still hadn't figured out her mother's involvement in this: she'd acted averse to the idea of Tess taking on the job, but that's exactly what it was, an act. Her mother definitely wanted Lacey found too, although she'd obviously been concerned that Tess would be the one to go and look for him, and Tess couldn't figure out why. When she met with Stella earlier, the young woman had given no hint, only that she'd tracked Barbara down through her dad's contacts in an old address book she'd discovered in his apartment, in the vague hope that she'd spoken with him recently. Apparently it was her mom who'd raised the subject of Tess being a private investigator and put the notion into Stella's head about hiring her. A major issue for her was why her mom's number was in Aaron Lacey's contact list, after all these years. In fact, as she recalled, it was her grandfather who'd been Lacey's patrol partner, and there had never been any love lost between her parents and the arrogant young patrolman. Again she flashed back on the memory at her granddad's graveside, and Lacey comforting her while her mom and dad dropped roses into the grave . . . but the memory didn't end there. Her dad returned from the graveside, and literally tugged her from Lacey's arms with a snarl of animosity. No love lost whatsoever. Who knew: perhaps afterwards they'd straightened out whatever issue existed between her dad and Lacey, and they'd reconnected later, sharing

contact details after her parents moved the family north to
Portland. Without asking her mom about it, Tess had no
way of knowing if they'd kept in touch during the passing
years, and if Lacey had been considered an old friend. When
her dad succumbed to cancer so many law enforcement
officers had attended his funeral that Aaron Lacey could
have been among them, but she couldn't recall. At the time
she'd been crushed by grief, and the faces of mourners at
the graveside were indistinct in her memory at best.

'We might have another tail,' said Po and growled a curse
under his breath.

In the last minute she'd thought about two funerals, and
had to give a mental shake to rid herself of the morose scenes.
She checked her side mirror, to see if she could spot what had
alerted Po. They were in heavy traffic, having cut through
midtown back towards Stella's hotel. She had no idea which
of the dozens of vehicles behind them had caught Po's attention: this time there was nothing as obvious as a panel van
with blacked-out windows.

'The black Chrysler,' Po pointed out, 'four cars back. It's
been with us through three different turns now. I've given it
an opportunity to close the space between us twice, but the
driver's deliberately sitting back.'

'Is it the same guy you pushed over?'

'Couldn't say,' Po admitted, but took a longer look in his
rear-view mirror and changed his mind. 'Don't think so. This
driver's head isn't as fat as that blowhard's was. Plus, this
time, he's making an effort at stealth.'

'Could you lose him?'

'In a heartbeat.' His head cocked as he squinted sidelong
at her. 'D'you want me to lose him?'

'Do your stuff.'

Po's teeth flashed.

TWELVE

A city block ahead, the black Mustang cut across two lanes of traffic, inviting angry responses from other drivers: brake lights flashed and horns blared, and somebody cursed out of an open window loud enough for Hayden James to hear. Before anyone else got moving again the Mustang took a left turn and sped away and the traffic lights overhead turned red. Hayden snorted at Villere's daring manoeuvre, a waste of time in his opinion. Sticking to the redneck's ass was unnecessary when he already knew where he was going. Villere and his partner were returning to Stella Dewildt's side, and Megan was still in place to observe their arrival. Hayden could take his time.

The abrupt attempt at losing his tail was contradictory to the manner in which Villere had reacted to the physical threat at Elite's HQ. Back there, Villere had employed economy of motion and a subtle application of leverage, attacking the smallest of joints to defeat a bigger foe. He appreciated the skill and ease by which Villere had dispatched an enemy who was no stranger to extreme violence, and the brief display had taught Hayden much about the man. Nicolas Villere, as Hayden had figured on first spotting him, was genuinely dangerous, and should be handled with caution. The big dope that'd ended up on his ass, nursing an aching finger and bruised ego, deserved everything he'd got, and Hayden felt no pity for the man. Perhaps Hayden should have urged him to be more cautious, but then he wouldn't have seen the rare display of Villere's skill from where he'd remained seated in the van. Hayden had sent in Mitch Burnett as a test, to gauge Villere's response – a literal pre-emptive poke before he met personally with him. Had Burnett been CQB trained, as had Elites' most skilled operatives, he'd never have set himself up for a fall that way, but Burnett came from another wing of the company that supplied scary-looking guys to act as doormen and stewards at rowdier, booze-fuelled events. Burnett's proclivity was for beating up drunks and boisterous youths, he employed his bulk and the red haze of violence to dominate, but had no close quarters battle skills and was therefore ill equipped to handle a sober and skilled fighter. Burnett had approached Hayden on more than one occasion, begging for a job with one of Hayden's protective services teams, so had willingly answered the summons when Hayden offered him the task of ejecting some unwanted visitors: he'd spectacularly failed his job interview, but Hayden had expected nothing less.

It pleased Hayden that Villere had made an assumption – figuring Burnett was the one to have shadowed his movements from the van – indicating that Villere was fallible. Having protected his identity, it gave Hayden a second bite at the cherry. Though he must ensure he switched rides again; he had decamped from the van to the Chrysler to continue the chase, only to be made almost as quickly by Villere as before. He drove on, ignoring the left turn taken by the Mustang, and called up Megan to arrange a rendezvous point near Dewildt's hotel. He warned her that Villere and Grey were en route, and this time urged caution, as, unlike Burnett, she wasn't cannon fodder. Megan assured him that the extra manpower he'd requested earlier had been mobilized, but she was loathe to back off from Dewildt before they arrived: her target was currently seated in her hotel lounge with Megan sequestered close by.

'You've about five minutes, then you need to get outta there,' he warned her. Holbrook had already informed him that Megan had been made, and the PI, Tess Grey, had demanded she be withdrawn.

'Blondie can go fuck herself,' Megan snarled. 'If she doesn't like it, I'll gladly fuck her over myself.'

'Holbrook wants this handled differently.'

'I don't give a damn . . . This is personal, Hayden.'

'No, Megan, it's not. Retrieving the data comes first, your beef with Lace second, and the rest of humanity third. You get me? If that doesn't suit, I'll pull you the hell off the job, and see how you get on without our resources behind you.'

Megan fumed silently for a moment. Hayden was under no illusion. Megan was resourceful enough to find – and kill – Lacey without support from Elite, but she was also wise enough to take the second option. Besides, if she went rogue, she wouldn't get paid, and beyond her thirst for vengeance she was greedy for cash. 'Don't worry, I'm still with the program, Hayden, but I'm telling you this: Lace is still getting it, and no blond bitch gets to waltz in and keep me from him.'

'I hear you, but be cool. There are ways and means to get this done without more complications we could do without.' Covering up Jacob Mathers's death had been taken care of – his body was in a sunken container out in the north Atlantic – but having been washed downstream to fetch up short at Squantum Point had meant there was no chance of a clean-up regarding Ethan Prescott. Up until now, Elite had managed to avoid any connection with Prescott; all his employment records had been expunged from their systems, and the man himself personally disavowed as if he'd never been on their books. A determined investigation would uncover his connection with the company, but fortunately – incentivized by Holbrook – the investigating detectives had kept Elite's name out of their reports and written off his death as a mugging gone wrong. However, Holbrook couldn't steer a police investigation where third-party players were involved. The involvement of Grey and Villere in the hunt for Aaron Lacey was a wrinkle, but one that could be smoothed without Elite's apparent inclusion. 'Like I said Holbrook's on it, and there's an alternative solution in motion. For now, I need you to fall back and let the other team take over—'

'Wait one, her cell's ringing,' said Megan. 'I need to get closer.'

'I said back off, goddammit.'

'Yeah, yeah, but you also gave me five minutes' grace.' Megan cut the call.

Hayden shook his head, more the way a long-suffering

parent might disapprove of a naughty child's antics than with any genuine displeasure. Megan had a rebellious streak as wide as her dislike of beautiful people. How she'd ever managed a six-year military career without losing everything through her inability to follow orders was beyond him. Then again, he supposed she was correct: he had told her she had five minutes before she needed to back off.

He drove with a touch more urgency, arriving at Huntington Avenue within a few minutes, and fed a parking metre in view of the public library and the chain hotel where Dewildt first met with her friends from Portland. Stella Dewildt's hotel was two blocks north beyond the library, plenty distance for him to approach unobserved from. He donned a baseball cap and an unobtrusive dark brown jacket, to help blend in, as he crossed the junction towards Copley Square and came within sight of Stella's hotel. Valets were busy parking visitors' cars and hailing cabs for others: he doubted Villere would hand over his Mustang to them, and reckoned he would have parked elsewhere, so wasn't concerned by its absence. He was confident he hadn't misjudged Villere's destination, so took care not to be spotted; the damn redneck had proven to have the vision of a bird of prey. He called Megan on his cell.

'Sit rep,' he demanded the second she picked up.

'Made it out by the skin of my teeth,' she said. 'Stella's friends are here, they're all chatting over coffee in the hotel lounge.'

'Villere too?'

'Is that the redneck? Yeah, he's there. Least he was last I saw of him.'

'Be wary of him, Megan; he might look like a dumb hick but you know how looks can be deceiving.'

'Amen to that,' she growled.

'The call Stella took?' he prompted, to get her back on track.

'Wasn't from her dad,' said Megan, 'it was Blondie asking where to meet. I suppose in hindsight we should've known we wouldn't get that lucky.'

'Sooner or later we'll catch a break. Either Lace will surface, or the PI will lead us to him. Holbrook had our analysts do a background search on her. By all accounts Tess Grey gets results, at least she has done in the past coupla years. Before that she'd an unremarkable career with the Sheriff's department. Word on the street is she's been "unofficially" hooked up with this "Po" character – that'd be Nicolas Villere – for the last two years and maybe it's no coincidence her fortunes changed with him at her side.'

Megan grunted in scorn. 'You sound like you respect him.'

'I do. If he applied for a job I'd give him a position on my team, no questions asked. That doesn't mean a thing when it comes to our mission: if he gets in our way, I'll show him the respect he's due, but it won't stop me shooting him in the face if need be.' Hayden paused for a beat. 'Let's hope it doesn't come to that.'

'If it comes to it, I'll happily do them both, him and his bitch.'

'You're forgetting what I said about wanting no further complications . . . if we kill 'em, we'll have the job of burying them, and that's time and effort I'd rather spend on getting Lace. Besides, if we kill them, Stella Dewildt will have to go too: who knows how many others know they've spoken with Holbrook; Elite will be immediate suspects in their murders. It's too messy, Megan.'

'We don't have to kill them, just get the team together, work them over and warn them who they're messing with. I'd bet a dollar to a dime they'd run home with their tails between their legs.'

'From what I've heard they aren't easily frightened. They took down some crime lord and his demented brother, not to mention a bunch of other assorted maniacs since, and recently some heavy hitters from right here in Boston. They won't back down from a fight. Like I said: too messy, too many complications, and our priority's getting back the data before the shit hits the fan and things get messier.'

'What exactly is this data Lace stole?'

'I've told you before, that's above your pay grade, Megan.'

'I'd like to know if it's going to affect my liberty if it gets out,' she said.

'It will bring Elite down in flames,' Hayden warned, 'and

that should be enough motivation to concentrate on getting
it back.'

'What if Lace releases it before we get him . . . have you
got a contingency in place, Hayden?'

Hayden said nothing.

'Thought so,' said Megan. 'Maybe I should invest in a one-way
ticket to a country without an extradition treaty with the US,
huh?'

'If Lace intended on releasing the data, he would've done
it by now.'

'Maybe he hasn't been fit to do much except lay low.
Judging by the blood we found, he didn't get off scot free
with Mathers, and I'm betting Ethan didn't go down too easy
either. Would be a shame if he's already dead, and he floated
downstream with Ethan all the way to the sea. It'd mean I
won't get to kill him a second time.'

'If he's out in the bay then good, the data will be beyond
salvageable. But neither of us believes that, Megan. So we
stay focused, and we get it back.'

'Like I said, I'm still with the program.'

'Are the others in place?' Throughout their conversation
Hayden had been watchful, both for Elite operatives and for
Villere, but had seen neither.

'Johnson and Nicholls are on them in the lounge. Seung and
Aiken are covering the doors. I've repositioned to the foyer.'

'Get yourself outta there, it's too close. Villere had eyes on
you this morning, and I bet he's got a memory for faces.'

'Faces like mine, you mean,' Megan rasped.

'Get over yourself, Megan. Come meet me out in the square.'

'I would, but we've got movement. All three targets.'

'Get your damn head down then, and make sure you
aren't made.'

'No worries there, boss,' Megan said, 'they don't have a
line of sight on me. OK. They're heading for the exit, you
should see them in three, two . . .'

'One,' said Hayden, and true to her word, spotted Villere,
Grey and Dewildt exit the hotel. They huddled a few seconds
outside the doorway, the two women talking animatedly, while
their male companion used the opportunity to light a cigarette

while scanning the area. Hayden had found an observation point in the lea of Trinity Church, and was largely obscured from view by people milling about as they boarded their ride at a bus stop. Trusting that Villere was watching for Mitch Burnett's ugly mug, Hayden didn't make any furtive movements, which were sure to catch an observant person's attention, but strolled to a point where pedestrians drawn to the stalls in a farmer's market surrounded him, offering an extra layer of camouflage. He didn't put away his cell phone, speaking on it looked natural, and gave him an excuse to stand in one spot. He observed the trio only in his peripheral vision, only noticing when a taxi pulled in at the curb that Stella was toting luggage.

'Megan,' he snapped, 'get Seung and Aiken mobile fast; Dewildt is about to leave in a cab and I want to know where she's going.'

'On it,' said Megan, and she cancelled the call in order to hail their back-up team.

By then Tess Grey was already waving off Stella, and Hayden cursed under his breath. His pulse rate quickened unexpectedly: hell, years had passed since he'd felt a spurt of adrenaline like it. He'd always maintained a cool head in combat, and it was only when his body responded to abject failure that he ever experienced the flooding of endorphins through it. The last time he'd reacted similarly was when insurgents pinned down his unit in a nameless Afghan *waddi* system and the prospects of getting out alive were slim. On that occasion he'd lost men, and also some of his own blood, and though his heroic actions in fighting off a greater force were later commended, he'd only felt the sting of failure; the cold wash of adrenalin through his body gave him another disquieting sensation now. In the face of it, losing Stella Dewildt was in no way tantamount to losing soldiers under his command to enemy fire, but shit, it was a failure all the same, and he did not like it.

Slow moving traffic, delayed further by a delivery vehicle blocking one lane, conspired to help Hayden out. Before Stella's taxi had cleared the curb, and joined stationary vehicles at a red light, he spotted a familiar vehicle feed into the queue half a dozen spaces behind. He could tell even from his distant vantage that Aiken and Seung had made it to their vehicle with seconds to spare. His pulse slowed, but his core still trembled. He rang Megan's cell again.

'Get Johnson and Nicholls on the PI, and remind them to keep a healthy distance, then you come join me,' he said without preamble. Next he rang Holbrook's number.

'Tell me you've got a lead on Lace,' said Holbrook.

'Nothing's changed there, sir, but we're still on his daughter, and hope he'll contact her soon.'

'That's not good enough. You need to make your own leads, Hayden, not wait around hoping for the best.'

'If you mean pressing Dewildt harder, there's no opportunity for that while her friends are in town. Not unless you want the cops coming down on us.'

'I know that and don't need reminding. They're a damn inconvenience showing up like this. However, they shouldn't be in the way too much longer.'

'The contingency's up and running then?'

'Yes. All I need from you is to keep me informed of Villere's location. Whatever happens next I trust both he and the private eye will have too much on their plates to trouble us again.'

'They'll suspect Elite is behind it, and involve the cops, are you certain you want to follow this extreme route, sir?'

'They can blame us, but it won't make any difference. I'm not stupid enough to leave a direct trail back to Elite and the police will only look at the obvious . . . I'll see to it that it's all they'll do. So that I can uphold my end of the plan, ensure none of our people are involved when it happens; whatever the outcome nobody steps in to assist.'

'Roger that, sir.'

'Oh, and, Hayden?'

'Yes, sir?'

'Need I remind you how important it is that you stop Lacey from releasing any of that data?'

'No, sir, I know exactly what it will mean for us all.'

'Good. I'll leave you with that thought in mind.'

Holbrook killed the connection.

THIRTEEN

When Tess first spotted that Stella was under observation she'd elected not to tell her friend for a couple of important reasons: Stella would have been tempted to look for the surveillance team and her subsequent actions would have been dictated by anxiety, or perhaps outrage. Until Tess could determine who and why Stella was being followed she didn't want Stella to react irresponsibly and give the game away. Caution was redundant now, so Tess had informed Stella about Elite Custodian Services' unhealthy attention, and counselled the wisest course of action. Stella needed to return home to New York; otherwise her presence in Boston would only impede her search for Aaron Lacey. Their limited resources – her and Po – couldn't be split between conducting an investigation and protecting Stella from intrusion by Elite's operatives.

Stella had been loath to go home, believing she should demand direct answers from Holbrook and Glenn, and at first wouldn't listen when Tess argued it would be useless. Stella was brim-full of indignation, adamant she could force answers from the security consultants, until Po reminded her she might be the one forced to answer by them instead.

'But I don't know anything,' Stella rebuffed.

'They don't know that, and they could make things intolerable for you before they're satisfied you're ignorant to your dad's whereabouts.'

'Intolerable in what way?'

'Threat of torture,' Po said.

'They wouldn't dare!'

'Maybe they'll skip direct to the torture,' he decided.

The blood drained from Stella's features. Tess scowled at her partner. 'Po, you're frightening her.'

'Just saying it as it is.'

Tess reached for Stella's hands. 'If you go home, I can't

guarantee you won't be followed, but it's less likely. If we stay here and continue the search, I'm positive that they'll waste their manpower shadowing our movements instead of bothering you.'

'Why shouldn't I call the police and let them deal with them?'

'You could, but I'm not confident your dad will want that. It could push him to go further underground.'

'You make it sound as if my dad's the bad guy in all this,' Stella said.

'Stella, as hard as it is to hear, your dad *could* be the bad guy. Until we know otherwise, it's best you have as little involvement as possible in this.'

'What if you're wrong, Tess? Not about my dad, but about Elite. What if they do follow me home to New York?'

'How much of what's going on is your husband aware of?' Tess countered.

'Paul? Why, he knows I'm here because my dad's gone missing. I spoke with him earlier on the phone and told him I'd employed you to find him . . .'

Tess nodded. She'd heard enough. 'Is your husband home?'

Stella shook her head. 'He's over in Los Angeles on a business trip. He won't be back for another three days.'

Tess's face shadowed. Sending Stella home to an empty apartment could prove problematic. She glanced at Po and saw he had the same reservation about compromising Stella's safety. Then the corner of his mouth curled up and the wrinkles round his eyes crinkled. 'Paul ain't the jealous type is he?' he asked.

'No. We have a steady and trusting relationship: we have to when his work takes him away from home so often. Why do you ask?'

'How'd your husband feel about you sharin' your home for a few days with a strange man?'

Stella's look of horror told him everything.

'I should have said a strange gay man. And by strange I mean eccentric.'

Tess smiled at the suggestion. Then, while Po wandered away to speak into his cell, Tess encouraged Stella to book a seat on the first flight home out of Logan International Airport. Within minutes they'd abandoned their coffees and headed out to hail Stella a cab, Tess all the while assuring her that their friend would meet her at home before evening, and that – despite appearances – she would be in the safest of hands with Pinky Leclerc. 'He's an oddball,' said Tess, 'and speaks kind of funny, but he's no fool. I'll give you half an hour with him and you'll fall in love with him the way I did.'

FOURTEEN

P o lit up a cigarette. Scanned the immediate area. Nothing untoward raised his hackles; unlike the couple he'd spotted inside that were trying too hard to blend with the hotel guests in the lounge. They were a freckle-faced ginger-haired man and an Asian woman; there was nothing wrong with interracial pairings, in Po's estimation, but their relationship appeared strained – for one they rarely looked at each other, and only then for an instant before their attention gravitated back to what was going on at Stella's table. They only exchanged conversation out of the sides of their mouths and at a whisper too. Both were in their prime and solidly built under unassuming clothing. Po had made them as Elite operatives within seconds of their arrival in the hotel lounge. Also he'd spotted the swarthy woman from earlier, who'd turned away too quickly as they walked out into the lobby, and raised a hand as if scratching her forehead to cover her profile as she feigned interest in some tourist brochures next to the checking-in desk. In the briefest of times before she concealed her face, Po noted a vicious scarring of her cheek that hadn't been obvious when he last saw her at a distance. Where there were three operatives, he assumed there were more. He allowed his casual gaze to range further. There was no sign of the big lummox he'd dropped back at Elite Custodian Services' HQ: his brutish mug would've stood out in any crowd, but Po hadn't expected him again. In hindsight, the fool had fallen

too easily to a simple pain compliance technique, and if
Clarissa Glenn's boast was to be believed, their close protection operatives were skilled in unarmed combat. No bodyguard
skilled in close quarters battle would have presented himself
square on, stuck out his chin or offered a finger to be wrenched
off. Ergo, the big guy was not the same man who'd previously
exercised precaution, and was instead a sap sent in to test Po's
response to a direct threat. He fully expected that the man
from the van was out there somewhere, having ditched the
black Chrysler he'd used to follow them across town. Po's
gaze ranged further.

In the shadow of the Gothic spire of a church across the
busy street, he spotted him. This man was of a similar build
to Po, tall and rangy rather than muscular, long-limbed
and almost casual in gait. He wore a baseball cap, but Po
could make out a short hairstyle beneath it and a weathered,
clean-shaven face dominated by sharp cheekbones and aqui-
line nose that belied his age. Po put him in his late thirties,
but guessed most of the latter two decades had been spent
under desert sun and mountain winds. The man made no
attempt to look directly at him, but there was a fractional tilt
of his head that gave away the lie: he was observing out of
the corner of his eye, while talking into a cell phone. All
around him pedestrians moved at pace, and by his cool
demeanour the man stood out from the crowd, the way a
prowling wolf would pretending to be part of a flock of milling
sheep. He moved towards a market at the perimeter of a park
adjacent to the church, still talking, and Po made himself a
bet it was to the scarred woman, his second.

A cab pulled in to the curb, and Tess assisted Stella in with
her luggage, the women still talking, but their words were lost
on him. His attention was on everything else. Across the street
he noted the sudden tightening of the man's features, and
though his lips couldn't be read, it was apparent his words
were clipped and urgent: commands. Tess waved off Stella's
cab, and it filtered into a row of slow-moving vehicles all
manoeuvring around a parked delivery truck, Stella peering
back at them in a mild state of shock. Incrementally Po turned
and saw the ginger man and Asian woman exit the hotel and

walk nonchalantly a few paces, until they were certain they went unnoticed when they hurried for a car parked at curbside. They clambered inside and the woman, who was driving, almost bullied their way into the traffic. Po was unconcerned. They were following Stella, yes, but it was unlikely they would even approach her given she'd have the protection of airport security around her when next she left the cab. Po flicked ash, drew on his cigarette; to anyone observing, they'd think he hadn't a care in the world.

The man opposite was talking into his cell again, and his slightly bent stance belied his status, where he nodded frequently, an unconscious reaction to taking orders. When the call ended, he straightened again, and made the fateful mistake of looking directly at his quarry, and was caught and held by Po's turquoise stare.

'I see you,' Po whispered under his breath, but enunciated the words clearly so there was no mistaking his meaning.

For a fraction of a second, the man looked as if he wanted to glance away, to feign disinterest, to continue the charade, but then he came to a decision and raised his head, and met Po's stare. He echoed Po's words back at him. Around both men the rush of humanity was never stilled, but they were frozen, locked together. It was as if they existed in a parallel dimension once removed from the real world, where only the other mattered. Tess's gentle tap on Po's arm broke the tether, and the noise and movement impeded on him again.

'Have you finished blackening your lungs?' she asked.

'You ex-smokers are always the most judgmental,' he replied, and took another defiant pull on his cigarette. Across the way, their observer had disappeared, retreating, Po supposed, into the park beyond the market stalls. It mattered not that he'd lost sight of him, because one thing Po was certain of was he'd see him again. In what manner he'd reappear was a matter of conjecture, but during their silent stare down there'd been a promise the meeting could be final.

His Mustang was parked on an adjacent street. Tess bustled to reach it without checking he followed. Behind her, Po walked with no sense of urgency. He was only partially alert to his surroundings, his thoughts also on self-analysis. His recent behaviour was out of character. He was used to conflict, and was unafraid of it when it raised its ugly head, but he'd never been a troublemaker. Yet he was spoiling for a fight, and he'd deliberately made an enemy of who could prove to be an otherwise decent person. The man he'd recently stared down had most assuredly served their country in an admirable way Po could never claim, and now continued to serve as a protector, working in the security industry. Intrinsically, the guy could be one of the good guys and Aaron Lacey the villain of the piece; and without clarifying the situation Po could have aligned himself on the wrong side.

No, he decided, *you've aligned with Tess, not Lacey.* He was there to support and protect her, and yet his challenging attitude could place her in unnecessary danger. His gaze lit on her as she led the way: Tess was strong, wilful and intelligent, and could be a fierce defender in her own right, the last to need mollycoddling and would probably elbow him in the ribs for thinking such chauvinist thoughts, but never would he apologize. Almost from the beginning, despite their differences, he'd known she was the one for him, but of late he'd begun wondering if her feelings for him had been dulled. He hadn't as yet gone down on one knee, but had suggested she make her move to his home a permanent one and that was tantamount to a proposal in his mind. Maybe he'd read too much into things, but recent comments she'd made about his habits had unexpectedly stung: the stuff about his grey hair, his wrinkles, the crack about him suffering a mid-life crisis – even his smoking too much – all hinted at a growing disillusionment in him. It had to be said, that was why he was spoiling for a fight; he had to prove his viability to her, and that he wasn't over the hill.

He grunted in mirth at the notion, but even it was tinged. Damn it if he wasn't apportioning his own insecurities on her. It wasn't Tess who was growing disillusioned with him, quite the opposite. *Face it*, he told himself, *age is creeping in, as it does for everyone, and Po Villere isn't immune, however hard you try to stave it off.*

Growing old, he reminded himself, isn't a guarantee for all, nor is it a privilege to be taken for granted. Inviting trouble could be the premature death of him, or worse the woman he doted upon. Immediately he dropped the maudlin attitude and was once again fully conscious of his surroundings.

Tess had to wait at the car for his arrival. He zapped the doors open from ten yards distant, but she didn't get in, only waited.

'What's wrong?' she asked.

'That's the thing,' he said, 'I haven't made up my mind yet.'

'Sometimes,' she replied, 'you're far too enigmatic to figure out. Other times you're less subtle than a redneck in a monster truck. What's troubling you?'

'Coming here might've been a mistake.'

She nodded, then instantly shrugged off her agreement. 'I'm here for Stella, and, I guess, for my mom. Whatever part Lacey plays in this isn't an issue for me right now, and can be dealt with when the time comes. First we find him.'

'It'd foolish to hang here . . .' His words were loaded with double meaning. 'For one thing, Holbrook hasn't pulled the surveillance teams.'

'The couple that followed Stella's cab: ginger guy, Asian girl? Yeah, I noticed them too.'

'There are others. A mixed-race woman with a scarred face –' he touched his cheek – 'and the guy from the van earlier.' He described the man in brief brush strokes only. 'There are probably more I haven't spotted yet.'

'Well, if that's the case, it's their time and manpower to waste if they want to follow us.'

'Where are we going next?' Po walked around the car to the driver's door.

'It occurred to me that Lacey must have had a place to stay here in Boston when he wasn't on duty. While you were smoking I asked Stella and she said he kept a room at a low-rent motel down near Mattapan Train Station. Yeah, if you recall, that's very close to where the gunshots were exchanged and the police suspect Ethan Prescott went into the water. I want to go take a look in his room, see if there's any clues to where he might have run.'

'Sounds like a plan. Let's go.'

As Po drove them away, Elite Custodian Services operatives Johnson and Nicholls followed in individual cars,
switching positions when required so neither vehicle was
constantly reflected in the Mustang's mirrors.

FIFTEEN

'Y'know, y'coulda saved some cash if you'd let me download those files direct to the Cloud,' Si Turpin
announced in a nasal whine. He placed three identical
thumb drives on the counter, then finally set down the original
given to him by Aaron Lacey, sheathed once more in plastic
and surrounded by rice.

'I prefer something tangible I can hold onto,' Aaron Lacey
said, and fluttered a dismissive hand overhead, 'not floating
around in the wild blue yonder. I want the info on 'em right
here when I want 'em.'

'That's the thing, Lace, you can access the Cloud anytime
you want, s'long as you have your phone with you.'

That was the problem: Lacey had ditched his phone, a
veritable tracking device that would lead his hunters to him.
He shoved the packaged original device away safely in a jacket
pocket, then reached across the counter and touched each of
the duplicates in turn. 'So each of these are copies of the
original, right? They can all be accessed from any computer?'

'Yah. I've bypassed the passwords and encryption of the
original. These're click and go, Lace. Even you should have
no problems bringing up the files.'

'Good.' He stuffed the three copies in his shirt pocket.
'That's great.' Lacey was the definition of 'anachronistic',
being an analogue man at odds with the digital age. He grasped
the basics, could use a smartphone to call his contacts, or
answer his emails, but beyond that he was largely lost; he had
an account with an online movie streaming company, which
had been set up for him so he only had to point and click his

TV zapper to bring up his favourites; and he'd a basic savvy of computers that allowed him to download files to a flash drive, but when it came to more intricate procedures he'd be outdone by any modern five-year-old child. His daughter Stella gifted him a 'smart' kettle last Christmas: it could be controlled by an app on his cell phone. The fault in Lacey's mind was it couldn't damn well fill itself from the faucet, so after doing so he still just hit the switch on its base, exactly the way he would any other mundane electrical appliance, which, to him, was far less effort than going through the controls on the app.

The trio of flash drives made a comfortable weight close to his heart. Fuck the Cloud! He feared that his account could be accessed by any of Elite's analysts, all of them more know-ledgeable at this 'hacking stuff' than even Si Turpin was. Si was almost as old as Lacey, and most of his computer banditry days were behind him; he'd wager that the younger MIT graduates at Elite would smirk at Si's inept and outmoded skills the way he did at Lacey's. One time he'd called a young analyst a 'hacker' in earshot, and the guy had put him straight: 'Hackings what you do with a blunt axe, what I do is more about finesse.'

Si Turpin lacked finesse. He was grubby and unkempt, clad in a stained New York Jets shirt and shapeless denims, and about one hundred pounds over his ideal weight, a flabby guy whose thighs rubbed together when he waddled around his workshop. Apparently he'd been a boxer in his youth, but not a very good one if his flattened nose was anything to judge by. The crushed nasal bridge gave the man his whining tone, and his nickname. His actual given name was Bruce, but everyone called him Si, shortened from 'sinus'. He wasn't the type Lacey would usually associate with, but the tech guy served a purpose, and he knew how to keep his mouth shut. They'd met back when Lacey investigated him for receiving stolen goods, a charge that could've easily stuck if they hadn't come to a certain accommodation. Although he was a person living in the past when it came to technological advances, Lacey had never been short on foresight: he knew that buying stolen property was the lesser of Si Turpin's crimes – through creating false identities the fat dude wasn't averse to ripping

off lonely spinsters of their savings – and he'd told Si he'd
keep his suspicions to himself in return for the occasional
favour. This was not the first time he'd pulled on their deal.

'How much do I owe you?' Lacey asked.

Si rubbed his squashed nose with the back of a hand,
weighing his options. 'You've never paid me before . . . not
for anythin'.'

Lacey tapped his breast pocket. 'These gotta cost you to
buy in.'

'Yeah, a coupla dollars each. I wouldn't insult you by askin'
for six bucks, Lace.'

'Good of you, Si, but what about your time?'

'I'd charge you by the hour, but not when I just left things
running and got about my own business.'

What Si was really saying was he hadn't poked around the
files he'd downloaded, but Lacey didn't believe him. He was
unconcerned that Si might have spotted the crucial evidence
that'd bring down Elite Custodian Services and one of their
most valued clients, because without knowing where to look
and cross-referencing facts hidden in different files there would
appear little untoward.

Lacey slapped down his final ten-dollar bill on the counter.
'Have a beer on me, at least. Oh –' he leaned closer, squinting
hard, so that Si was under no illusion of his seriousness –
'but don't go sayin' who your benefactor was, right? In fact,
if anyone comes around here askin' about me, you haven't
seen me in months. Understand?'

'A deal's a deal, Lace. It's been good for how many years
now?'

Lacey shrugged the question off. In truth, Si had no real
reason to uphold the bargain they'd made almost ten years
ago, because they'd long passed a point where any evidence
Lacey held about his scams could be used against him. Si
might be an immoral son of a bitch when it came to ripping
off lonely women, but he valued that bullshit about honour
among thieves. 'Y'know,' Lace said after a moment's consideration, 'I do trust you, Si. In fact, play your cards right, buddy,
and I might throw some more work your way, and you can
bet it's gonna be lucrative for the two of us.'

'How lucrative?' Avarice shone in the tech guy's eyes.

'Put it this way, you won't be buyin' a lousy beer on me, you'll be poppin' the cork on the best bottle of champagne. You interested?'

'Is this work illegal?'

'Would it bother you if it were?'

'Nah, man. Just makes it more interesting.'

Lacey winked, then backed out of the cramped workshop through a door so narrow Si must turn sideways to fit through. A short flight of metal steps, shielded from the elements by rusted tin sheets, disgorged him onto a greasy sidewalk on West 56th Street in Hell's Kitchen. He could smell spoiled garbage, raw fish from a nearby sushi restaurant and who knew what from the adjacent property, a sex den masquerading as a massage parlour. His mouth tightened in distaste. He wasn't sniffy about the services on offer behind the faded façade of the parlour, and had been a past customer of the establishment. However he didn't think his wounds would stand up to a rigorous "massage" just now, and besides he couldn't pay for a girl having handed Si the last of his cash.

The weight in his breast pocket was comforting, the one in his butt pocket not so much. He pulled out his billfold, flicked it open, in the hope that something miraculous had occurred where he'd missed a high denomination note tucked away in a corner. No such luck. He'd weighed Si's computer skills against the team at Elite, and the fat man had come up wanting: but had the younger wiz kids the ability to set up alerts on his bank account and credit cards? He was certain that they could, but was still of the opinion that if he used them at some random ATM in the sprawling city, they'd still have no way of pinpointing him to a location. Manhattan covered a big area in which to hide, but he couldn't be too careful. He decided to triangulate his use of the cards, but nowhere near where he currently lived. Which meant he'd a walk to the first ATM, so that it was a distance from Hell's Kitchen. His fucking knees! They were more troublesome than the gunshot wound and knife slash times ten over, but there was nothing for it. He dry swallowed some of the painkillers supplied to him by Doc Grover, determined that once he'd replenished his wallet he'd damn well take taxi rides to the next. If everything went to plan, he'd be back with Si Turpin soon enough, because he'd just thought of a way to set things in motion without compromising his whereabouts.

SIXTEEN

Tess and Po followed a scruffy, skeletal man past a row of sketchy rooms to the final one in a block of ten, which faced an identical row of shabby rooms across a cracked and pitted asphalt parking lot largely devoid of vehicles. It was mid-afternoon, and custom was slow, although come evening Tess would bet things got a bit wilder. She assumed that patrons of the Shady Pines motel generally rented rooms by the hour, but she'd learned from the concierge that Aaron Lacey had planned on using its less-than-salubrious facilities on a regular basis while working in Boston. He'd paid up a month ahead, so he still had a few days to run before his belongings would be bagged up and slung in the dumpster out back – after, the skeletal man didn't add, the choicest of morsels were picked through. It was standard practice, the concierge said, because some of their clients often took flight and never returned for their stuff. To which Po had muttered something about Norman Bates making similar claims, but the reference went right over the man's scabrous head.

While the guy hummed and cursed under his breath as he sorted through a set of keys, Tess and Po exchanged glances of disgust. Aaron Lacey obviously was not a man of fine taste. The motel was as dilapidated and unkempt as its concierge. Beyond Lacey's room was a small patch of untended lawn from which jutted the rotting stumps of felled trees. The pines in the motel's name were a distant memory and there was little by way of shade either; its owners should be reported for trade description infringements.

Before the correct key was found, Po leaned past the guy's shoulder and shoved two fingers against the door. It swung inward, and the concierge again cursed under his breath, this time at the splinters of wood, and the lock housing ripped from the frame, which lay on the carpet. 'That's coming out of your dad's breakages deposit,' he growled, as he peered closely at the damaged doorframe. 'You can tell him that from me.'

Tess didn't deign to reply. The man hadn't made a faux pas. She'd arrived at the concierge's desk on the pretence that she was Stella Dewildt, to collect the belongings of her father whose work had unexpectedly taken him away from Boston. She'd expected to be interrogated further, and asked for identification, but the guy seemed to care less who she was than he was happy that the room was free to rent again to customers willing to pay an inflated price for an hour of no-questions-asked privacy.

'I guess housekeeping don't make too many visits a week?' Po said.

'Only after guests check out, otherwise they might prove unwelcome distractions.' The concierge displayed the gaps in his brown teeth in a lurid grin, before he caught Tess's disapproving frown and muttered an apology. 'Not that I'm suggesting your dad got up to any of that funny business.'

'Do you know much about what he did here?' Tess countered.

The man swiped a palm over his mottled pate. 'I tend towards discretion, ma'am. It's none of my business what any of my guests do in their own time, so I tend not to inquire.'

'OK, bra, we'll take things from here.' Po moved the man aside with a hand on his shoulder.

'I should check the rest of the room; see that there's no other damage. That deposit might not cover everything—'

'Here.' Po palmed the man a twenty-dollar bill, that'd never go through the books. 'That should cover everythin', including your ongoing discretion. We'll let you know if anything's in need of repair after we've cleared out Mr Lacey's stuff. See you back at your desk.'

Po's tone gave the concierge no opening for argument, and to enforce his point Po blocked him from the room, holding him under a baleful stare. 'Sure, sure,' said the man, 'just pull the door to when you're done. Don't want any burglars finding their way in before that lock's fixed.'

It's a bit late for that, Tess thought, because she severely doubted Lacey had broken the door. With that in mind, she squeezed past Po and into a room as horrible as she'd expected. It looked as if it had last been decorated circa 1970, and each passing year could be read on the stained walls and carpet. The once white ceiling was the colour of caramel, as were the tops of the walls, testament to ten thousand cigarettes having been smoked without a window ever being cracked open. Po, she suspected, could get his next nicotine hit if he merely stepped inside and inhaled deeply: if he licked one of the disgusting walls he'd probably overdose! The bed was one of those coin-operated vibrating monstrosities she'd only ever seen in comedy movies: it was doubtful it still worked, otherwise it would have been adapted to take cash of larger denomination than quarters. The bedding had been pulled off it, and piled randomly at the foot of the slightly offset mattress. The curtains were shut. An outdated TV sat on a cabinet opposite the bed, and the only other items of furniture was an easy chair set cater-corner to the TV and a flimsy wardrobe with badly hung doors. She didn't need to check to assume that the TV showed pay-per-view movies of a certain ilk. A door led to a bathroom. That was all. Except for some items of clothing and papers strewn on the floor.

'The room's been ransacked,' Po said over her shoulder.

'Yeah, and we know who searched it.'

There was the slimmest of chances that a burglar had broken into Lacey's room, but her bet was on Elite. Whether the break in occurred prior to Lacey fleeing – and was the nucleus for him doing so – or after in search of him or something else was open to conjecture.

'So what now?' Po asked. He hadn't advanced beyond the threshold.

This was the point where the police should be informed. It was not proof that Elite had overstepped the law in their hunt for Lacey, but firmly suggested so and could be enough to initiate an investigation into his disappearance. If the connections were made between this break in, the reports of gunfire nearby and the subsequent discovery of Ethan Prescott's corpse, then the cops were duty bound to follow it up. In fact, as a licensed private investigator, Tess was also duty bound to report her suspicions to the police: withholding information about a crime was an offence for which she could be made to pay dearly. She should call it in. But what then? Earlier she'd cautioned Stella about making a similar move, suggesting that by involving the police they could push Lacey deeper into hiding, especially if he was treated as a suspect in Prescott's murder. She wasn't naïve; she fully believed that the man had died during an altercation with Lacey, but under what circumstances? The very fact that Holbrook and Glenn refused to admit knowledge of Prescott meant that they were hiding something – and it was probably their culpability in the incidents leading up to his death. Holbrook admitted Lacey's disappearance had caused them some embarrassment with a client, and that they'd like to resolve the matter 'without injury to our reputation'. If Elite operatives were responsible for ransacking the motel room, then it had to be for one of two reasons: first, they were seeking clues to where Lacey might have run; second, looking for the evidence that'd injure the company so it could be secured. If they'd discovered either, then why waste their resources surveilling Stella, and now them, in a hope of catching Lacey?

'I'm going to have a look around,' she announced.

'If I were you, I wouldn't touch a damn thing,' Po counselled, though it wasn't for fear of leaving behind incriminating fingerprints, 'not unless all your shots are up to date.'

He had a point, the room was crummy and who knew what kind of bugs lurked in the darkest corners, but largely Lacey's belongings looked well cared for and clean, before they'd been scattered. She moved among them, only paying attention to the paperwork and any items of clothing with pockets. She patted the latter down, before turning out each pocket where possible, but found nothing except for lint. She moved to the wardrobe and used her sleeve over her fingers to grasp a door handle and opened it. She found empty coat hangers, and a few random pieces of underwear and socks lying in

an untidy pile, through which it was apparent they'd already
been searched.

'You're taller than me,' she stated the obvious. 'Anything
on top?'

Po moved closer, could see only dust bunnies. 'Nothing.'

'Help me move it away from the wall, will you.'

Between them they jostled the wardrobe clear of the wall,
and Tess checked that nothing had been taped to the back.
Clear. She crouched and fed her hands under the bottom and
felt about but couldn't reach far. She wasn't prepared to crawl
on the musty carpet for a look underneath. 'You're going to
have to tip it for me.'

'Damn thing will fall apart.'

'I only need a quick look, just tip it far enough so I can see.'

Po did as asked, and the wardrobe creaked and swayed,
threatening to come apart, but Tess was quick about it. There
was nothing taped beneath, and she nodded for him to set it
upright again. This time Po jostled it back to its original position, while she paid attention to the TV and cabinet. She
visually checked behind the TV, and then under it, and finally
crouched to check the cabinet drawers. Inside one of them she
found a random stack of menus from various restaurants and
take-out joints, and a few business cards for local escorts and
prostitutes: she was tempted to retrieve the latter. Who knew
if Lacey had taken refuge with one of the working girls he'd
met here in Boston, but no, she doubted it. She left the cards
where they were. The cabinet stood on legs, so she'd no need
for Po's muscle to check under it, and there was enough of a
gap behind that she could see there was nothing hidden there.
The chair was quickly looked over and under. She turned to
the bed and grimaced.

Lacey was a divorced man with his own set of needs, but
she didn't want to think of him lying there with a succession
of prostitutes, let alone the countless other previous inhabitants of the room whose DNA was absorbed into the stained
mattress. Whoever had beaten her to the search had already
checked the bed, but she couldn't be neglectful. Cringing
inwardly she made a fingertip search of the mattress and
base, paying particular attention to the stitching, looking for

somewhere where an item could have been inserted inside it. Again there was room to check behind and under the bed, and it was enough to tell there was nothing hidden. She even checked the coin-operated mechanism, and found it out of order, the cash box removed, and nothing concealed in the void it had left.

Having gotten over his aversion and joined the search, Po reappeared from the bathroom. 'Nothing in there.'

'Did you check inside the cistern and behind the bath panel?'

Po said nothing and she shrugged an apology. Of course he'd checked the most obvious hiding places. She turned to rooting through the various pieces of paper deposited around the room, in particular on the look out for receipts, tickets or itineraries that could point towards any travel plans Lacey had made. That of course was expecting too much, and besides, it was obvious that he'd fled on a spur-of-the-moment decision not after carefully planning his route. She felt he hadn't returned to his room after what had occurred to send him running, but she'd be a fool if she neglected a full search.

She knelt over a picture frame lying face down on the carpet. Flipping it over, she yelped.

'What's up?' Po moved in.

The frame held a photograph of Stella Dewildt. She'd posed for the shot and was beautiful. It was unsurprising that a dad would keep a picture of his beloved daughter close, even when he was away from home, yet it wasn't the photo of Stella that'd shocked her, but another old Polaroid jammed into one corner of the frame. In the faded picture stood a smiling blond-haired woman and her equally fair daughter hugging her around her knees.

'Oh,' said Po, because even though they were around three decades older now, he recognized both mother and child.

Tess stared up at him, her mouth open in silent question.

Po vocalized it for her. 'What's Lacey doing with a photo of you and your mom?'

Any answer was unforthcoming: out in the parking lot a vehicle screeched to a halt, and in the next instant Po flattened her to the floor as gunfire blared and bullets ripped through the room.

SEVENTEEN

C hunks of plaster and glass rained, splinters of wood flew, and even the material of the curtains lifted and danced as each projectile tore through them. The only saving grace for Tess and Po was that the gunmen outside couldn't see them and had made the initial mistake of firing high. Tess was still kneeling, in a state of mild shock when Po leapt on top of her and squashed her beneath him. Immediately he enfolded her in his arms and rolled with her and jammed up against the base of the bed, covering her with his body.

More bullets punched inside, the noise horrendous. Outside somebody was using an assault rifle to disassemble the motel's structure, perhaps in the hope it would collapse on those inside, or by simply firing enough rounds at it he was guaranteed to hit his targets. The front wall was no barrier to the bullets. Unhindered they passed through the back walls too. In the bathroom, porcelain shattered and tinkled. The unsteady wardrobe collapsed, thundering across the floor. More bullets stitched a pattern across the bed's headboard, the angle of fire now descending. There was no aversion to handling the grubby mattress for Po now, who dragged it off its base, and used it to shield them from the bullets and flying debris. The mattress wouldn't absorb all the bullets, but was better than nothing.

He exchanged a look with Tess.

'We can't stay here,' he whispered.

Tess nodded in agreement.

Any second now the gunmen would advance on the room, and the open door and shattered window gave them a clean view of its interior. The mattress wouldn't save them from sustained or directed fire.

The assault rifle fell silent. A handgun continued to fire, the sharp cracks echoed by the sounds of impacts in the wall above them. Dust and fragments of plaster caught in their hair.

The handgun ceased fire. Both gunmen were reloading, and if they were experienced in weapons then it would take only seconds before they moved in to end things. Their window of opportunity was very slim.

Po rose up, pushing aside the mattress. He jabbed at the door, and Tess scrambled for it, throwing it to. It wouldn't stop a gunman entering, but might stall him a second or two, better still divert him. She grabbed the TV cabinet and shoved it and the television against the door: immediately she went to her hands and knees and propelled herself away. Bullets holed the door behind her at the same time as more glass clattered and the trailing curtain was yanked aside, and the barrel of a rifle poked inside: the shooter with the assault rifle was about to turn the interior into hell.

Two things happened simultaneously. From her low vantage, Tess grappled the barrel of the assault rifle, encumbering it with the tatty curtains, and Po emitted a wordless shout as he hefted up the easy chair and charged.

In response the gunman tried to wrench back control of his gun, to bring it to bear on Po, but Tess wasn't letting go. He depressed the trigger and even through the material shroud, the heat of the barrel scorched Tess's palms. She gritted her teeth and held on, even as the gun flashed and roared, almost blinding and deafening her. She fancied she felt the heat of each bullet searing the air directly above her head. Then the chair slammed into the man and both disappeared outside the window frame: both made heavy thumps as they hit the sidewalk. Tess still held onto the barrel gamely, eyes scrunched tight and ears ringing. She felt the gun pulled from her grasp, and knew to let go. Po tore it and the curtain fabric out of range of the man outside, and swung the stock to his shoulder.

The other attacker took a couple of wild shots, but he was hollering as he dumped his handgun and retreated, reluctant to continue the fight now he was outgunned. Another voice joined his – the downed gunman scrambling to escape and bleating in panic – and Po galvanized him by roaring a challenge. He was taking a reckless chance by showing himself in the window, let alone vaulting through the broken glass and menacing their assailants with the assault rifle from the side-walk. Both men, faces masked behind impromptu scarves wound around their lower features, had already leapt into their car, a beaten-up old Ford sans a license plate. Terrified, and believing Po was about to tear them to pieces, the driver threw the car into reverse and it powered backwards. Po pursued a few steps, never lowering the rifle. The Ford hit a skid, and the back end mounted the sidewalk before ramming into one of the rooms halfway down the block. Ducking in anti-cipation of a face full of lead, the driver threw the car forward again, driving blind, and left behind the rear fender as the car hurtled out of the lot.

Behind Po, Tess edged open the pocked door, and stared at his back. He still had not lowered the gun. His stance spoke of unrequited murderous intent.

'Po,' she cautioned, but he didn't relax until the roar of the escaping vehicle was lost among the distant city sounds. Only then did he drop the magazine and deport the unspent shell from the rifle. He placed the three component parts on the sidewalk and stepped away from them. Tess moved in and hugged him, barely able to breathe.

'You OK?' he whispered into her hair.

'Burned my hands, but I'm glad that's all.'

Po bled from a few insignificant scratches on his face and hands, but was fortunate not to have cut himself worse when jumping through the broken window. Hell, they were both fortunate they weren't full of bullet holes.

Some Shady Pines guests had vacated their rooms now the shooting had halted. They stood gawping from a safe distance. Two of them, a man and woman – quite possibly not spouses – had no intention of being caught up in the aftermath and ran to their car; they sped from the lot with almost as much urgency as the would-be killers a minute ago. The concierge, his bony limbs barely able to support him, staggered along the sidewalk towards Tess and Po, but faltered in his step and halted. He stared in abject dismay at the ruination of not one but two of his rooms. Slowly his vision focused on them, then dropped to where the disas-sembled gun lay among a scattering of broken glass shards, before it drifted to the upended easy chair lying five feet distant. 'What?' he croaked.

Tess and Po both turned and regarded the destruction.

The concierge stumbled forward another few steps. He blinked in confusion. 'What happened?'

'Would you believe you had a gas leak?' asked Po. 'That room was primed to blow.'

He received another series of rapid blinks in reply.

'We don't know what happened,' Tess tried. 'Do you have a problem with random drive-by shootings around here?'

'This had nothing to do with you guys?'

'Why would it? We only came to collect my dad's stuff.' Tess nodded towards the few visible items inside the room, all of them dusted with debris and glass or chewed by bullets. 'I think we can all agree that we'd be wasting our time now.'

The man's bottom lip worked in and out. His shoulders rose and fell. 'I . . . I'm going to have call the cops.' He ran his hands over the sparse hairs on his head, then, with not a little fear in his eyes, added, 'I'm also going to need you to wait here till they arrive.'

'That twenty bucks I gave you isn't enough to buy your discretion, then?' Po offered him a conciliatory grin.

When the concierge gawped at him in disbelief, Tess held up her hands and said they'd stay. In reality they'd no option but wait. Leaving the scene would only cause them undue trouble from the police, particularly when Tess had lied about her identity and reason for being there. If the cops tracked Stella to her home in New York, she could show she'd an alibi, but that would lead the cops to digging deeper into her dad's business. It was better that they come clean, she decided, albeit with a little obfuscation thrown in for good measure. Before the cops could respond, she ducked back inside the room, and retrieved the only item that had made an impact on her during the search. She tucked the faded Polaroid away in an inside pocket. If she and Po were subsequently searched she could argue the photo belonged to her, and anyone looking at the likenesses of the mother and her now grown-up daughter couldn't disagree.

When she stepped outside again, she trembled from top to toe. She was unsure if the response was to an adrenalin rush after surviving the recent life-or-death fight, or to finding the photo among Lacey's possessions. She knew for certain which of the two troubled her most, and wanted nothing more than to get things over with the cops so she could make an urgent call home. Barbara Grey had some tough questions to answer. The thing was, Tess wasn't sure how much she really wanted to ask them let alone hear her mom's explanation.

EIGHTEEN

From the safe distance of a parking lot adjacent to a family-run diner, Hayden James frowned as the Ford skidded out of the Shady Pines motel, forcing other road users to brake and swerve before it fishtailed away, gathering momentum and volume. He could understand the recklessness and urgency; even at a distance he could make out Nicolas Villere standing there like the hero of an eighties action movie with the stock of the liberated assault rifle to his shoulder, as if prepared to light the Ford up. Yes, he could understand why the shooters had fled the scene, but he was no less pissed at their ineptitude. But that was what came of subbing out a hit to street-level hoodlums. Shit, if he'd taken on the job, he'd have approached stealthily, entered through the open motel door and taken down both Villere and Grey with two controlled bursts before either knew he was there. Nerves, and maybe a little overzealousness for the task, had driven the shooters to bad judgment, and it had come back to bite them severely. They were lucky to have escaped with their lives: if the roles were different and he was the one left holding an M16 he'd have riddled the Ford and those inside and damn the consequences. Villere's reticence to shoot told him something else important about the man: he was a badass, quite possibly a killer, but not a cold-blooded murderer. He shelved away that nugget of information for the time when they would inevitably meet.

'Told you, Hayden, you should've let me do it,' said Megan. 'This has turned into a clusterfuck!'

'No. It's win-win whatever way we look at it,' Hayden replied, despite his own misgivings. It was well known in the criminal underworld that Villere had a beef with some of Boston's lowlifes. It was why Holbrook's contingency plan was to put out the word that Villere was in town and let Hayden's team lead those punks to him. 'Sadly the guys Villere's up against sent a couple of dipshits instead of doing the job themselves, but you have to admit . . . things turned out more spectacular that way. Villere and his woman live to fight another day, but you can bet most of *this day* is ruined for them. They're going to be stuck answering awkward questions for the foreseeable future.'

'Yeah, maybe so, Hayden, but how the hell does that help us . . . seeing as we hoped they'd lead us to Lace?'

'It frees us up to get on with our real job instead of playing at spies. I'm of the opinion he's in the wind. He isn't here in Boston anymore, and I think we're all wasting our time chasing each other's tails. Villere and Grey too, they aren't going to find him here, and I think they know it. At least by tying them up like this, we get a head start.'

'That's only helpful if you know where to go.'

'Where do you want to go?'

'Well, it's been obvious from the start he'd have run back to Manhattan.'

'Exactly.' Hayden smiled. 'A wounded animal will always try to crawl back to its den. I told this to Holbrook and Glenn, but they wanted to draw Stella into the hunt and use her as bait, and now she's gone back home. It's been a waste of our time and resources. We know that Mathers wounded Lace, and Prescott will have gotten his licks in too, so Lace will have needed patching up. He's practically a stranger to Boston, wouldn't have any contacts here to help stitch him back together, but that's different back in Manhattan. Christ, to hear him brag about it, just about every criminal and miscreant on the island owes him a favour.'

'So that's your plan, Hayden: speak with every piece of shit in New York till somebody gives him up?'

Hayden grunted, but she wasn't being serious, it was simply in her nature to be sarcastic. 'No, we start with clinics, and not those of the reputable kind.' Medics were bound by law to report patients bearing gunshot wounds to the police, so Lacey could not have sought assistance through ordinary avenues, but gone instead to one of the many quacks plying their trade to ne'er-do-wells and illegal immigrants. The list of back-alley physicians could be long but not exhaustive.

'He hasn't showed up at his apartment yet,' Megan pointed out – Elite had a surveillance team keeping a close watch on his and his daughter's registered addresses. 'D'you think he's lying up in some doctor's basement somewhere, too sick to do anything with the info he stole?'

'He's too much of a son of a bitch to die and do us all a favour.'

'He'll die, it's just a matter of when.' Megan focused on the distant trio of figures conversing amid the scene of recent destruction. 'Those two as well,' she said, ignoring the skinny-assed concierge.

Hayden held her in the corner of his vision. She wasn't only bitter; she was damn well vicious too. Saying that, many of those he'd worked alongside, in the military and later in the private security industry, had chosen their vocations because it suited their anti-social dispositions, and gave them outlets through which to vent steam and occasionally a murderous bent. Megan had always been hot-headed and talked a good fight, which, to be fair, she could also back up with actions, but she was beginning to get on his nerves. She'd fixated on avenging Ethan Prescott's death, but if she weren't careful it was going to get her killed, and maybe Hayden by association. Hadn't she just witnessed what Villere and his partner were capable of: shit, there weren't many unarmed people faced by overwhelming odds and heavy firepower who could come out of a fight unscathed. Hell, not only were they unscathed they'd gotten the upper hand.

The cops would be en route soon. They should make themselves scarce, and so too should Johnson and Nicholls who'd tracked the PIs to the motel, all the while updating Hayden and Holbrook via a conference call facility on their phones. Multitasking, Holbrook was on a separate line to a man named Bryce Chapel, who had a serious bone to pick with Nicolas Villere, and who'd outsourced his vengeance to his underlings. The Elite people had no way of knowing that Chapel was still in recovery from his last meeting with Nicolas Villere. He'd undergone surgery to mend the crushed vertebrae in his spine: he wasn't permanently crippled, but as yet was unfit for a fight. Despite his serious injuries, Chapel had come off better than the other professional hitter employed by Jimmy Hawkes to take down Villere; he'd only been struck once by the baseball bat Villere wielded, whereas his partner, Dylan Murphy, had been beaten like a drum at a heavy metal concert.

Megan patched in to Nicholls and then Johnson, both of whom were parked close by, and passed on Hayden's instructions to get away before a police cordon caught them in its snare. Hayden took one last look at Villere and Grey, and saw the woman emerge from the motel room, discreetly shoving something away in a pocket. Had she found something important they'd missed when he and Megan made a search of Lacey's belongings the day after he'd given them the slip?

If she had, he'd have to wait and discover what it was she'd retrieved another time. Holbrook's instructions were that his team took no part in the contingency plan, to ensure Elite stayed a few steps removed from the shooting, and that would include not being caught up as potential witnesses when the cops began casting their nets. He started the Chrysler and pulled out of the diner's lot, heading in the opposite direction that the Ford had disappeared in.

NINETEEN

Jerome 'Pinky' Leclerc was a busy man, but not too busy to drop everything concerned with the pursuit of illegal money when it came to assisting his closest friends. In fact, if he'd to be entirely truthful, he'd probably sounded like an excitable kid when replying to Po's request for help. His business centred on supply and demand, where he acted as a middleman in the receiving and redistribution of 'desirable commodities' – though never in narcotics or human flesh – everything from luxury motor vehicles, down to the varied contents of shipping containers, warehouses and trucks stripped. Pinky, of course, had his standards, and would never deal with street-level criminals, house burglars who'd boosted a TV, laptop computer or somebody's family heirlooms; he'd no time for bottom feeders who preyed on their neighbours and loved ones. Lately, and it was all down to previous times when he'd helped Po and Tess, he'd suffered a paradigm shift in his mindset, and some of the stuff he used to touch had also become anathema to him. There was a time when he'd dealt almost exclusively in the acquisition and supply of specially ordered weapons, but though he mostly respected the constitutional right to keep and bear arms granted by the Second Amendment, he'd been sickened by the rise in mass shootings currently blighting his beloved country. He hated to even contemplate the idea that the specialist weapons he'd distributed had fallen into the wrong hands and he'd helped facilitate the mass murder of innocents, but it was a firm and soul-wrenching possibility.

Pinky was black, gay, and, due to an imbalance in his endocrine system, he suffered an affliction that often caused a debilitating bloating of his lower body and limbs. To some prejudicial types, that made him a nigger, a queer and a fat cripple, any and each a target for their hatred. Pinky's rise to criminality had originally been in response to those offensive tags used to define him, his intention to rise above those who'd demean him, to make them so reliant on his favour they'd have to kiss his fat-queer-black-ass. Eventually he got so deep into the criminal world, he forgot those intentions. Money became his driving force, and with it came a lax attitude toward what he referred to as his clientele. For some years now he hadn't been selective when accepting orders, and through short-sightedness or in a blasé attitude to the consequences he'd supplied to isolationists, right-wing paramilitary groups, and apocalyptic-end-of-the-world nutjobs: many of them the very kind who'd despise him and wish him dead simply for what he was.

Well, no more.

In a fit of contempt he'd shut up shop when it came to supplying illegal weapons, despite the discord it had caused among those involved in his network, not to mention his workers reliant on him for their ill-gotten wages. He'd prover-bially thrown his toys out of the cot, and there was a scramble by those who'd pick them up. He was sick of the moaning and the bickering of those grasping after his scraps, so an unscheduled trip north was a very welcome distraction. Who could say: the short break could be the prompt he required to make a permanent one.

He took a Delta flight out of Baton Rouge, by way of a connection in Atlanta, to LaGuardia Airport, took a cab along the Grand Central Parkway and onto the island and rang the doorbell to Stella Dewildt's apartment before full dark had shrouded Manhattan.

'I'm Pinky, me,' he announced into her intercom, and raised his head to beam a toothsome grin at the security camera scrutinizing him from above. In whichever way Tess or Po had primed her, he obviously fit the bill, because Stella buzzed him inside without question, but an amused exclamation: 'Wow! You're exactly as I pictured you!'

TWENTY

Before the first responding patrol car arrived at the Shady Pines motel, Tess had put a contingency in place. She called Stella's phone just before she'd boarded her flight back to New York, instructing her that if she received contact from the Boston police she should confirm she'd asked Tess to be her agent in collecting her dad's belongings on her behalf. Keep things short, and say nothing about your dad being missing, Tess had added. When Stella worriedly asked what was going on, Tess played down the attack on her and Po.

She said the police had been summoned after a slight confrontation, and she must give a valid reason for being there, one
that shouldn't raise suspicion. If she was right, the attempt
on their lives had nothing to do with Elite, and everything to
do with Po's handling of the extortionist who'd dared to muscle
his way into Portland. There was little reason to think Stella
was in similar danger, so why concern her needlessly?

As it turned out, she needn't have placed the call, because
her explanation wasn't challenged and the detective questioning her made no move to follow up on it. Their alibi for
being at the scene was only questioned after the concierge
claimed Tess to be the daughter of his guest, causing some
confusion, but Tess kept a straight face and convinced the
detective that the man must have misheard when she announced
she was there on behalf of Stella Dewildt, and identified
herself as a private investigator from Maine working for Stella
on a private family matter. Her claim that she had no idea
why they'd been caught up in a gun battle did, however, raise
a sceptical eyebrow, but she stuck to her story, and in the end
gained kudos from the Boston PD for her bravery and quick
wits that had definitely helped save her and Po's lives, and
who knew how many more innocent victims the gunmen could
have turned on next.

A trip to the local police station was unavoidable. Po, who
had handled the assault rifle, was checked for gunshot residue
to show if he'd been an active participant in the gunfight. Once
he was confirmed innocent in that respect, his fingerprints and
DNA were taken to eliminate him from the forensic examin-
ation to follow. It helped that Po showed he'd disarmed the
assault rifle, and laid the parts out for collection by the police
on their arrival, not to mention a number of the witnesses at
the scene, the concierge included, stated that he'd never fired
the gun, even when being threatened by a man armed with a
pistol. Everything they'd done was deemed in self-defense.
Tess and Po gave descriptions of the gunmen and their vehicle
to the best of their recollection, and it matched with the statements from the others. The police treated them afterwards as
victims in the wrong place at the wrong time, caught up in
what was probably a case of mistaken identity. After that the

Shady Pines motel came under more scrutiny about the types of guests it accommodated. It wasn't the first time the local cops had responded to shootouts between opposing gang members on its premises. By the time they were released to go on about their business, it was too late to drive down to Manhattan, so they took a room at a more appealing Sheraton hotel with good access to Interstate 90, of a mind to get some rest before setting off the following morning.

Tess's first task was to soothe the burns on her hands. They were minor, and some cooling antiseptic cream calmed down the sting in her palms. She washed her face, then combed out the tiny slivers of glass and plaster caught in her hair, deciding to shower later once she was out of her dirty clothes. She went to check on Po, but was distracted by something else.

'I don't believe it,' she said, causing Po to lift his head off a pillow to appraise her. Fully clothed, he'd stretched out on the hotel bed while she'd pottered in the bathroom, and been dozing by the time she'd come out and made the casual glance at her tablet.

'Whassup?' His tongue was thick with sleep.

'This is totally unexpected,' she went on, which engendered a grunt of indifference from Po, who was in danger of sinking back into the plush pillow again: his own reaction to the previous near-death experience they'd gone through. She sat next to him, shook him by his shoulder. 'Here, take a look.'

He roused enough to prop himself on an elbow as she angled the screen towards him. He blinked to clear his vision, moved his head back an inch or two for clarity. Without his reading glasses, purposely left at home at Presumpscot Falls, she suspected, it was doubtful he could make out the screen, let alone the information displayed on it. 'It's the program I left running on Lacey's credit cards,' she explained, 'it's got a hit. In fact, that's an understatement. While we were dodging bullets, and then tied up at the police station, Lacey's been on a spending spree all over midtown Manhattan.' She took a closer look at the data. 'Correction: he hasn't been spending, he's been withdrawing cash from ATMs.'

'Liquidating and stockpiling,' Po suggested.

'Raising cash in order to run again?'

'That much cash won't take him far. I'd guess it's for somethin' else.'

A quick tally showed that between two credit cards, and his checking account, Lacey had collected two thousand dollars, each in smaller withdrawals of two and three hundred dollars per transaction, from no less than nine different locations.

'It's not an excessive amount,' Tess said, 'so why not just draw it from a smaller number of ATMs?'

'Maybe that's his limit on each account . . .' Po shook his head. Lacey had put in more than twenty-five years with the NYPD, his pension should be good, and not to mention the pay he'd been earning from Elite before his sudden flight. When he was in Boston, if the Shady Pines motel was anything to judge by, he wasn't extravagant in his spending. Therefore, he shouldn't be short of a dime. 'No. This is more like obfuscation.'

Po was right, Tess thought. He'd visited a number of different ATMs spread across a wide area so his actual location couldn't easily be determined. She mirrored the tablets screen to her smart phone, and on the larger device switched to a mapping app. Lacey had visited machines throughout midtown Manhattan ranging between Eighth Avenue and Park Avenue, north as far as Central Park and south to a bank in the shadow of the iconic Flatiron building on 23rd Street. If she roughly estimated a central point as Lacey's hiding place, she'd place him within a few blocks of the intersection of Sixth Avenue and West 42nd Street, but she wasn't fooled: Lacey wasn't an idiot, and knew his accounts were probably being monitored, so had laid a false trail.

Po had come round enough to focus on the map. 'Where'd he first start off?'

'Near the corner of Eighth and 56th.' For clarity Tess pointed at a pin marked on the map. 'Wells Fargo Bank.'

'And the final one?'

'Here at Seventh and West 26th.'

'And the last three withdrawals were all in multiples of three-hundred bucks, before that all were two hundred?'

'Which suggests he was tiring of the charade,' said Tess, 'so sped up the process.'

'Or he was getting physically tired. He was on foot, I'd assume, but didn't Stella tell you he suffers from arthritic knees these days?'

Smiling at his astuteness, she nudged him gently in affection. 'You've just earned another merit badge on your way to becoming a fully-fledged detective, fella.'

Without saying so, Po had more or less pointed out that Lacey had cut a corner to make his way back towards his starting point. Tired, hurting, he'd had enough of plodding around Manhattan and wanted only to get back to wherever he was laying his head. She touched the map again, this time outside of the circuit of ATMs in the region of Hell's Kitchen.

'We could be wrong,' Po said, playing devil's advocate, 'it could be a bluff and he only wants us to think that's where he's hiding . . .'

'Or a double bluff and that's exactly where he is,' Tess finished for him.

Po swung his feet off the bed, and stood, stretching and yawning. 'So I guess we should get moving. I can drive us there in a few hours.'

She was also keen to get moving, but they must be pragmatic. 'We need to get cleaned up, and then rest. There's nothing we can do if we arrive in Manhattan in the early hours we can't do tomorrow morning.'

'It's the city that never sleeps, ain't it?'

'That may be so, but *we* need to sleep.' She gently patted his cheek, felt the rasp of whiskers under her tender palm. Dust clung to his hair, and tiny spots of coagulated blood marked where breaking glass had pricked him. 'You need to sleep. Why don't you shower, have a shave, and then get your head down for a few hours? We can leave after.'

He watched her in that enigmatic way that had once perturbed her, but had come to recognize as him searching his own soul rather than hers.

'What?' she prompted.

'I've been a damn fool.'

Confused, she only waited.

'Back there,' he said, 'at the motel, I coulda gotten you killed.'

She shook her head. 'You saved my life, Po,' she corrected, 'when you jumped on me like that, otherwise I'd have been shot.'

'That's beside the point. I shouldn't have put you in danger in the first place. You know who those guys were, and why they were there. They were after me, because of my beef with Chapel and Murphy, and I ain't gonna lie . . . I expected them to come. I *wanted* them to come, because I had a point to prove. Not to them, to . . . well, to myself. My damn insecurities coulda gotten you killed.'

'Wow, I'm surprised.'

'That I don't want you killed?'

'No, that you feel insecure. Po, you're about the most confident, self-assured person I've ever met in my life. What have you got to be insecure about?'

He grunted, stuck for words.

'Oh, I get it.' She touched his cheek again, allowed her fingertips to linger. 'When you said you'd a point to prove, you really meant you'd to prove it to *me*?'

He rolled his neck, said nothing. He had no wish to state the obvious. He turned away, hooking his thumbs in his belt.

'What do you need to prove?' she asked.

He didn't look at her, perhaps realizing how pathetic his words sounded. 'I'm not an old coot, Tess; I'm not over the hill yet. I'm older than you are, yeah, but—'

'You're not too old for me? You really believe that's what I think?'

He glanced at her, his lips writhing, but then he looked away, embarrassed to admit the truth.

'This is about me moving in with you—'

'Or *not* moving in, for that matter.'

She thought she'd explained her reticence to living with him full time at his ranch, thought he understood it had nothing to do with a lack of love for him, but the baggage she carried from her previous engagement to Jim Neely. Her need to prove to herself that she was capable of independence without any man holding her hand, to succeed in a career where she'd only been met with doubt before . . . and, well, she also needed to prove it to her mom.

'Po . . .' She didn't know what to say to ease his concern.

Abruptly, he changed the direction they were taking. 'I just don't think hangin' around Boston much longer is a good idea. After they failed to kill me earlier, what's to stop Bishop or Murphy trying again? I don't want you caught up in my bullshit a second time.'

She allowed him his out. The last thing she wanted was to contemplate their relationship just then, when to her she already believed it was solid. 'Maybe you're right,' she conceded and moved to hug him. 'Unlike at that other cesspit, this hotel room's far too lovely to get shot up. However –' she dusted down his collar – 'I still think we could both do with freshening up. Go on. You take the shower first, there's something I've got to do before it gets too late.'

He knew to what she referred. Neither of them had mentioned it since she discovered the decades-old photograph in Lacey's motel room, but its presence there had lingered in her thoughts, and become more troubling than being shot at again.

'I'll give you some privacy. Tell your mom "hi" from me,' Po said, kissed her briefly and then closed the bathroom door between them.

She waited until she heard the shower at full blast before she picked up her cell phone, closed down the search app and brought up her mom's number. Her finger hovered over the call icon. Did she really want to know the truth? Of course, she did. She was a detective, and to her a puzzle was to be solved, a mystery to be determined, even if she didn't like what she found. She must ask her mother the most difficult of questions . . . despite how her answers might change everything.

From her inside pocket she took the Polaroid. She stared at her mom's face, then at her own. She wondered whom the photographer was, whom it was they both smiled at. Face flushing red, feeling sick with anxiety, and trembling with another wave of adrenalin, she pressed the call button.

TWENTY-ONE

'Mom,' Tess said, worried how she should pose the most difficult question ever, 'there's something very important I need to ask you, and you're not going to like answering.'

Her mother had apparently anticipated her call, spending the evening working herself up. She was more abrasive than usual. 'I think you've something to answer to first, young lady: why you've hared off to Boston without a care for me!'

'Don't pretend you're surprised.'

'Oh, I'm not. I'm used to your wilfulness, but that isn't to say I'm disappointed. Damn it, I'm more than disappointed, I'm furious!'

Her anger was a defensive mechanism, and wasn't unexpected, even if Tess had hoped for a calmer, more heartfelt conversation.

'I suppose I should've expected something like this when you expressly went against my wishes,' Barbara went on. 'I asked you not to take on this job, Teresa, and now look at where it's got us.'

'I don't want us to argue.'

'Oh, don't you? Well that's good. You can listen to me instead, and maybe in future you'll—'

'Mom,' Tess cut in. 'Please stop right there.'

'I certainly will not stop! I knew no good could come of you contacting Estelle. Why you took it on your back to run off to Boston, even when I asked you not to, only shows you don't care for my feelings! I told you to decline the job, to put Estelle in contact with a local detective, but as usual you totally ignored me!' Barbara had grown strident, her response to panic. 'Why do you never do as I ask, Teresa?'

'You never ask, Mom, you only tell.'

'Don't be so damn facetious.'

'I'm not, Mom, only trying to show you the awkward

position you always put me in. Your exact words were "I don't want you taking this case, but the final decision's yours". In other words, I've to do as you say or you won't be pleased. I'm damned if I do and damned if I don't.'

'I'm not pleased.'

'Well, I'm sorry, but that's nothing new.'

'I only want what's best for you, Teresa.'

'No, Mom, you want what's best for you.'

'What's best for me is keeping you safe. Look at what happened when you joined the sheriff's department against my wishes: you were almost killed!'

Her hand had almost been severed, and she could have died within minutes had a colleague not been there to shoot her knife-wielding attacker and staunch her blood. Tess couldn't argue Barbara's point. Her injury was a contentious issue that had often peppered their arguments where Barbara never accepted her assertion that she, or anyone else, could be killed crossing a street. Besides, she hadn't called her mom for another round in their ongoing battle.

She took a deep breath, controlled her next delivery.

'Mom, you claim you want to keep me safe, and I do believe you. It's why you were conflicted when Stella contacted you out of the blue, right? You didn't want me digging too deep because you feared I'd learn something that would hurt me.' Tess halted, allowing the silence to do its work, hoping her mother would fill it. All she heard was Barbara's ragged breathing.

Tess was pacing the hotel room, back and forth with the cell phone clamped to her ear, conscious of the sound of streaming water from the bathroom: Po couldn't stay under the shower forever. She sat on the far side of the bed, held the phone under her chin to ask what was troubling her most. 'Did you cheat on Dad?'

'I *loved* your father.'

'That isn't what I asked, Mom. I asked if you cheated on him.'

'How could you even think that?' Sadly, her mother's tone was too defensive.

'Memories from when I was a child,' Tess replied. 'They

are from Granddad's funeral. I remember Dad being angry with Aaron Lacey at the graveside, and telling him to stay away from *his* family.'

'And *that* makes you think I was having an affair with Aaron?' Barbara coughed in scorn, but again it sounded faked.

'I remember how he reacted when Dad told Aaron he was unwelcome there; Aaron looked at you to . . . I don't know . . . to stand up for him.'

'He was your granddad's patrol partner. Aaron had a right to be there, to pay his respects.'

'Not at the expense of upsetting my dad. It was obvious, even to me as a child, that he didn't want Aaron anywhere near. I remember almost being yanked out of Aaron's arms by my dad. He was seething with anger, and at first I thought he was angry with me.'

'That's the thing you're missing, Teresa. You were only a little girl. You're recalling events through a little girl's eyes but juxtaposing an adult's take on those memories now.'

'My most vivid earliest memories are those of trauma. I remember when I first fell off a swing and broke my collarbone, and when Alex threw a Frisbee at me and cut my forehead; I remember trapping my fingers in the car door that time we vacationed at Cape Cod; and I remember dad yanking me out of Aaron Lacey's arms with such force and anger that I cried for an hour after.'

'You make it sound as if you had a terrible childhood.'

'That's not what I mean. I do have happy memories too, but they're fuzzier; they didn't make such a lasting impression on me. As humans we're wired-up to remember the things that hurt us most, so that we don't repeat our mistakes; it's how we learn.'

'Spare me the psychology lesson, Teresa.'

'Mom, stop dodging the question. Just tell me the truth. I need to know if you ever cheated with Aaron Lacey.'

'No!' Barbara's reply rang sharp. 'Is that good enough for you, or are you going to continue making these hurtful accusations?'

'Did something else happen between you then? Is that it?

Was he interested in you even if you never reciprocated his advances?'

'He was your granddad's patrol partner,' Barbara stated, 'and a friend of the family. We often had occasion where we met, but no, there was nothing *funny* going on. By God, Teresa, how on earth did you get the idea I cheated on your dad?'

'If you didn't have a thing with him, can you explain why Aaron should keep a photograph of you next to his bed? You never . . . you know, after my dad died . . .'

'I have not laid eyes on Aaron, as I told you before, since we moved from New York. And, no, I cannot, and will not even try to, explain why he'd have a photo of me. To be quite honest, Teresa, I'm tired of defending myself, and am not prepared to do so any longer. I'll speak with you when you're home, and you'd best get these silly notions out of your head before I see you.'

Barbara canceled the call.

Tess dropped the phone and cupped her face in her palms.

If she could weep, she would have, but no tears would come. Her mind and heart felt equally hollow.

Po exited the bathroom, came round the bed and sat alongside her. His bare arm slipped around her shoulders. He waited in respectful silence until she was ready. Finally she raised her face an inch, took his fingers in her right hand and gave them a gentle squeeze.

'I guess that didn't go so well?' he said.

'I'd say it went *horribly right*, and I wish to God it hadn't.'

'Tell me.'

'I've interviewed enough people in my time to tell when they're lying. My mom was lying through her teeth.'

'I wasn't tryin' to eavesdrop, but, well, you got kinda riled up, and these hotel walls are thin. Are you sayin' that your mom and Lacey did have an affair?'

'Yes. I don't believe my mother's lies, any more than I did Holbrook's earlier.' Her voice grew reed thin. 'What if . . . I don't even want to think about it, but what if I've been lied to all my life?'

'In what way?'

'Po, you know what I'm saying.'

His embrace tightened around her shoulder. 'I don't see it, Tess. You and your brothers, you're the spitting image of each other.'

'Alex and I look alike; we both have our mom's colouring. But Alex also looks like my dad, he's got his height and build, his mannerisms, and Michael Jnr is Dad's mirror image. But I don't recognize anything of my father when I look in a mirror. With her hair dyed blond these days, I see more of me in Stella than in either of my brothers.'

'You're not Aaron Lacey's daughter. Get that idea outta your head.'

'That's the thing, Po, I'm finding it difficult.' She showed him the Polaroid, even as she once again replayed the events at the graveside through her mind, where it was almost as if she was a possession being fought over. 'Lacey didn't only keep a picture of my mom close to hand, I'm in it too.'

TWENTY-TWO

With a thick wad of bills in his pocket, Lacey returned home to his apartment, too tired to conduct counter surveillance techniques. He was under no illusion: using his cards to withdraw cash was about the most stupid thing he could do, but there was no other option. If he'd been ten years younger and fitter, and not carrying wounds, he might have taken a different approach to refilling his wallet. Back in the day, there were times when he'd rolled drug dealers for some of their takings rather than arrest them, and not a damn one of them had dared make a complaint when they'd have been incriminating themselves. He was never greedy, he only skimmed a wedge off the top and let them keep their product, but it only took a few shakedowns per week to earn him some walking round money his wife was unaware of, or to keep up the rent on his hidey-hole. Back then he'd been extremely careful about keeping his lair a secret, and he was even more so now he was in real danger. But after tramping all over

Midtown, spreading his ATM visits wide enough that he could be hiding anywhere on the island, he was fit to drop and wanted only to lie down and take the weight off his knees. Elite's analysts might be able to monitor his credit card usage, but they weren't the NSA. Even if they were on to him right that minute, analyzing where he'd used the cards, they didn't have a fucking spy satellite overhead to track him home. They'd have to mobilize their assets, put boots on the ground, and that would take time. He was confident he needn't have to worry about a team running him down this evening, and it'd be some time after before they looked for him on his side of town. By then, his get-rich plan would be in play, and he'd be long gone.

As he'd walked he'd chugged down more of the pills given to him by Doc Grover, but their painkilling efficiency didn't equal the exertion, and the ache in his knees had become a red haze of agony spreading from his legs to his throbbing skull. He was hot too and sweating, and wasn't fully sure if that was through effort alone, but more to do with a fever. The wounds in his side were tight and itchy, and damp: he was bleeding again.

Doc Grover had warned him about overexertion, but people who wanted his head weren't currently hunting Grover, and neither had the doc been down to the last few brown cents in his pocket. His energy output would be tested again this evening, because he fully intended a second visit to Si Turpin's workshop. Now he had some considerable green in his wallet, he felt he could entice the hacker to join him in his blackmail plot better than the promise of decent alcohol could.

At the same convenience store as before, he bit down on his discomfort while he bought supplies, as he hadn't consumed anything substantial since the glugs of Mountain Dew earlier. A good meal and a hot drink inside him and he would feel much better for the trek back to Turpin's place. Leaving the store, he made a half-assed attempt at covering his tracks again, completing a shambling circuit of the block, before dipping into the stairwell of his building and trudging upstairs to his apartment. He set his groceries down and collapsed on his couch. That bells-and-whistles smart kettle Stella bought him would have come in handy just then, because he'd barely the energy to rise again and get some water boiling, but it was gathering dust over at his official family home. He'd fill the plastic kettle he kept here in a minute, once he'd rested his sore knees, and put something in the microwave to heat up, he decided, and instantly fell asleep, his snores rattling the windows in their frames.

While he slept in blissful ignorance, other players in his story moved towards him, Tess and Po by road, Hayden James and his team by air, following separate trails of breadcrumbs, all of whom were more than a step further ahead than he could have known and, worse still, Lacey should have promised more than champagne to a guy who couldn't tolerate the stuff.

TWENTY-THREE

It was one thing playing nice to Aaron Lacey's face, treating him as if they were old buddies, but that couldn't be further from the truth. Lacey's relationship to Si Turpin was based on a debt Si was never allowed to pay off. He'd been kept on the bastard's leash so he could be snapped to attention whenever Lacey called. They acted pleasant in each other's company, but Si was under no illusion: the ex-cop thought he was a dirt bag and he'd be tossed aside when he was of no further use. Yeah, both of them smiled and played nice, but each thought the other was shit. He didn't buy Lacey's parting promise of throwing more work his way, none that'd prove lucrative to him at any rate. For sure, Lacey's fingers were dug deep in somebody else's pie, but Si wouldn't get as much as a lick of the ex-cop's dirty fingers afterward. Lacey would screw him on the deal, squirreling away any percentage of an illegal take promised to Si, and how could he ever complain?

Allegedly Lacey still held onto historical evidence of Si's

illegal activities, but so fucking what! They were so dated most of the old spinsters he'd scammed of their savings were probably dead, or their memories too scrambled in their dotage to call as witnesses if ever a case was brought against him. When he thought about it, any leverage Lacey held had lost its efficacy when he'd retired from the NYPD. He bet if he'd called his bluff before this, Lacey would've had no option but cut his losses, walk away and never darken his workshop again. He didn't owe Lacey any loyalty, and certainly no respect. In fact, Lacey was due a fucking-over for the way he'd squeezed Si's balls all these years.

Years ago, Lacey must have engaged another hacker to gather the info he'd subsequently used to blackmail Si into being his tech bitch, because the fucker didn't have a clue when it came to technology. So, when he'd shown up, clutching that thumb drive as if it were a winning Lotto ticket, Si had instantly figured there was something on it he intended using to blackmail somebody else. The stupid analogue dinosaur had no idea that it was as easy for Si to make himself a copy of the files as it was to download onto those cheap-assed flash drives he'd handed over. He'd barely been able to contain a smile of triumph when he lied to Lacey about removing the passwords and encryption from his copies. In fact he'd inserted into each, as well as the original, a self-destruct virus that'd corrupt the data the instant they were slotted into any device.

After Lacey limped off down his stairs, Si had instantly shut up shop for the day, and brought up the files ripped from the original flash drive. When Lacey, or whoever he'd coerced into helping him, downloaded the raw data, they hadn't been selective; they'd just copied everything held on a particular server. Whatever there was of importance was hidden among reams of irrelevant crap he had to sift through. There were audio and video files, and also data logs recording the relevant dates, times and duration of each, plus serial numbers cross-referencing to further connected files, some of them recording subsequent follow-up communications.

In the dimness of his workshop, Si scrutinized various files, growing quickly frustrated. He felt like a voyeur with a fetish for the mundane – until he stumbled over a certain audio file bearing a person's name that tugged at him in familiarity. Initially he thought the name couldn't be that of the man he was thinking of, that it was simply a coincidence. But these files had been stolen from a security consultancy that probably had equally important clients on their list.

Not a little star-struck, his nerves trembling throughout his body, Si adjusted his earphones and turned up the volume, and heard the first bleats of a Hollywood superstar better known for on-screen tough-guy roles. At first Si struggled to associate the panic-stricken squawk with the testosterone-fuelled on-screen persona he'd grown used to from a series of back-to-back action blockbusters, but . . . Holy shit! That *was* A-list movie star Jon Cutter, begging some guy called Holbrook to collectively save his career, his reputation and his ass from serious jail time!

He grew jittery as he listened to the call, and was sick with trepidation by the time it ended. That, of course, didn't stop him from sorting through the cross-referenced files and pulling them all together in one place. He clicked on a video file, but dithered over letting it play. Once seen, it couldn't be unseen. But Si Turpin was a guy who'd witnessed the worst that the Internet could offer, and he couldn't halt the impulse. He hit play . . . and afterwards knew he'd never be able to enjoy a Jon Cutter movie again, not now that his heroic status was tarnished. Fuck tarnished! His image had been painted pitch black.

Si checked the date embedded in the file: the damming video had been recorded on the cusp of Cutter's rise to superstardom. Had its contents been leaked, he'd have been destroyed, and so too would have the multi-billion dollar machine he'd subsequently grown into. That's where Elite Custodian Services had stepped in.

Ben Holbrook had made the threat to Cutter disappear, but it was at a heavy cost. A 'consultancy retainer' amounting to ten percent of Cutter's gross income between the conspirators, and Elite had grown wealthy as Cutter's star power exploded into supernova.

Si's left arm tingled. There was a sharp constriction of his chest. His heart fluttered. For years he'd been warned to lose a few dozen pounds, to avert the cardiac arrest written in his future, but his physiological reaction wasn't to a failing heart or blocked artery, it was fear. The magnitude of what he'd learned was alarming, but also . . . exhilarating. There was nothing that excited Si Turpin more than being the recipient of a windfall that'd change his miserable life. Earlier he'd sneered at the thought of Lacey holding a winning Lotto ticket, but – by fuck! – Si had just snatched the winnings out of the bastard's dirty fingers.

That was, supposing, Si had the courage to make an enemy of the ex-cop. To hell with Lacey! If Si played things right, he could disappear to somewhere hot, where he could laze away his days sipping ice-cold mojitos – Lacey could shove his champagne up his ass – out of reach of anything Lacey could do or say to hurt him in revenge. The question was how to work this to his advantage?

Some of the newspapers or news syndicates would pay dearly to break this story, but that'd mean blowing the story worldwide, and that did not protect Si's anonymity: he wanted to spend his new wealth without the intrusion of cameras and journalists. He could go direct to source and blackmail the shit out of Jon Cutter, but who knew the kind of complication that might bring down on him. No, his best move here was to go back to source: he'd bet Ben Holbrook would pay a finder's fee to anyone who could save his company from burning by returning the incendiary evidence.

He considered avenues through which he'd make first contact; an email from an anonymous Hotmail account; an encrypted voicemail message; but decided those methods were too slow for his timetable. He had to strike before Aaron Lacey got his dumb ass together and set to extorting Elite. From the clutter he kept in his workshop he selected a burner phone, an old cheap model cell, certain that Ben Holbrook would welcome a personal call from one who'd end his troubles at a bargain price.

TWENTY-FOUR

'Come here and show me some love, Pretty Tess. It has been far too long!'

Pinky Leclerc enfolded her in an embrace, squashing her against him as he danced in place. It was his manner to be magnanimous with his affection. Tess hugged him in return, but even she could sense the tenseness in her frame. It had been too long since last she'd seen Pinky, and there was a part of her that was overjoyed by his presence, but the recent discussion with her mom played heavily on her. She'd yet to meet Stella's smile of greeting, for fear she saw too much of herself smiling back. Pinky set her down, and held her under his gaze. He cocked his head to one side.

'What's wrong, you?' he mildly scolded. 'You look like you've lost ten bucks and found a nickel, instead of the ton of gold that is Pinky, me!'

She forced him a smile. 'It's wonderful to see you, Pinky. It's not you; I'm just extremely tired. It's been a couple of trying days.'

'I blame that brutish oaf Nicolas, he's no good for you, him. I beg you again, leave him and run away with Pinky. I know how to treat a lady, me.'

'I might need readin' glasses but there's nothin' wrong with my ears,' Po announced as he carried in their overnight bags. 'I hope you haven't been flirtin' with Stella like that since you arrived; I'm not sure her husband will be as under-standing as me.'

'I'm always the model of a gentleman, me,' Pinky claimed, before aiming a grandiose wink at Stella, 'unless you fancy an affair with a bad boy, eh? Haha!'

Stella's chuckle and corresponding wink said Pinky's flam-boyant and shameless manner had ingratiated him with her – as Tess promised it would. Pinky grinned, and had Po in a hug before he could even set down their bags.

'Thanks for comin', bra,' said Po the second they parted.

'Hey, try keeping me away, you. You now there's nothing more I love than the company of beautiful women . . . and one boorish Cajun in particular.'

'Any trouble?' Po asked.

'Only if you count finishing the incredible meal my lovely hostess cooked me; y'know, I'm watching that one, Nicolas, I'm sure Stella's fattening me up for the kill.' He cupped his belly and jiggled it up and down for effect.

Po appraised him. 'You've lost weight.'

'Have not.'

'Have so.' Po studied him squarely. 'You're looking a little pale, you haven't been overdoin' things lately?'

'Nicolas, I'm fat as a bull and black as night; you need to throw away those glasses and wear a stronger prescription, my friend.'

Their friendly jibes would sound insulting to anyone who didn't know them, but Tess was used to their ways. Except this time she wasn't fully convinced that Po was joking. Pinky's features looked slightly drawn, with spots of grey in the hollows of his cheeks and there was less animation in his brown eyes than usual. She'd say something was troubling him and had been for a while. Ordinarily she'd try to get to the bottom of it, to help take the weight off his mind and alleviate his concern, but her own thoughts sapped her energy. She wanted only to sleep, hoping that when she woke again her mom's lies could be consigned as figments of a lucid and discomfiting dream. After speaking with her on the phone the notion of resting was impossible, and Po's suggestion of immediately driving down to Manhattan had seemed like a better idea than before; it had given her time to mull things over as he concentrated on the roads: her mind had got to a point where darkness settled in at the edges, but it hadn't helped blunt the disbelief or, yes, the disappointment, at what she'd concluded about her mom's faithlessness to her dad. If she rested now, she expected any sleep would be fraught with similar disturbing thoughts.

Stella's Upper East Side apartment was spacious and sumptuously dressed. Although she and Paul Dewildt were yet to start a family they'd planned in advance, despite the extortionate mortgage rates in their neighbourhood, so there was ample room to accommodate her extra guests. It was past two a.m. but Stella wasn't put out, and gladly set about preparing a light supper for them, while Po updated her and Pinky about the goings on in Boston, and the hits Tess had gotten on Lacey's ATM usage. It went without saying that Elite's operatives wouldn't be far behind them, if not already there.

'I've scouted the block a couple of times and seen nothing suspicious, but that isn't to say we aren't being spied on,' Pinky reported, the seriousness of the situation taking the edge off his strange speech pattern.

'I didn't spot anyone when we arrived,' said Po. For Pinky's benefit, he described the tall operative who'd returned his stare from Copley Square in Boston, the scarred woman, the ginger-haired man and the Asian woman. 'There were others with them in Boston, and I'd bet there was a team already on the ground here in New York.'

'Well, if they're here, they're keeping their distance for now,' said Pinky.

Stella shook her head in disbelief that she'd become the target of a concerted surveillance operation. 'What is it my dad's supposed to have done?' she asked, her question not as rhetorical as it sounded. Tess had explained Holbrook's assertion Lacey could cause embarrassment to Elite and one of its clients, but beyond that the clues to the extent of his supposed wrongdoing were few and far between. Neither Tess, or Po judging by the way he crinkled his eyes, was about to suggest her father could be responsible for smashing Ethan Prescott's skull in, but then it was Stella who'd originally raised his name.

Tess rubbed her face, enlivening it as best she could. 'My guess is he's in possession of some information that could harm this client, and the repercussions could also prove harmful to Elite. Before this, before he went missing, how often were you in contact with your dad?'

'Rarely.' Stella was embarrassed by the confession, and quickly explained. 'That wasn't because of me, I often reached out. But, well, my dad's very much about himself. Not exactly selfish or self-centred, just, I don't know, he's a bit detached. We'd occasionally speak on the phone, but rarely in person. I'd invite him over for dinner, he'd politely decline, and then turn my offer around telling me not to worry, that he's still capable of feeding himself without my mom being there. If you ask me, he's going through a bit of an identity crisis, and wants to prove he's capable of independence.'

Tess and Po exchanged a glimpse, each for personal reasons.

'I know little about him as a person . . .' Tess paused, changed her emphasis, '. . . as a dad and husband.'

'All I can say is he was good with me, always loved me, but even when I was growing up I remember he was slightly aloof with my mom. We lived in the same house, but it was as if they coexisted at a different beat. Dad's shift patterns didn't help, but it was as if they lived separate lives that rarely converged. I'm not naïve, even as a kid I was aware that they loved each other but in their own way – kind of a marriage of convenience because they shared a child – but they lacked affection for each other, and I know they found intimacy elsewhere, especially my dad. I told you already my mom got to a point where she'd had enough of his cheating and that's why she filed for divorce.'

Tess couldn't respond, it was as if she'd swallowed a baseball. She coughed, pulled at her collar, and used the moment to turn away to compose her emotions, and blink back the tears pricking at her eyes. She noticed Po subtly gesture Pinky, and they sloped away on the pretext of checking the perimeter. When she returned her attention to Stella, she feigned tiredness, but Stella frowned at her reaction. Tess changed the subject.

'I was unable to identify the client Holbrook alluded to: during recent conversations with your dad, did he mention who he was looking after?'

Stella paused over the makings of supper, her bottom lip nipped in as she thought. 'He was part of a team that floated between jobs, rather than being part of a dedicated protection detail. The way Dad had it, they were troubleshooters, or they went in when extra bodies were needed, say for instance at a public event or such. Many of the clients were business people, some sportsmen and women, and now and then a celebrity.' She laughed, as if even she couldn't believe it. 'He mentioned looking after Beyoncé, but I think he was pulling my leg . . . I checked her tour dates and there was nothing mentioned about a show in Boston. But, yeah, he did do some protection work for that actor . . . y'know the one who makes all those brainless action flicks where he's a super spy: the *Death Before Dawn* series?'

'Jon Cutter?'

Stella again shook her head in disbelief, but this time at her opinion of Cutter's acting abilities. 'He's so wooden, I can't believe he's one of the highest-paid movie stars.'

'He's also gorgeous,' Tess said.

'Yeah, well, there is *that*.'

'Was Cutter in Boston promoting his latest movie?'

'Yes and no. He was attending a premier showing of *Death Before Dawn IV*, but it was also a homecoming for him. He originally hails from Boston, and apparently a lot of the movie was filmed on location in town, so his promoters were using that as a hook. From what Dad said, Cutter keeps a place in West Roxbury for when he's home from LA.'

'Where's West Roxbury in relation to Mattapan?'

'I couldn't say, I'm unfamiliar with Boston. Why'd you ask?'

Tess shrugged off her question.

Except Stella recalled where she'd heard the name of the other neighbourhood before. 'Isn't Mattapan where the police think Ethan Prescott might have gone into the river?'

'Yes,' Tess admitted. 'I'd have to check, but I've a feeling that something could have happened at Cutter's place, and it ended up with Ethan's death not far away.'

'My dad has his faults,' Stella said firmly, 'but he isn't a murderer.'

'Perhaps not, Stella, but we do have to consider it.'

'No. If Prescott was killed, it wasn't by my dad's hand, or if it was, it was an accident.'

'There aren't many reasons people kill,' said Tess, 'but the circumstances leading up to them can be varied. I'm not going to prejudge anything about your dad until I know the truth.'

Her words held double meaning, but Stella was unaware of her second misgivings about Aaron Lacey. 'Take my Po for instance: he was convicted for murder, but he killed during a fight with the man who'd murdered his father. How you stand ethically with that I don't care, but in my opinion he's no murderer, just a son avenging his loved one. He was a convicted killer, but I also know he's the best of men.'

Tess prepared for a backlash from Stella: how could she bring a murderer into her home? Except, Stella's response proved sanguine, as if hearing the truth of Po's past resolved some concern over her dad's hand in Prescott's death. Nevertheless Tess changed tack again.

'Where in New York was your family home?'

'Here in the Upper East Side. I'd've thought you knew that from going to school with me.'

'And you've always lived here?'

'Since birth,' said Stella.

Tess knew already where Aaron Lacey's official address was, but had hoped to hear he had connections to Hell's Kitchen. 'I don't recall from my childhood, but my grandfather and your dad were patrol partners, I'm unsure of the neighbourhoods they were stationed in . . .'

Stella reeled off the 19th Precinct in neighbouring Lennox Hill without a second's thought, and after a further moment's consideration added the 6th Precinct. 'He was there before transferring to the Nineteenth.'

'Where's that?'

'Down in the West Village,' Stella said.

Tess mulled over the location of the 6th Precinct. It wasn't a million miles from the ATM near the Flat Iron building, but it was a long walk back to where Lacey had made his first withdrawal at Eighth Avenue and 56th Street. It was possible that her assumption that his initial trip to an ATM was close to his hideout was wrong; perhaps Lacey had cleverly began at the furthest point so when returning to the West Village he wouldn't have too far to walk, and yet, that was supposing he had reason to be connected to a neighbourhood he'd patrolled many years ago. No, she decided, Hell's Kitchen felt right to her, and she should centre her search there . . .

After all, it's where her parents lived before she was born, before they too had moved to the Upper East Side to be closer to her dad's work – also at the 19th Precinct – and where Tess attended school alongside Stella.

When next she looked, her old friend had set down her cooking utensils and was staring in open question. 'What is it, Tess? What aren't you telling me?'

'I'm only trying to get some background on your dad; something that'll give me a clue where to look for him next.'

Stella didn't buy her explanation. She came out from behind the kitchen counter, indicating for Tess to take a breakfast stool with her on the opposite side. The situation resembled the way Barbara bid her to sit when first raising the subject of Lacey's disappearance. She stalled, until Stella patted the stool and asked her again to join her. Reluctantly, she sat.

'There's something on your mind, something you're not happy with.'

'I'm just tired.'

'Tess, I barely know you these days, but even I can tell you're a different person to the one I spoke with yesterday morning. Since you arrived here you've looked preoccupied . . . sad . . . or maybe guarded and struggling to say what's really on your mind. Have you learned something about my dad that's given you second thoughts about looking for him?'

'No, that's not it,' she blatantly lied. 'I didn't tell you before, but when I rang you earlier about that trouble at the motel I wasn't wholly truthful with you. I played down the incident because I didn't want you to worry, but Po and I could have been killed. We were attacked by some guys armed with an assault rifle.'

'What? No way! How on earth did you survive?'

'Thankfully luck was on our side, and our attackers weren't very experienced with their weapons. We managed to get the rifle away from them and they ran away.'

'What you're saying is that they weren't employed by Elite then?' Stella hadn't forgotten that Elite's employees tended to be ex-servicemen and women, who would know their way around weapons.

'It was more due to a personal grievance some local

criminals have against Po. But it hasn't escaped either of us that somebody working for Elite tried to use it against us and set them on us; otherwise they would've had no idea we were even in town. If it's true, Elite could be more dangerous than any of us first thought, and who knows what they'll try next.'

'Those thugs were sent to stop you from finding my dad? Are Elite so determined to get their hands on him first they'd have the competition killed?'

'We have to consider it.'

'Which suggests he's in real danger from them.' Stella deflated visibly, and her eyes glazed over with fear. 'All of us are. My god, Tess, if I'd been the one attacked like that I'd have just curled up and died. No wonder you look so troubled.'

'Yeah,' said Tess, thankful for Stella's misinterpretation of her mood. 'It's become imperative that I get to your dad first and find out what he's hiding, before Elite can silence him.'

TWENTY-FIVE

It was deep into the night, but in a city that suffered insomnia, it didn't slow Hayden's hunt to find whoever had treated Aaron Lacey's wounds in the aftermath of the gun battle with Mathers. He didn't personally trawl the streets for actionable intelligence, but had set up a forward operating base in a hotel room only a few blocks west of where Stella Dewildt entertained her guests. From there he coordinated the search, collating the info fed back to him by Elite's New York team, whose numbers had been bolstered by the arrival of Seung, Aiken, Johnson and Nicholls. If not for the fact Megan Stein must be held on a tight leash, he'd have sent her out with them to probe the locals for information, using their connections to the NYPD to glean more in-depth leads on suspected back-street doctors, or even Lace's whereabouts if they were lucky. Instead he kept Megan close, and he could tell she was torn. She was antsy, spoiling for a fight, but also feeling self-important because Hayden had declared her second-in-command of the op.

She occasionally cursed under her breath, and clawed distractedly at the puckered flesh marring her face, but she'd assumed the role of his secretary without argument, inputting names and addresses on a tablet as they came in. Hayden had previously doubted the list of doctors willing to forego legal procedure would be exhaustive, but he'd reappraised his estimate after possible leads began trickling in: at this rate they could easily become a flood. People were corruptible. Lace could've engaged the services of any number of otherwise innocent medical professionals, who'd stitch his wounds for the right price. Neither could he discount veterinarians, med students, nurses, paramedics, morticians or fucking taxidermists! Hell, anybody with a basic knowledge of first aid could've field dressed his wounds for him and kept him on his feet.

Hayden hadn't slept much since Lace's disappearance, and neither had the rest of his team. They'd had no shut-eye since early yesterday morning, but for a few minutes each on the flight down from Boston on Elite's corporate jet, but they hadn't been refreshed. He told Megan to get her head down for an hour, and she could spell him on duty when she woke. She swore at the perceived inconvenience, but stretched out, boots and all, on the bed. She was asleep in seconds, and Hayden stood over her a moment. In repose her features relaxed; if that girl didn't constantly screw her face in hatred, she'd realize she was pretty, despite her scars.

He kept going on black coffee and adrenalin, and the allotted hour's rest he'd given Megan extended to three. The list grew longer, but, with the remote assistance of one of the analysts back at HQ, he'd already began whittling out many of them, choosing to concentrate his resources on medics known to have come into contact with Aaron Lacey during his latter days as a cop. They didn't have access to the NYPD databases, but news websites proved helpful and often liberal with their details. One story in particular caught Hayden's attention, where Lace's quick and fearless actions had saved a medical practitioner's life after a psychotic patient had taken him hostage in his clinic. With a scalpel held to the doc's throat, the aggrieved patient had demanded drugs in exchange for the doctor's life, but instead had been disarmed and then beaten senseless with a tubular steel IV stand wielded by the off-duty cop visiting an injured colleague. The papers differed in opinion. Some painted Lace's actions as an example of police brutality but others applauded his heroism: if he hadn't intervened Doctor H. G. Grover's injuries would've proved fatal.

A man who owed Lace his life might feel beholden to return the favour.

Follow up enquiries found a home address for the now retired physician, but that was not all. In subsequent years the doctor had been implicated in a case involving impropriety when it came to issuing prescription drugs – dredged up was the possibility that Grover's crazy attacker had been one of his aggrieved customers refused his illicit meds when he couldn't pay – but the case against Grover had been dropped after crucial evidence was allegedly 'mislaid'. Tarnished by the scandal Grover had retired from practice, citing illness as his reason. Hayden had to wonder: was Lace's reason for being at the clinic at the opportune time genuine, or had he and Grover been in cahoots and sharing the proceeds of his drug dealing? Was Lace also responsible for making the evidence against the questionable doctor disappear? Owing that kind of debt, the doc might be trusted to keep Lace's treatments under the radar.

He checked the clock, and confirmed things with a glance between the blinds. The night was over, the roads and sidewalks teeming with people heading to work.

He shook Megan awake, and she startled up from a deep place, grabbing at the comforter for stability as she surged off the bed.

'Morning Sleeping Beauty,' Hayden announced.

'There's no need to be snarky,' Megan countered, misconstruing his greeting. 'Shit! How long have I slept? What time's it, Hayden?'

'Not too early to pay a sick man a house call,' he told her.

TWENTY-SIX

'Daylight's burning,' Po announced with a gentle shake of Tess's foot.

Against the odds, Tess had slept soundly. Fatigue caught up with her after eating the light supper prepared for her by Stella, and she'd stumbled to a spare bedroom assisted by Po's guiding hand. He hadn't lain down beside her, intending to spell Pinky on guard duty for a few hours, but helped her slip out of her shoes and jacket, and covered her with a sheet. Her sleep was dreamless and complete, but that only ensured her mind was once again engulfed the instant the dawn light filtered through her eyelids and brought her back to reality. She was partly grateful for the rest, partly disappointed because she hadn't subconsciously mulled over her worry and come to terms with it. Often the solution to a problem had come to her while her brain was uncluttered by her waking thoughts, but she struggled up from the bed with no idea how to deal with her mom's possible infidelity, or how that affected her . . . or her hunt for Aaron Lacey.

Po didn't rush her, only helped when she cast around for her shoes by toeing them towards her.

'Did you get any rest?' she asked.

'Coupla hours in a chair.'

'Then you should sleep now.'

'I've had coffee. Now I need to smoke. I'll check around the block while I'm at it, while you freshen up.'

'What time is it?'

'Twenty after seven.' He didn't check his watch, but it was no mysterious divining trick, he must have taken note of the time prior to rousing her. 'Stella and Pinky are already up and about.'

'You should've wakened me before now.'

'You needed to sleep. Your body crashed after the crap that happened yesterday.' He didn't only mean the shooting at the Shady Pines motel. 'Make sure you eat somethin', and drink somethin' sugary, it'll help.'

'Maybe you should follow your own advice. You can't subsist on coffee and nicotine alone.'

'I've eaten,' he said, but without conviction. 'Now I need a cigarette or you'll see a side of me you won't like.'

She asked for her overnight bag and dug out her toothpaste and brush. 'I've got to do this before I eat or drink anything,' she said, 'my mouth tastes foul.'

He leaned in and planted a kiss on her lips. 'It doesn't taste too bad to me.'

He left and Tess saw to her ablutions in the guest bathroom. She brushed and flossed, but when she joined the others in the kitchen she could still taste pennies in the back of her throat. Stella had dressed down since yesterday, choosing sneakers, jeans and a pale blue sweater, and she'd pulled back her blond hair in a ponytail. Tess's stomach turned over when it struck how much they looked alike; the coppery taste flooded her mouth. She sat down heavily at the breakfast counter, even as Pinky shoved a jug of coffee towards her. The Polaroid tucked into her shirt pocket burned against her heart, demanding she show it to Stella. It stayed put, and would until necessary.

'Isn't Po back yet?' Tess asked the obvious.

Pinky mimed blowing smoke towards the ceiling. 'He's multitasking: smoking *and* looking for trouble.'

Tess checked the clock on the microwave. It was approaching eight a.m. and it was as Po had said: daylight was burning. They should get on, start knocking on doors in Hell's Kitchen, but she hadn't the drive to get moving yet. While Pinky and Stella chatted like lifelong friends over their breakfasts, she was silent and only once the buzz of caffeine perked her up did she stand and again look for Po. What was keeping him, anyway?

She went to the window and peered down onto the street. She could see his Mustang parked in Paul Dewildt's allotted spot, but there was no sign of her partner. She took out her phone and called him.

'All's quiet,' he announced.

'Where are you?'

'Thought I'd widen the perimeter,' he explained, 'see if those asshats had pulled back after Pinky arrived, but I haven't spotted anything suspicious.'

'That's worrying,' she said.

'F'sure, means they're busy elsewhere, right?'

'Maybe they've finally realized it's pointless wasting their resources staking out Stella's place.' Hearing her name, Stella shot a look of alarm her way, and Tess gestured that everything was OK. 'Are you going to come up or should I join you?'

'Pinky's OK with babysitting duty?'

'I assume so,' she said. 'He's got his feet planted under the breakfast bar and doesn't look ready to get up yet.'

Pinky was close enough to hear both sides of the conversation. He waved a strip of bacon. 'Hey, Nicolas! I took your comments to heart last night, me. You needn't worry about me losing more weight; I'm happy to stay here and work on getting back into shape. Ho ho!' He chomped down on the bacon and chewed like a mad man so Po got the entire message.

'I'll come down,' said Tess.

She briefly updated Stella and Pinky with her game plan, which she conceded didn't amount to much.

'Why Hell's Kitchen?' Stella asked.

Tess didn't want to go into a full explanation of how they'd plotted Lacey's ATM usage, from which she and Po estimated where he was hiding on the island.

'Just a hunch,' she admitted. 'But it's as good a starting point as anywhere. If anything happens –' she meant a return of the Elite surveillance team – 'let us know immediately and we'll be back.'

'Don't worry, I won't keep all the fun to myself,' said Pinky, and she read the undertone of his words. He was desperate to join the hunt with his best friends, but alas, he better served them watching over Stella for the time being. She gave his hand a conciliatory squeeze, then turned to leave. As much as she loved him as a friend, she had something to do that she didn't want overheard by anyone but Po.

She joined her partner at the Mustang. 'Take the drive over

easy, Po,' she instructed, 'I'll see if I can narrow down the search a bit.'

Once seated in the car she steeled herself with a couple of deep breaths for round two with her mother.

TWENTY-SEVEN

The tinny strains of unfamiliar music jolted Si Turpin out of sleep. It wasn't the first time he'd conked out in his workshop. He often worked into the wee hours on difficult repairs and by the time they were finished he lacked the will and energy to shamble the five blocks home to his apartment. On those occasions he usually made it to a camp bed in the storeroom before passing out. This was a first for him: falling asleep at his work counter, with his hand cupped over the cell phone he'd stared at for hours before sleep took him. Startled awake, his hand snatched away, and he floundered a few seconds as his brain attempted to make sense of where he was, and why. The ringtone – no longer muffled by his palm – was loud and annoying. Yet he didn't immediately pick up the phone to answer. After his resolve to beat Lace to the punch and get rich yesterday evening, he wasn't confident he'd done the right thing by contacting Elite Custodian Services. If – when – he answered the phone his life would be changed forever, for good or . . . more worrying . . . for bad.

Initially he'd decided to call direct and demand to speak with Ben Holbrook, but had dithered. He wasn't the most erudite speaker, his profound nasal drone made it difficult for him to make his point clearly, and there must be no confusion when making his demands to ensure he was taken seriously. So he'd chosen to message Holbrook instead, using an anonymous email account. In the email, he'd left his instructions to call him with the brief notation that 'Nobody need die before dawn', a clever, he felt, play on words most associated with Jon Cutter. If ever it fell into the hands of law enforcement nothing in the message could incriminate him, but its recipient would understand exactly to what he was referring.

The phone continued ringing.

Si's stomach gurgled, and deeper down he felt a loosening of his bowel. It was one thing scamming desperate or vulnerable women out of their savings, another when it came to a potentially dangerous foe. He almost hit the cancel button, with a mind to breaking the phone and burning the SIM card. But greed won out.

He depressed the answer button and held the cell to his ear.

'Am I speaking with Si Turpin?'

Si almost dropped the phone, emitting a croak of dismay.

'Please don't hang up,' said the voice. 'You might as well speak considering we already know who you are.'

'H-how?'

'You took pains to make anonymous contact with us, Mister Turpin, via the Hotmail account and what we imagine you consider a burner phone. All we can advise is, in the future, should you attempt a similar stratagem you should be more careful how you source your product.'

His error came to him in a flash of disappointment: he'd made a fool's mistake. He'd crowed to Lace about buying flash drives in bulk, and he'd done the same with his goddamned supply of SIM cards. The purchase was linked directly to his business account. Ordinarily his scams went off without a glitch, because his victims lacked the technical ability to connect a cell number to a corresponding SIM, but Holbrook's people evidently could.

'I sense your embarrassment,' the voice went on, 'but never mind. We can all make mistakes, Mister Turpin; the important thing is that we never repeat them, eh? For instance, should you attempt to record this conversation, you should know it has the probability of coming back to bite you.'

'Uh, I'm not . . . uh, not making a recording,' Si spluttered.

'That's good. I can also confirm it's a practice we're no longer engaged in.'

'Uh, yeah . . . bite ya. Right.'

'I take it from your carefully selected wording that you believe you've something we want from you.' The tone was incredibly sarcastic, and at Si's bumbling response rather than his original message.

'I want to speak to Ben Holbrook directly,' he said, forcing a little grit in his tone.

'Yet you are speaking with me.'

'You're Clarissa Glenn,' Si stated. *Yeah, you Limey bitch, two of us can play at that game!* 'I want to speak with your business partner.'

'You've done your research. That's good.' Glenn waited a moment before dropping her next bomb. 'Then you should be aware that we are not amateurs. We know who and where you are.'

'Is that some kind of threat?'

'Yes, Mr Turpin. Wasn't I clear?'

'There's no need for threats. I made contact with you because I can give you what you want; I'm prepared to give you it. We can come to a reasonable agreement, right?'

'How much?'

'A million.'

'Goodbye, Mr Turpin.'

'No! Wait! Don't hang up.' Si scrubbed a hand over his face, his unshaven bristles rasping under his fingers. 'I'm prepared to negotiate an agreeable price.'

'Then go ahead. Try again.'

'Five hundred thousand.'

'No.'

'Come on, that's a pittance compared to what you've made off—'

'Don't mention his name.'

Both their names had been spoken, why did she care if Jon Cutter was mentioned?

'You're worried somebody else could be listening in?' he asked.

'No, Mr Turpin, as unlike you we have followed the proper channels to decrypt this conversation and to ensure it can't be traced back to us. I simply ask you don't mention his name as it turns my stomach to hear it.'

'You don't like him, but you don't mind skimming the cream off the top of his income.'

'That's as it may be, but as a woman I can't conscionably abide him or the actions he pays to conceal.'

'As a dude, I can't either,' Si admitted.

'Ah,' said Glenn, and Si realized he'd been sucked blindly into a trap. 'Then you have viewed the surveillance footage?'

He was caught, and lying would only weaken his position in the negotiation. 'If it gets out, he's going to prison, and so are you and Holbrook. Your cash cow will run dry, and your company will crash and burn. Does five hundred thousand still sound a high price to pay for my silence? In fact, fuck that, I'm not going to budge from my original demand. It's a million bucks straight, or the deal's off the table.'

'We are not giving you a million dollars.'

'You will or I'll release the footage to the press. All I need do is press a key on my computer and it's gone . . . and you're all finished.'

'Mr Turpin, something has been irking me since first we spoke: did you eat supper at your counter last night?'

Si was stunned into silence.

'You might have cleared away the debris after you finished your pizza and wiped that unsightly glob of melted cheese off your shirt.'

Horrified, Si glanced once at the pizza box delivered last night while he awaited a response from Holbrook. He rubbed at the streak of cheese on his football shirt, even as, open-mouthed, he tried to spot where he was being surveilled from. His gaze lit on the tiny web camera embedded in his personal computer screen.

'You've hacked my system?'

'Of course we have. We wouldn't trust you to delete all those files, even if you did hand over the physical copies you've undoubtedly made. Therefore we've already done that for you, as well as the poorly worded email you drafted offering the files to the highest bidder in an online auction with the media. Had you sent that email already, we would not be speaking now, nor would I be enjoying the stupid look of defeat on your face.'

In a panic, Si reached for his computer.

'I wouldn't do that. If you try switching it off, in fact if you were to press any key now, your entire system will be fully wiped, except for the images of child pornography we've planted on your hard drive, which I'm certain any reasonably adept tech guy at the NYPD will be able to recover.'

'You're fucking bluffing!'

'Being a reasonably adept tech guy in your own right, I'd tell you to check, but doing so will initiate the self-destruct of your computer, and your life.' Glenn's triumphant smile could be heard in her voice. 'Before you threaten to give the files to the police and claim you are the victim of a hack, hear us out. You earlier mentioned coming to reasonable agreement. Well, we've heard your demands, now you can listen to ours. You hand over every copy of the files, for which we will not give you a cent in compensation. However, there is something more you can do for us we will reward you for. Interested, Mr Turpin?'

'How much are we talking about?'

'You're more interested in how much rather than the task we're about to set you?'

'I'm not an idiot: you want me to give you Aaron Lacey. How much for me to put him in your hands?'

'Ten thousand dollars.'

'Fuck you.'

'Animosity will get us nowhere. How much would you like?'

'I told you my price and I'm not budging.'

'You have no leverage and you will budge or get nothing. You can lead us to Lacey a little quicker than we can find him at present, but it's inevitable we *will* find him and the clock is ticking down. This is a time sensitive deal, Mr Turpin. Give us Aaron Lacey and we will pay you twenty thousand dollars . . . but if you dally it will be too late.'

'Fifty.'

'Twenty-five.'

'What will you do with him?'

'Why should you be concerned?'

'I'm not. He's a piece of shit. Twenty-five you say?'

'I'm feeling generous today. Thirty, Mr Turpin.'

'What do you want me to do?'

'You have a way in which you can contact him.'

Si supplied Lacey's burner phone to him: of course he could contact him.

'Call him. Have him meet with you at your workshop,' Glenn instructed. 'Don't try to warn him; remember that we are watching and listening.'

'Trust me, I'm not going to warn him; I want that son of a bitch out of my hair.'

'That's what we all want, Mr Turpin. Once he's in our hands you'll be richer to the sum of . . . oh, why not? Fifty thousand is a pittance skimmed off that cream you mentioned.'

TWENTY-EIGHT

Hayden James held up a finger.

'Try to keep things down over there, huh?'

Megan, her face set in a rictus, craned her captive's spine over the back of his easy chair, hissing to convey the demand for silence. 'You heard him, asshole, one word and you're toast.'

Hayden frowned at her rough-handed tactics, but admittedly they got what he wanted. The old doctor, so frail he was ready to snap under the manhandling, wheezed in agony, unable to speak. Hayden listened intently into his phone.

Ten minutes earlier they'd gained access to Dr Grover's home on the pretence that Megan was injured. She'd feigned a dislocated shoulder, gritting her teeth in pain as she supported her elbow with her opposite hand, and allowing Hayden to assist her over the stoop. The charade was unnecessary, because once he'd answered his door, the old man couldn't have stopped them from entering. Immediately they were inside, Megan straightened, swore at her miraculous recovery, and Hayden heeled the door closed behind them. Megan grasped the lapels of Grover's plaid shirt and propelled him backwards into his sitting room.

'What's the meaning of this?' Grover demanded. To his

credit, he was more outraged by the invasion of his private residence than afraid.

Megan slapped his face. 'You don't ask the questions, Herb, we do.' Her hands grasping his collar again, she swung him around and parked him in the easy chair. She gave way for Hayden, who offered the elderly man an apologetic shrug.

'I'd prefer we didn't have to do this, but I'm afraid I need some answers from you and haven't all day to get them. Please answer me quickly and truthfully and I swear my associate will not lay another finger on you.'

'Get out of my house,' Grover snarled.

Hayden crouched in front of him, reached out a questing hand. Doctor Grover batted it aside.

'Megan,' said Hayden.

She slipped into place behind the chair, grasped Grover's head in both hands and forced his skull into the headrest. Crying out in dismay, Grover's legs and arms flailed. Megan adjusted her grip and tilted up his head, so Hayden had a good view of his whattled throat. He nodded at the line of paler flesh cutting obliquely from below his left ear towards his collarbone. 'Half an inch to the right and you wouldn't have survived that wound. I bet you're thankful to the man that came to your rescue, before that psycho fully sliced your throat with your own scalpel?'

'You're here because of Aaron Lacey?' Grover halted his pitiful attempt at escape. His hands dropped in his lap, curled upward. To Hayden, the arthritic fingers, stained orange with cigarette tar, were like the legs of a sickly spider. He took no pleasure in torturing the weak old man, but needs must.

'I'm glad you got my prompt so quickly. Now we're on the same page, how's about we cut out any more necessity for the rough stuff and tell me where I can find him?'

'I have no idea.'

'Megan.'

She twisted Grover's ears so savagely the cartilage collapsed in one of them. Grover yowled, and his limbs flailed anew.

Still crouching, Hayden's eyelids flickered at how close Grover's feet kicked but he held his position.

'This can stop,' he reminded the old doctor, 'the instant
you obey my instructions. Quickly and truthfully: where can
I find Aaron Lacey?'

'I told you! I've no idea.'

'But you have treated him?'

'Yes! Yes, I tended to his wounds, but I don't know where
he is. He came to me with a bullet wound in his side, and a
cut to his neck.'

'A cut to his throat, huh?' Hayden aimed a smile at the old
scar on Grover's throat. 'As bad as yours?'

'Bad enough. It required suturing.'

'Do you hear that, Megan? You were right: Ethan did get
his licks in before Lacey killed him.'

'Wh-what?' Grover's rheumy eyes bulged from their sockets.
'Lacey killed someone? He told me he was mugged, and was
injured trying to run away.'

'But you didn't buy his story, did you? You're an intelligent
man, you know when the exit wound's out the back that he
wasn't running away.'

'He told me he was backing off . . .'

'And you didn't believe him. But hey! That's OK. You owed
him your life; I don't blame you for trying to help him out.
The thing is, you've repaid your debt to him, right? You don't
owe him a thing now. So do yourself a favour and don't suffer
on his behalf.'

'Look,' said Grover. 'He came to me and I dressed his
wounds, gave him some meds and advice . . . I didn't ask
about where he was staying.'

'What did he talk about with you?'

'Nothing much. Small talk.' Grover craned to see Megan,
who still gripped his skull. 'Please, there's no need to do that.'

Megan twisted his abused ear, making him yowl again. 'I'll
decide what I need to do, you old fart.'

Hayden snapped a scowl at her, and waited until the retired
doctor shuddered his way past the intense pain.

'Think,' said Hayden, once he'd Grover's attention once
more. 'He must have said something about where he was
staying.'

'I only assumed he was at home. All I know is he has an

apartment in the city, and has lived there alone since his divorce. But I never learned his address. The nature of my practice—'

'Yeah, yeah, it's mostly anonymous because it's off the books. Lacey hasn't been back to his apartment; we know that for certain. It means he's hiding someplace else.'

'A hotel . . .'

'Perhaps but doubtful. Too many questions would've been asked of a guest showing up with gunshot wounds and a slashed neck. C'mon, Doc. Think! He must have said something.'

'He didn't.'

'Megan. Jog his memory.'

She yanked the old man out of the chair, dragged him unceremoniously out of the way while Hayden straightened. With one hand at his throat, and a fist under his nose, she snapped: 'I'll make you remember you senile old bastard.'

Grover sneered at her contorted face, his gaze tracking the scarred flesh from top to bottom. 'I can guess why someone would want to throw acid in your face,' he spat.

'This wasn't from acid,' Megan growled. 'This was from a Haji with a petrol bomb. Call yourself a fucking doctor?'

It was while Megan was correcting his mistake, digging her fingers into his cheeks and forcing his spine backwards over the chair, that Hayden's cell phone rang and he raised a finger for silence. Megan hissed for silence, and showing some spunk Grover told her she needed to make her damn mind up. She knocked him down, planted a sole on the back of his head and jammed his face into the carpet. She looked at Hayden expectantly, but couldn't see his face. His answers were short affirmations. He ended the call, turned and saw she'd pinned Grover to the floor.

'Let him be.' He pitied the old man's plight, but was also a pragmatist. 'We don't need him now.'

'What do you want me to do with him?'

Hayden gave the situation scant thought. Having abused Grover, he would report the home invasion to the police, and he could give good descriptions of both, plus Megan's first name. Not that her name would pick her out from a crowd, but her scarred face would. Ordinarily, putting the fear of a return visit in a man's heart would be enough to ensure his silence, but they hadn't time for that. Hayden couldn't allow a police hunt to bring theirs to a halt.

'You know what you have to do,' he said.

For the first time since Lacey and Mather drew their guns on each other Megan's smile was genuine. She raised her heel, poised to stamp.

'Megan,' Hayden cautioned. 'Show some restraint, will you? Make it look like a goddamn accident.'

TWENTY-NINE

P o stepped out of the Mustang at the first available parking space he found adjacent to Wells Fargo branch where Lacey had used the first ATM, and stood with his elbows on the roof while he smoked and observed. His pose served dual purpose; he could keep an eye out for a tail and give Tess a modicum of privacy. Neither of them expected the improbability of Aaron Lacey randomly walking past, so his no-show was unsurprising. As Tess sat and spoke into her cell phone she had a good view of Po's torso through the driver's window and little else. She never turned her face towards the sidewalk for fear a passer-by would note her stricken features and wet eyes: she kept her voice low, but it was loaded with conviction.

'I'm not giving in until you give me the answers I need, Mom,' she warned, 'so you may as well be truthful and get it over with.'

'Are you calling me a liar?'

'No. Perhaps. You said before you only want to protect me; I think you're withholding the truth so it doesn't hurt me. But, Mom, don't you see? I'm already hurting.'

'Because you've got some ridiculous notion in your head that I . . .' Barbara couldn't repeat the words.

'That you slept with Aaron Lacey. Yes.'

'I loved Michael . . . I've never stopped loving him.'

'Mom, that's one thing that was never . . . isn't now in doubt. Right up until the end, when his cancer took him, anyone could see how much you loved each other.'

'I still love and miss him now, Teresa.'

'I know, Mom. We all do: you, me, Michael Jnr and Alex.'

'Then why are you making these horrible accusations?'

'Love is rarely the driving force behind an affair.'

'What is it you want to hear? That I was a young mother, struggling to raise two boys, while your father was always at work? That I was a woman whose life was an endless loop of dirty diapers and sleepless nights? That I was lonely, feeling out of shape and undesirable and fell into bed with the first man that showed me the attention I craved because your father was never there, and when he was he was too tired to think straight let alone make love? Is that *really* what you want to hear, Teresa?'

Tess's throat constricted. 'Is that how it happened?'

'Teresa—'

'Mom, you wouldn't be the first who cheated then regretted it after. Even if I don't agree with it, I can understand why you might have sought some excitement away from the drudgery; you were vulnerable, feeling unattractive and Aaron was handsome and had a way with the ladies; at the time you weren't thinking straight, certainly not about the possible consequences of sleeping with another man.'

'Is that really what you think of me?' Barbara's tone had gone from disbelief to anger in the space of seconds. 'That I was some kind of whore who didn't appreciate how hard your dad worked to keep a roof over our heads and food in our mouths; that I'd betray him for the sake of a few minutes of *dirty sex* with his father's friend? How dare you judge me like that!'

'I'm not judging, I'm trying to put myself in your shoes, so I can understand why—'

'If your father was here now, he'd be so mad at you, Teresa.'

Tess waited a beat; her next words would be the most hurtful. 'That depends on who my real father is.'

'What? I don't believe you said that. You know who your
dad is!'

'I'm not asking about my dad, the man that raised and
loved me, and who I loved in return. He'll always be my dad,
and nothing will change. I'm asking about my biological
father. I've a right to know the truth.'

'Michael is your dad, and your father. How could you ever
doubt that?'

'Until very recently I didn't. But now . . .'

'Michael's your father, Teresa.'

'I desperately want that to be true, Mom. I really do. But
the alternative is eating at me. That photo of us: why would
Aaron keep it after all these years? Why did Dad grab me off
him and tell him to stay away from *his* family?'

'Dear Lord, Teresa! You've based this madness on an old
photograph you found, and one fight you were too young
to understand at the time. I have no idea why Aaron has a
photo of us, but the reason your dad was so mad with Aaron
wasn't because we were having an affair! He blamed Aaron
for your grandfather's death, for not being there to back him
up when he needed him.'

'Why? Granddad died when he was off duty.'

'Yes, he was, but Aaron was in the store with him when
he was shot trying to stop the robbery.'

'I, uh, didn't know that.'

'No, you didn't. There's a lot you don't know, but have
made up your own mind on. But you're wrong, Teresa, so
very, very wrong.'

'Then why does Stella look so much like me?'

'Huh! Listen to you! Next you'll be accusing your dad
of having an affair with Estelle's mother.' Realizing what she'd
just suggested, Barbara emitted a squeak of self-admonishment.
'No! Before you damn well ask, that did not happen either.
To my knowledge we both stuck to our vows, and damn you
for ever doubting us, young lady!'

Tess dashed tears from her cheeks. Her relationship with
her mother had never been easy, and now she'd made things
worse. What she'd accused her of might prove to be unfor-
givable, but it had to be done. She wasn't fully convinced

of her mother's explanation, and worse still, she'd been unable to push her for a lead as she'd hoped. She wouldn't apologize, but she should try to mend the rift somehow. 'Mom, look, I'm going through some *things* at the moment. Maybe I'm not thinking clearly. Actually there's no *maybe* about it. All these distractions, they're affecting my ability to do my job. I can't concentrate, and because of that I'm not getting any closer to finding Aaron. I need your help Mom, but if you didn't—'

'I didn't.' Barbara relented a little. 'I don't know the circumstances of Aaron's disappearance, but I'm neither naïve nor stupid. This case you've taken on, it has turned into something you never expected, hasn't it?'

'Yeah . . . and then some. I'm not going to say why, but it's imperative that I find him, Mom. Except, I've come to a dead end and don't know where to look next. The trail's led me to Manhattan.'

'You're in New York now?'

The question was rhetorical, but Tess clarified. 'Aaron left Boston and returned home. The thing is, he hasn't showed up at his own apartment, and I suspect he's lying low somewhere else. My investigation has brought me to Hell's Kitchen. From when you were younger and still friends, can you think of anywhere here that Aaron might have hidden?'

Silence reigned for a long count. Barbara was uneasy about saying anything that might prompt another accusation from her. She sighed. 'Are you with Estelle?'

'Not at the moment, there's only Po with me and he has stepped out.'

'Good. It's best that Estelle doesn't hear this . . .'

'What is it, Mom?'

'As far back as we knew him, Aaron wasn't the most faithful husband . . . but *not* in the way you thought he was involved with me. He had an unusual relationship with Estelle's mother; these days I suppose you'd say they had an *open marriage*?'

'Estelle's mother knew he was cheating on her even back then?'

'Yes, and she didn't object, albeit she did set certain rules. She did not want to hear about his affairs and she did not want anything happening under their own roof. Personally I thought his behaviour was disgraceful, but who am I to say what other adults can get up to?'

Tess bit her tongue.

'It's funny that you should be in Hell's Kitchen,' Barbara went on, 'and it might surprise you to hear that you might possibly be closer to him than you thought. I remember over-hearing your dad and granddad talking about Aaron's second apartment, the one he kept strictly for his extra-marital activities, and mentioning it was in Hell's Kitchen. Before you ask, no I don't know where exactly, but haven't you some way to narrow down the list somehow?'

'There are ways, yes, but things are a little time sensitive here.'

'Teresa, you won't say why you need to find him so quickly, but you don't have to. Aaron's in some kind of danger, isn't he?'

'It could be a matter of life or death, Mom,' she admitted.

Again Barbara fell silent, and Tess could almost picture her wringing her hands in turmoil. When finally she came back on the line it was apparent she'd lost an internal battle because her voice was a whisper of remorse. 'It'd be terrible if anything happened to him . . . for Estelle's sake. Look for him near De Witt Clinton Park, on one of the streets off Eleventh Avenue.' With that she canceled the call, and Tess knew it was because she did not want to be pressed on how – despite all her previous denial about sleeping with him – she knew the location of Lacey's love nest.

THIRTY

A tinkling noise set Lacey's teeth on edge, and he groaned and swiped his hands over his ears. His efforts failed to banish the annoying music, and finally forced him to open his eyes and stare blearily about him for its source. His brain was wrapped in a thick woollen blanket, and for a long confused moment he would have had trouble recalling his name, let alone figuring out where he was or his reason for being there. Finally he flopped out an arm and it struck the floor. He pushed his knuckles into the carpet, propping himself to help rise, but his arthritic shoulder gave him hell and he gave up. He had to jack his body, worm onto his side, and then allow gravity to counterweight his feet and aid him to raise his torso. He swore at each small pull and twist of his body. He sat for another long pause, head in hands, his face hot and clammy against his palms . . . all the while the music never stopped.

He stood up, swayed in place until he was confident he wouldn't collapse down on the couch again, and scanned the room. He'd never progressed further than the sitting room of his apartment last night, and his supper had gone uneaten. He vaguely recollected sitting down, promising himself a minute's rest before putting his meal in the microwave, but beyond that he was oblivious. Sleep must have taken him, and he'd slumped down on the couch fully clothed and hadn't moved since. Daylight lanced in through the cracks in the window blinds, and he averted his gaze.

'What time is it?' he mumbled aloud.

Never mind the time, what day was it? And where the fucking hell was that music coming from?

The living space was open plan, with one bedroom and adjoining bathroom separated from it by partition walls erected to afford a modicum of privacy. One corner accommodated the galley-style kitchen. All in all, a few stumbling steps could take him from one end to the other, so there weren't too many places where anything could get lost. Whatever was making the noise defied his first sweep though, and he stood again, swaying, cocking his ear to pinpoint the source. Feeling stupid, he slipped a hand in his jacket pocket, and withdrew the burner phone given to him by Si Turpin. The ringtone was on its factory setting, the volume on full blast. A number was displayed on-screen though Lacey didn't recognize it. He hadn't given his contact details to a living soul yet, so assumed the caller had misdialled or wanted to sell him something. He canceled the call and dropped the phone on the settee.

His bladder ached to be relieved. His left shoulder was almost locked in place and he folded his weakened arm like a chicken's wing across his abdomen. Both knees felt as if splinters of glass had been inserted between the cartilage and bones and the muscles of his thighs were hot and swollen. None of his discomforts were new, but they'd all been compounded by the effort he'd put in walking the wide circuit of ATMs yesterday.

Shit! It struck him that the daylight was slanting in from the wrong direction: it wasn't dusk, it was the goddamn morning of another day. He'd slept for more than twelve hours, oblivious and vulnerable, every hour of it allowing his hunters to close in.

The phone rang again.

Originally he'd intended using the anonymous phone to make first contact with Ben Holbrook, but his plan had changed when deciding to use Si, and his tech-savvy, as his middleman to make his demands. His plan of a return visit to Si's workshop last night to set things in motion had gone to shit. It was the damn fever caused by his infected wounds; it sapped his energy and will. He peered down at the screen. Same number as before. A small pop-up box told him he'd missed three previous calls. Whoever was on the other end, they were determined. He scooped up the phone.

'Who is this?' he rasped.

'Lace. It's me.' Further clarification wasn't required, because the nasal drone was enough.

'What the fuck you doin' calling me on this number, Si?'

'It's the only one I had for you, buddy.'

'So now I'm your buddy?'

'I know. It's a stretch. But I think we can be.'

Lacey grunted, but didn't dash the idea completely. After all, he needed Si's expertise, so shouldn't alienate him.

'What's this about, Si?' He worked some life into his frozen shoulder, unconsciously clenching and unclenching his left fist.

'I expected to hear from you sooner,' said Si, a quaver entering his voice.

'Why?'

'C'mon, you know why. You said you had some work for me. The impression I got was it was something you wanted to get started on straight away.'

The blood drained from Lacey's head. 'You snooped around those files didn't you?'

'I'm not gonna lie to you, Lace. If we're gonna be workin' together, I think it's best that we're open with each other, right? So yeah, I snooped.'

'You said you didn't look at what you copied for me.'

'I'm a conman at heart, Lace; whaddaya expect?'

There was no arguing with his logic, but Lacey was still pissed. 'So, what do you know?'

'Not a lot.' Soft rasping sounds came down the line, as if Si had adjusted his bulk. 'I guessed that you've got something on somebody they might want back at a price you're gonna set.'

Lacey sniffed.

'When you said you had some work for me, of the illegal type,' Si went on, 'it got me thinking. You're in the market for someone who can set up an exchange for you, but the list of people you can go to is limited. In fact, it's narrowed down to one: Me.'

'You've an overinflated opinion of your worth, Si. You're not the only hacker I can go to.'

'Yeah, you probably have other dudes by their balls too, I don't doubt it, but you came to me first. Tells me you don't trust any of those others with what you have.'

'No offence, but I chose you 'cause you're the dumbest of a dumb bunch.'

Si laughed nervously. 'No offence taken. Listen, Lacey: those thumb drives I gave you, I've a confession to make . . .'

'Oh, yeah?'

'I'm guessing you intend keeping one of them after you hand over the original . . . as security against any come backs. Well, sorry buddy, but they're no good to ya.'

'What did you do, you son of a bitch?'

'Nothing unfixable, just corrupted them so they wiped if anyone tried to play them. I did that, well, I did that in revenge for the shit you've held over me for years.'

'You fucking did *what*?'

'Lace, hear me out, man.' The nasal drone had risen to a high-pitched buzz as Si tried to wheedle his way back into

Lacey's good graces. 'I saw the error of my ways. After you offered me some work *lucrative to the two of us*, I realized I'd shot myself in the foot. I've sat up most of the night figuring out how to make this right again, and in a way you'll be able to trust me in the future.'

'I wouldn't trust you as far as I can throw you, and that ain't far, you fat tub of shit.'

'I get ya, man, and don't blame you for being sceptical. But you can trust that I want that lucrative shit to come true, man, and it ain't gonna happen if I don't put things right.'

'How'd I know you ain't trying to fuck me over again?'

'What's in it for me to do that? Lace, unless I remove the virus from those devices they ain't worth squat. Fact is, I've taken away any leverage you had over whoever you've planned on squeezing.'

'They don't know that.'

'It'll take them seconds to check and when they realize the files are corrupted they'll refuse to pay you.'

'You bastard,' Lacey snarled as he realized the truth of Si's words. 'I ought to come over there and beat the living shit outta ya!'

'I want you to come over. Not to kick my ass, but so's I can repair those files.'

'Fuck you! I've still got the original. I'll get copies made by somebody else.'

'No, Lace.' Si paused, and it was because he was about to make another confession. 'See, I also programmed the virus into the original. You need me to remove it or it's toast.'

Lacey's hand crept back to his chest, though this time resting his painful shoulder wasn't the reason. His palm cupped the flash drive in his shirt pocket. Yesterday it had felt like a winning Lotto ticket, a fucking gold nugget, now it was just a useless piece of plastic.

'You'd better be able to save it,' he warned, 'or so help me, you're the one who'll need saving.'

'Just come on over, Lace. I'm waiting to make things right with you, man.'

'I'm coming,' Lacey promised.

THIRTY-ONE

S i Turpin ended the call, raised both palms to the couple menacing him across his workbench, signifying their plan was in motion. He kept his hands up, in surrender. The hard-faced woman didn't lower the suppressed pistol she'd aimed at his sweating face from the second after she'd arrived. Her male companion nodded at Si.

'Was that true?' the guy asked. 'That you've corrupted all the drives?'

Knowing his life depended on how he answered Si shook his head. 'No, man, I was just feeding him a line to make sure he came over here.' He desperately hoped the lie was convincing, because it'd mean they'd keep him alive at least until Laccy's arrival. When they had their hands full with Lace, he hoped to slip away via the fire exit out back. His dream of being made fifty thousand dollars richer had died the instant the couple pushed inside his workshop and the guy turned and slipped the locks behind him, despite his exhortations to the British woman on the other end of the phone that he would honour their deal without being bullied. Why the fuck hadn't Lace answered the damn phone when first he called, instead of making him wait for almost an hour as he repeatedly rang his number?

'If it was a lie, then we don't need you,' said the man.

His features weren't as stern as the Korean woman's threatening to shoot him, but were scarier for their nonplussed expression. His red hair and freckles almost made him boyish, but Si knew a dangerous son of a bitch when he saw one.

'You'll want me to confirm that Lace has brought the original, and all the copies I made, before . . . well, before you do whatever you will to him. Look, buddy, this isn't my problem, OK? I got caught up in some business that I had no stake in, and, yeah, greed got the better of me when I contacted your bosses.' The British woman had sold him a lie, conning him with the promise of fifty grand when she was only buying time for these gunmen to arrive. He'd been played as easily as he used to manipulate widows and spinsters: Karma had bitten a chunk out of him. 'I'd rather just wind back the clock and wish Lace never showed up at my door. You don't have to worry about me speaking about this with anyone; trust me, I know when to keep my mouth shut, OK.'

'Says the fat punk who just gave up his friend,' the Korean sneered.

'Are you kidding me? Lace isn't my friend; the son of a bitch has been the bane of my life for years! The sooner he's outta my hair the better . . . you get me?'

'Pipe down,' warned the red-haired man, because Si's drone had grown strident: he sounded like a desperate wasp seeking egress, and beating itself to death against a window. It was still early morning, and the adjacent massage parlour was yet to open for business, but there were still pedestrians on the street that might overhear and decide to investigate, or worse, call the cops. 'Nothing's gonna happen to you if you keep calm and do as we say.'

'So put down the gun! I can't concentrate with it stuck in my face like that!'

'The gun stays, and just remember, I can shoot faster than you can scream for help.' The Korean held no trace of a foreign accent; she was all-American.

'You need to unlock the door,' Si pointed out, as if trying to be helpful rather than widening his possible escape routes. 'If Lace gets here and the door's locked, he's gonna know something's up.'

'I'll unlock it once he tries the door,' said Red-hair. 'By then, even if he does smell a trap, our guys will be behind him. So don't you worry, Mr Turpin, he isn't going to get away.' Unbeknown to Si, Johnson and Nicholls were already in place across the street watching for Lacey, while Hayden and Megan were closing in fast after their visit with Doc Grover was cut short by Ben Holbrook, who'd redirected them while Clarissa Glenn kept Si busy on the phone. Red-haired Grant Aiken flicked a glance at his partner, Vera

Seung, an instruction: they'd worked together so long that spoken words were rarely necessary. She lowered the pistol, and retreated the few short steps to the door, listening for footsteps on the metal stairs outside. Si didn't know how far Lacey had to travel from his hiding place, but assumed it wasn't too distant. He'd noted Lacey's pained gait as he left his workshop yesterday, and a quick glance out of the window afterwards showed the ex-cop limping away on foot. He should arrive soon enough. Si prayed every step was filled with agony, and each took an age to complete, because there was a very real possibility his life could be measured in seconds after Lacey's arrival.

He should have realized the jeopardy his greed could place him in. A company willing to cover up a murder, and subsequently blackmail the killer, wouldn't flinch at protecting their income. Elite had shown their determination to find Lacey, no less than in tracing Si, and remotely hacking his system, so he had to believe that once Lacey was in their clutches they wouldn't make do with taking away the flash drives and reprimanding him with a slap on his wrist. Anyone party to the cover-up involving Hollywood's latest Golden Boy had to be silenced. He was going to die.

Si didn't want to die.

His life was shit, but compared to the alternative, it was still life, and he clung to it with every iota of his being. He wasn't a coward, but neither was he beyond begging for leniency.

'Look, man,' he whined, aiming his plea at Aiken. 'I'm just a guy trying to get by, same as you, right? When you took this job, it was probably only ever intended to earn you a living, and I bet the thought never entered your mind that you'd end up here . . . doing this. I mean, c'mon, surely you never expected to be called on to hurt a poor Joe scraping a wage from repairing cast-off cell phones and outmoded laptops? Please, man, you guys –' this time he purposely implored Seung too – 'surely you aren't prepared to hurt me just so's Ben Holbrook can continue lining his pockets?'

Aiken leaned forward, placing a finger to his lips. 'Mr Turpin, I asked you once to pipe down. I won't ask again. You

do realize that every time you flap your lips you're digging
yourself deeper into a hole? Now, do as I said, keep quiet,
and everything'll work out just fine.'

'Fine for you . . .' Si's features were awash with beads of
cold sweat.

A sharp tap grabbed his attention. Seung raised the pistol
from where she'd knocked it against the doorframe, and
placed the silencer against her pouting lips. He was unsure
if she was miming Aiken's request for silence or promising
the kiss of death.

While most of Elite's employees were hardworking,
decent, law-abiding citizens, it wasn't true of a select few.
The four operatives bolstering Hayden's team since Boston
had been hand-picked for purpose: appealing to their better
natures was hopeless. They were Holbrook's troubleshooters
for good reason.

While Seung stood sentry at the door, Aiken moved to
stand behind Si. He too had a silenced pistol, but was yet
to draw it on his prisoner. A threat from a second gun was
unnecessary when Si was already terrified for his life. He
placed his hands on the fat man's shoulders and kneaded the
flesh. 'Relax, Mr Turpin,' he chided. 'I need you to think
clearly. The files have already been wiped from your server,
and from your cloud account. Beyond those you gave to
Lacey, did you make any more physical copies?'

'No!' Si was shamed by his child-like bleat of innocence.
He shuddered under Aiken's fingertips: the contact was far too
intimate for comfort.

'Can I believe you?'

'I swear I didn't make any other copies!'

Aiken's thumbs dug deeper, seeking the clusters of
nerves in Si's neck. The pain was deep and dull at first, but
the sensation grew torturous, and Si squirmed, hissing in
torment.

'Shhh!' Seung wagged her gun in warning from a few
feet away.

Aiken hummed, as if in self-admonishment. He stopped
digging and gently slapped Si's cheeks. 'I guess I do believe
you, Mr Turpin. Unfortunately my bosses aren't the trusting

types. But we'll get to that soon enough. Stand up and look at me.'

'Wh-why?'

'Because I told you to,' said Aiken, and bunched Si's collar in his fists and yanked up. Si's football shirt rose above his bulbous belly, and he struggled up after it, and turned to face Aiken as instructed. He was the taller guy, heavier, and not all of his build was comprised of fat. Aiken wasn't perturbed in the least. He dragged Si forward, bending him at the waist so their noses almost touched. 'Now, what I want you to do is grab any storage device you have here and pile them on the bench.'

'All of them?'

'All of them.'

'The packaged ones too?'

'I need to check they haven't been tampered with.'

'I rarely use flash drives or any other plug-in these days, I usually do my work online . . .'

'Then it shouldn't take you long. C'mon, Mr Turpin. Get moving. And don't hold out on me. I'll be doing a final sweep and if I spot anything you've *accidentally* forgotten, I'll rearrange your nose again for each one I find. Mind you –' Aiken laughed scornfully – 'by the look of things I might be doing you a favour.'

Si scowled. It was one thing having his life threatened, but did the bastard have to be so personal? He bunched his fists, and returned the stare, but he couldn't hold onto his resolve. His moment of steel hadn't gone unnoticed: Aiken snorted, and behind Si, Seung gave a scornful laugh. Aiken took a step back, invited Si to get moving with a wave of his arm.

As he riffled through the clutter of his workshop, collecting up all and everything that could be defined as a data recorder, whether or not it served that purpose, and delivered it to his workbench, Aiken watched him closely, perhaps expecting him to try to hide a device or snatch up a weapon. Si did neither, but edged nearer the door to the storeroom. If he could rush inside, and maybe jam the door in Aiken's face, he could somehow make it out the fire exit before they shot him. He took his time, sifting through electrical components, even dumping on the bench several busted shells of defunct cell phones and an old cassette recorder.

'OK,' said Aiken, 'there's no need to be sarcastic.'

'I like my nose the way it is,' said Si, and instantly regretted it, because that time he truly was being acerbic.

Aiken grinned, finding the retort funny. It didn't stop him from pushing Si against the bench. 'OK. Now I want you to load everything into that bag by your feet.'

The bag was Si's own satchel he used to carry smaller items to and from his apartment when he took a project home. He had to contort, and stretch uncomfortably to reach it, because Aiken didn't back off. The muscles between his ribs constricted in pain. He straightened, grimacing, and dropped the open satchel on the bench. Puffing air, he began scooping up the oddments and dumping them in the bag.

Seung abruptly raised her clenched fist, and craned next to the door.

'Quiet!' Aiken dug a knuckle into Si's lower back.

Si didn't move, even holding his breath.

From beyond the door came the unmistakable clanks of someone scaling the metal stairs. Instantly, Aiken snatched up his phone, just as it vibrated to announce an incoming message from the duo outside. He checked it, and nodded emphatically at Seung. She gently slid back the bolt, even as Aiken drew his suppressed pistol and stepped out from behind Si for a clear shot through the doorway.

Both Aiken's and Seung's attention was rapt, waiting the second when an irate Lacey shoved inside. It was now or never for Si.

Without warning he snatched up the satchel and swung it at Aiken's face. It was too light to hurt, but the sudden shock caused the gunman to turn away, protecting his eyes as the cloth whipped his face and the bag's contents showered him. Si lurched for freedom, one elbow wrapped around his head as he charged the door to the storeroom. He was big, he was overweight, but it added to his momentum. He crashed into the door without wasting time going for the handle, and almost took it off its hinges. He scrambled into the room, his first instinct to grab for the camp bed and upend it in his wake, just as he heard the subdued crack of gunfire. Something stung his left hip, but the pain wasn't enough to stop him. He barreled on, kicked his way through an adjoining door and spilled into a narrow corridor. Another bullet chased him, but he wasn't the priority target. From where he'd come, he heard the main door get yanked open, and a thunder of feet on the stairs, yelled commands. In all probability both his tormentors were engaged in bringing down Lacey, and Si was safe from immediate pursuit, but that didn't slow him. He slammed down on the push bar, and shouldered out the fire exit. A rusted set of stairs, in worse shape than those at the front of his building gave access to a tiny yard, filled to capacity with trashcans and a dumpster. Si fought through them, and burst into a service alley. He scrunched his head down into his shoulders, a pointless attempt at offering a smaller target, and fled with the alacrity of a man half his size.

THIRTY-TWO

If Aaron Lacey knew where he was going to die, he wouldn't go there. The joke, and his resolve, was wearing thin. In fact, it barely crossed his mind as he paused at the foot of the corroded staircase and peered up at the door to Si Turpin's workshop. However, he'd been a cop too long to ignore the feeling of unease that crept through his chest as he pondered going up. The stairs, enclosed beneath tin sheets, and guarded from the street by a wrought-iron gate, looked like a rat run leading to a trap. His mind was not as sharp as it should've been when first Si's incessant ringing had wakened him. Anger and disappointment, if not surprise, had propelled him over here, in pain every step, but he wasn't about to play happy families with the fat shit. In his pocket, he carried his old service pistol. He'd force the scumbag to put things right with the flash drives, and then beat his gratitude into Si's flabby head with the barrel of his gun.

With one last glance over his shoulder, Lacey pulled open the gate and climbed the first half-dozen steps. He halted. Felt for the reassuring weight of his gun. It gave him confidence to proceed, but he didn't shift.

What's in it for you, Si? Did he think Lacey would forgive and forget, and still bring him in on the scheme to blackmail Elite Custodian Services? He'd be a fool to expect as much as a cent out of the takings now. *What's in it for you?* The question had plagued him every limping step of the way, but now he'd reached the stairs and paused his cop's radar had pinged a final warning. Summoning him to the workshop felt more and more like a trap. For as long as he'd known him Si had always been about his self-preservation. The epiphany struck him as hard as a kick to the nuts, and Lacey felt his gorge rise.

The idiot had tried beating him to the prize, by making his own blackmail demands first. And Lacey guessed what had been offered in exchange. The bastard! He'd tried luring him into Elite's clutches!

Instantly Lacey reared around, and began lumbering down the steps for the open gate. Behind him there was a ruckus, barely muffled by the intervening door: a thump, a slap of feet and something being broken, the dulled retort of a suppressed gun. The door overhead was yanked open, and commands for him to halt pursued him down the last steps. A bullet caromed off the metal gate a few inches from his head. Without thinking, Lacey tore the pistol out of his pocket, and blindly returned fire as he ducked out the gate and onto the sidewalk. Rapid clanging indicated a swift pursuit.

Lacey was incapable of running far, even energized by fear. He swung back, planned on ambushing his pursuers as they exited the stairwell. A door clunked open on a vehicle posted across the street, and a stocky man raised his close-cropped head above its roof. Lacey recognized the pug face that followed: Sean Nicholls. Lacey hadn't personally worked alongside the thickset veteran before but was aware of his reputation as a no-nonsense tough guy, the very type Hayden James would recruit to fill the empty shoes of Prescott. So who'd filled the vacancy left by Jacob Mathers?

Brian Johnson blocked the sidewalk twenty paces ahead. Because of other pedestrians, he hadn't yet drawn his weapon, but his hand was poised to draw it from a shoulder holster. He held out his other hand flat, a warning to stop.

Lacey was at the centre of a converging triangle of armed opponents, and yet he still had an advantage. None were prepared to shoot him dead, not without first checking he had the flash drives on his person. Even those who'd shot at him from the workshop had aimed to miss. He wasn't similarly constrained, but if he fired, then the scenario would change and they'd be entitled to save their own lives.

Bracing his feet, he swung his pistol between Johnson and Nicholls, the latter of whom lowered his head to place the car between them. Lacey could still see him through the windows, and it was apparent the guy was preparing for the worst. Lacey snapped a glance at the stairwell. He spotted red hair as Aiken popped out for a glimpse, then ducked under cover again. A few seconds later Aiken came into view once more, this time with his silenced pistol aimed directly at Lacey's chest. Beyond him, Vera Seung appeared, also threatening Lacey with a suppressed pistol as she sidestepped to a position where he had no escape beyond the massage parlour, should he take Aiken out of the equation.

Pedestrians ran for cover, some dropping to the sidewalks and covering their heads with their arms. Some shouted, and a woman shrieked, calling out to somebody else to get away. None had any idea if they'd been caught up in a law enforcement operation, or if they'd stumbled into the middle of a criminal shoot-out. It mattered not who was involved, a stray shot could kill from any weapon. Cars screeched to a halt, and one driver threw his vehicle into reverse and backed at speed to get out of the line of fire. Others sped up and streaked by, momentarily offering cover to Lacey from Nicholls, but it wasn't enough. It was only a matter of time until the real police responded, and none of them, Lacey included, wanted to be there when they arrived. He backed away from Aiken and Seung, his gun wavering between the two.

'You're done, Lace,' Aiken told him. 'Give up now, nobody else needs to get hurt.'

'Nobody but me, eh?' Lacey shook his head, then swung to aim at Johnson, whose gun was now out, but held low by his side: he still held out his palm, an imploring look on his face.

'Lower the gun, Lace.' In contradiction, Aiken held his firm, two handed.

'Shoot me, and you'll be sorry,' Lace warned.

'I don't want to shoot you, but you're forcing my decision.'

'Do that and you'll lose the files.'

'Bullshit. You've got them with you. We know you were bringing them back to Turpin to be fixed.'

'You think I trust that lying sack of puke after he tried to fuck me over? I only brought one of them.' Lacey pulled a flash drive from his pocket and slung it down. It bounced, then slid between Aiken and Seung. The woman crabbed sideways and slapped a foot down on it. Without lowering her pistol she crouched and retrieved it, and immediately tucked it in a pocket for safekeeping as she rose. 'Take it,' Lacey went on, 'it won't do you any good when I've already arranged for the others to be sent to the press and FBI in the event of my death.'

'You're lying,' said Aiken. 'You never did have a good poker face, buddy.'

'Let's not play games, Aiken, you were never my buddy. Now back the fuck away, and let me go, or you're all finished.'

Johnson had moved in a few paces while Lacey was distracted. He came to an abrupt halt when Lacey swung on him again. 'Don't,' was all the man said.

'Yeah,' agreed Lacey, 'don't. Now back up, or I swear to God . . .'

Behind Johnson, a young girl pushed to her feet and ran, hunched, over for the nearest doorway. Across the street, Nicholls leaned over the roof of the car with his gun extended. He glanced repeatedly at Aiken for instruction: Aiken was the default leader of the pack for the time being.

'I'm surprised Hayden isn't here,' Lacey said, as he stepped off the curb onto the road, causing them all to adjust their trajectories. 'This is his op, right? I bet it's become kinda personal to him.'

'He's coming,' Aiken assured him as he shuffled forward. 'It's not him you should be worried about though. After what you did to her boyfriend, Megan's got a real boner for you, Lace.'

'Megan can bite me,' Lacey growled, although he was under no illusion: if the deranged bitch were here now there would be no stand-off, she'd come in with all guns blazing. Her imminent arrival made getting away more pressing, because she wouldn't care if killing him meant the files would be released. Why the others hadn't shot him dead already was apparent: Hayden had commanded that they take him alive – to negate the kind of bluff he was pulling now – and, conditioned to take orders, they were loath to shoot. Albeit, they weren't averse to disarming him and taking him down by force, which was the reason they inched in, closing the noose on him, and why he sought space to manoeuvre in the centre of the street. His action drew out Nicholls, who edged around the front of the car, even as Seung moved parallel to Aiken.

It was now or never, Lace realized, before they pounced on him like a flock of ravenous crows on road kill. His safe options were few, but far better than if they'd trapped him between them on the metal stairs, out of sight and sound of the public, as they'd originally planned. Next to Nicholls was the entrance to a dance studio. Lacey had spotted a couple of kids take cover inside when panic had spread among the civilians. If he could make it past the stocky gunman and through the doors, there was the possibility of finding an exit he could barricade behind him, and give him a few precious minutes to escape. Surely in an environment where there were probably more kids, the others wouldn't use their guns? But Lacey wasn't a complete shit: he couldn't be confident they'd hold fire and wouldn't put children at risk, not even for the sake of his own life.

He lunged towards Nicholls, and the guy crouched, spreading his stance, unsure whether to shoot or to grapple, and instantly Lacey danced back again, ignoring the flash of pain in his left knee that threatened to make his leg collapse. He rushed from the gap between Johnson and the gunman now behind him. Aiken and Seung leapt after him, even as Johnson lunged to cut him off: thankfully nobody went for a crippling shot to his legs, and he hoped that would last. He stuck his gun in Johnson's face, snarling in defiance, but the man wasn't deterred; he knew that to shoot meant engaging them all in mortal combat. Lacey jerked aside, twisting to check where the others were, and used the butt of his pistol to hammer Johnson aside. Johnson deftly avoided the swing of the gun, using his own pistol to bat it further away. He got a hand on Lacey's jacket and was trawled a few feet in his wake. Lacey elbowed at him, brought round his pistol and stuck it in the guy's ribs. He faced the other trio with his hostage between them. 'Stop, or he gets it!' he hollered.

Nobody stopped, not even Johnson, who squirmed away from the gun, and brought round his own. Lacey grappled his wrist, and the gun exploded, deafening so close to his ear, and the flash and stink of black powder filled Lacey's senses. Johnson clasped his other hand, flexing his hand outward, and locking it torturously close to breaking. Lacey kneed him in the groin, and the grip on his arm lessened, but already, through the black spots swimming in his vision he saw the others swooping in to grab him. He shoved Johnson aside, and braced to meet them. Ears ringing, he didn't hear his yell of challenge as he readied to fight them off, or the louder roar bearing down on him.

THIRTY-THREE

Even though he was a big guy, big-boned and thick with muscle, despite carrying a surplus of flesh, he wasn't a real match for almost four thousand pounds of steel and rubber. So when he hurtled blindly from a cross street and into the path of the Mustang, there was only going to be one outcome. He was swept into the air by the front fender and deposited on the hood, before he windmilled off again and crumpled to the ground. In that brief and startling moment before they collided and he stamped the brake pedal, Po got a snapshot look at the man's flat nose and eyes that bugged out of his sweating face in fear.

'Holy shit!' Po wheezed as he brought the muscle car to a halt. But already the big man had scrambled up, and lurched away across Eighth Avenue without a care for being hit again. If he was injured by the collision he didn't show it. Po looked over at Tess, who sat open-mouthed as she watched the guy disappear among the pedestrians waiting for the streetlights to change so they could cross safely. All those observing the lights stared in mawkish fashion at where the Mustang had been brought to a halt. Already, behind it, other road users were hitting their horns to get Po moving again, now that the drama was over.

'What just *happened*?' Tess asked.

'He's just put two hundred bucks worth of damage on my hood,' Po observed, trying to use humour to leaven the shock. He looked for the guy, but he'd fled the scene without a backwards glance. 'There must be a ninety-nine cents all-you-can-eat deal on at Wendy's,' he said with a nod at a nearby chain diner.

'Po, show some compassion. The poor guy could've been badly injured.'

'Yeah, he coulda been. Good job he ran when he did, or I might've slapped some road sense into the idiot.' He was still attempting to lighten the mood, as he had been since Barbara Grey ended her call with the direction to look for Lacey near De Witt Clinton Park. Tess had been sombre throughout the drive. Due to the one-way systems in place, the route had brought them back around via Eighth Avenue, where Po had been looking for a viable place to cut across town when the guy had unexpectedly lurched in front of them. Ahead the other cars had cleared the road as far as two blocks to the junction with West 57th Street. Between them and where Po got the Mustang moving again, other pedestrians began running across the street, fleeing some danger on 56th.

Tess exchanged a glance with Po. He squinted, observing the panic-stricken people running for cover. Cars pushed out on to the avenue against the lights. Po drew the buckled hood of his Mustang close to the corner, and they both scanned the street, wondering what lunacy was going on.

'I don't believe it,' Tess announced. 'It's him, Po!'

Po had only seen a photograph of the man they sought, lifted from his driver's license by Tess, but it was dated, and posed formally, so if he'd randomly met Lacey he might not have recognized him. This version of the man was older, heavier, had shaggier grey hair and had gone unshaven for a week. In his DMV ID, he had looked smug, on the verge of arrogance. The man surrounded on four sides by armed assailants projected desperation as he swung a pistol back and forward, trying to force a gap to escape through. Two of those advancing on him were more recognizable to Po, even with their backs to him: it was the ginger-haired guy and Asian woman who'd tailed Stella Dewildt from her hotel to the airport in Boston. The other two men, one tall and dusky-skinned, the second a bulldog with broad shoulders and thick arms, were strangers, but immediately identifiable as Elite operatives through their military bearing. Of the tall guy and scarred woman there was no sign, but that was likely to change. In the snap moment that Po took in the scene, he figured a trap had been sprung, but Elite's timing was off and Lacey had made it into the public arena before they could subdue him. Everyone had guns, but nobody was shooting, but that was apt to change. Either Lacey would be winged and brought down, or his desperation would grow and he'd respond with force, and the shit would really hit the fan.

Beside him, Tess's face was beyond pale as she stared at the man, and Po knew she was momentarily overwhelmed by competing emotions.

'Tess, they're going to take him if we don't move.' Po announced. Tess was licensed to carry back in Maine, but hadn't fetched her gun from the strongbox kept in her apartment on Cumberland Avenue. Other than his knife concealed in a boot sheath, they were unarmed. No, that was untrue.

'Climb in the back,' he said. His command was sharp; Tess

needed to snap out of it. She gawped at him, then back at the circle of assailants closing in on Lacey. Po shook her. 'Tess, get in the back now, and keep your head down!'

She nodded dumbly, but then a spark lit her gaze, as she understood Po's intention. She unclipped her belt and squeezed backwards through the gap between the seats and scrunched down across the rear bench seat. As Po gunned the engine she reached for the handle on the vacated front seat and flipped the backrest forward. 56th Street was one-way, and the traffic flow against them, but that was to their advantage. All other traffic had come to a stop a distance beyond the showdown, most of the driver's abandoning their vehicles as they ran for cover. Po had a clear run of twenty yards. He wasn't unarmed, he had almost four thousand pounds of steel and rubber that had proven its efficacy as a blunt instrument minutes earlier. He spun the muscle car through the No Entry signs, and hit the gas, and the Mustang roared as it burned rubber directly towards the group. Lacey and the dusky-skinned guy scuffled, and Lacey momentarily got control of the other guy, but didn't keep the upper hand. They jostled, and a gun went off. Then Lacey was locked at the wrist, but he kneed his opponent, and he broke free, only to be rushed by the others.

Po could mow down the entire group, but that would include Lacey. Not the result he hoped for. He took his foot off the gas, yanked down on the steering and the Mustang spun out. The rear tyres juddered on asphalt as the back end swung in an arc. The impact with a body much lighter than the big guy's earlier still rocked the car. The Asian woman was knocked reeling across the street, before she went down on her belly, a gun slipping from her flexing fingers. The ginger-haired man wasn't struck as severely, though he still stumbled away, and fell to his knees. Lacey was as stunned as everyone else, but he shook out of the fugue a second before they could recover, and he aimed a kick that hit the kneeling man square under the chin. By then, Tess reached and threw open the passenger door.

'Get in!' Po's shout snapped a glance from Lacey, but he was a stranger to the fugitive, and no trustworthier than any

of the four threatening his liberty. Lacey sought escape by
clambering over the top of the fallen ginger-haired operative,
only for the dusky-skinned man to lunge at him, and the stocky
bruiser to adjust his aim on the car. Lacey dodged back, and
again peered in abject hope at Po. 'Get in, goddammit!' Po
exhorted.

Lacey was still in flux.

The two able operatives were still armed, and there was
only one reason why they had not yet shot Lacey dead. They
needed to take him alive. The sentiment wasn't extended to
Po. The stocky guy fired and blew out part of the windscreen.
Shards peppered Po, who snarled in rage, and was about to
hit the gas: he wasn't about to let either him or Tess die for
the sake of an ungrateful son of a bitch!

'Aaron! Do as he says . . . *Get in now!'*

Lacey saw the face, and reaching hands beseeching him
from the rear seat, and was suddenly struck by recognition.
His features grew lax, and he stared for the briefest of seconds,
trying to make sense of his would be rescuer. Then he lurched
forward, and scrambled in over the tilted seat back, and Tess
grabbed and yanked his torso inside. His legs flailed a moment,
and were grappled by the taller gunman, who tried to drag
him out. The stockier gunman skipped nimbly around the
vehicle, his gun extended, but thankfully he didn't shoot again
for fear of hitting his colleague. Po hit the gas and yanked
down on the steering wheel, and the Mustang fishtailed back
the way it'd originally come, dragging the gunman with it.
The man's grip failed on Lacey's legs and he tumbled to the
curb. In frustration the only man left standing fired two shots,
one into the trunk, the other caroming off the back window.

Po ignored the red light at Eighth Avenue: all traffic had
come to a halt as people swarmed the intersection to observe
the lunacy in their midst. As the gunman let loose another
shot, they scattered and the Mustang had a free run along 56th
and away, with Aaron Lacey topping and tailing with Tess
across the back seat, while the open door flapped back and
forth until finally slamming shut with a bang louder than any
that had come in the preceding few minutes.

THIRTY-FOUR

B en Holbrook stared out of the window of his corner office, but was blind to the view across Boston Harbor, his thoughts hundreds of miles away.

'I had everything set up: how did it all go so wrong?'

He didn't respond to Clarissa Glenn, too caught up in his own disbelief to offer a solution to hers.

Earlier, they'd both been confident that the Aaron Lacey problem was about to be finalized when Glenn had set up the trap, luring him to Si Turpin's workshop where a team was already in place to grab him, and whisk him away in a non-descript van retrofitted for purpose. But look at where overconfidence got them.

Everything was spiraling out of control and unless Holbrook got a tight grip on the reins things would only get worse. It should have been an easy enough task to track and silence a washed up ex-cop, except Lacey had continually thwarted all their efforts and was still on the loose, and in possession of the damning evidence of their role in covering up a murder, and the blackmail plot that followed. Complication had piled on top of complication. Lacey must be dealt with, and now Si Turpin was on the run, and even if all the evidence was out of his reach, he could still squeal to the cops. If it were only Turpin's word to worry about, Holbrook would laugh it off. But after the incident at Turpin's workshop he'd be hard put to convince the police there was nothing in the guy's story: it'd put Elite under a microscope. Although he'd managed to hush up any involvement with the violent encounters in Boston, Holbrook had no sway with the NYPD.

Already the NYPD had launched a major investigation into the gun battle on 56th Street, which had culminated in Lacey's escape, and the burning down of Turpin's workshop. Grant Aiken, having returned for the rucksack and its contents, then took pains to cover up any forensic evidence inside by setting the place alight. Dozens of witnesses had observed his people make their escape in the two vehicles, a car and the van, and time must now be wasted in getting them out of sight, and his team mobile again. The only saving grace was that Hayden James hadn't gotten caught up in the clusterfuck, so was still able to move at liberty . . . That was supposing he couldn't be tied to the vicious assault on Herbert Grover; the retired doctor's murder was yet to be discovered, but was inevitable. Hopefully Hayden and Megan had gone unobserved entering or leaving the old man's home. Initially, Holbrook had been enraged on hearing about Megan's actions, and demanded to know why she'd been allowed to feed her appetite for violence, but Hayden had explained that to ensure they all escaped prison, they must clean up behind them. This Holbrook accepted begrudgingly, but where must things end? With the deaths of everyone who had the slightest inkling of what was going on. The list was growing longer: Lace, Turpin, Grey, Villere, and Estelle Dewildt, and who knew how many others they'd confided in; even some of their operatives, uninvolved in the original cover-up, were beginning to fill in gaps and coming to their own conclusions.

'Those bloody private eyes . . .'

Again, Glenn's words skirted past Holbrook.

'Ben? Ben! Aren't you listening?'

He turned and regarded the austere woman. She sat on a corner of his desk, arms folded across her chest, hawkish nose tilted towards the ceiling.

'I'm trying to think of a way out of this,' he snapped, 'but can't for all your complaints. For God's sake, will you just give me a break?'

Glenn pinched her lips, scolded him with her raisin eyes. 'I don't appreciate being spoken to as if I'm one of the help,' she said. 'I've as much at stake in solving *our* problem as you have, Ben.'

'So instead of asking why everything went wrong, help me figure out what we should do next.'

'I think it's apparent, don't you?'

'No.' Holbrook shook his head. 'It isn't apparent to me. Help me out here, Clarissa.'

'I was offering a solution,' she said, 'but you weren't listening. There's only one thing more important to Lacey than using the files to extort us: his daughter. We never worked that angle before, because we had no way of contacting him and making our own demands. That, I believe, has now changed. But we must act fast before those bloody private eyes convince Lacey to go to the police. Until we know otherwise, we have to assume the data's still salvageable and must ensure the devices are destroyed.'

Holbrook nodded. Turpin had allegedly input a malware programme into the devices in Lacey's possession, but they only had the conman's word to go on: they couldn't be certain he hadn't made up the lie when confronted by Glenn, his way of wheedling some cash out of them for helping to trap Lacey. Vera Seung had recovered one thumb drive, which was yet to be tested, but according to Turpin, he'd given another two copies and the original back to Lace: any, or all of them, could still be a viable threat to Elite.

Holbrook phoned Hayden.

'Bring the daughter here, and if anyone gets in your way, take Megan's lead and shut them up permanently.' He waited until he received Hayden's affirmation, then added, 'The instant she's in your hands let us know and we'll contact her father, oh, and Hayden, time is against us.'

'On it.' Hayden's reply was clipped, but held a great deal of promise: Holbrook should have lifted the non-combat constraints he'd placed on his right-hand man from the beginning. He had tired of third-party interference: Grey and Villere wouldn't have lived to snatch Lacey out of his team's hands if he'd sent Hayden to that crummy motel instead of trusting to local hoodlums to get the job done. Even if some miracle had saved them, those meddling PIs wouldn't have survived a second confrontation if he hadn't forbidden Aiken and the others from shooting to kill. His original order didn't extend beyond Lacey, but they couldn't

know he'd have happily rescinded the order when it came
to those two assholes. He wouldn't make the same mistake
again.

'Have the New York team take care of Turpin; we can deal
with Grey and Villere once they bring Lacey to us in Boston,'
he added.

THIRTY-FIVE

'Y ou can get off me now.' Lacey wasn't exactly a small
guy, and Tess was smothered. He was furnace hot
and his clothing damp with sweat: his odour was
unhealthy. She pushed and squirmed, so she could shift
around on the bench seat. He hissed and groaned, the act of
any movement an intense labor. Tess sat, squashed into one
corner while he manually dragged one of his legs off her.
She pushed her hair into some semblance of order, ran her
palms over her face, looked at something sticky on her palms.

'Blood! Were one of you hit?'

'Stung by a bit of flyin' glass, but I'm good,' Po reported,
then with a grumble, 'can't say the same for my ride.'

She studied the man beside her. He sat with his head thrown
back, eyelids squeezed tight, gasping for air. The ordeal had
taken a lot out of him. His hands were clasped above his right
hip. Blood leaked between his fingers. Tess almost lunged on
top of him this time.

'It's OK,' he croaked and fended her off with the gentle
shove of his shoulder. 'It's an old wound; things just got a bit
too strenuous back there . . .'

'Let me see,' Tess leaned over him a second time, reaching
to move his fingers aside.

'Don't worry about me, I'll be fine, just need . . .' He halted,
looking at her for the second time with confusion. 'Who are
you people anyway? For a second back there I thought you
were—'

'Stella,' said Tess, and felt the blood rush to her head.

'Yeah, you look a bit like my daughter.'

'We're private detectives. We were hired by Stella to find you,' said Tess.

'Yeah?' Again he studied her closely. 'But that doesn't explain why you look so familiar. Who are you?'

Before he could ask more, Tess peeled away his fingers and saw that beneath his jacket his shirt was sopping with blood. He immediately clamped his hand in place once more, and turned so he could regard her again. 'I can see you're not really like my Stella, the resemblance is only passing, and I guess I wouldn't have noticed at all if she hadn't took to dyeing her hair the same as you.'

Tess's colouring was natural, but she wasn't offended. And he had a point; with her natural auburn hair, Stella's passing likeness to her would be greatly diminished. Had she, as her mother more or less pointed out, been seeing patterns where none existed? It wasn't something she wanted to go into right then. 'We have to stop the bleeding,' she directed at Po.

'Can't help you from up here, unless you want me to pull over?'

'No, keep moving.' It was imperative that they put some distance between them and 56th Street: in fact, now Lacey was in their hands they should head directly to the nearest police station, but neither of them had suggested it yet. Plus, Lacey would be in disagreement, and she didn't want a wrestling match with him if he tried to escape the confines of the car.

'I'll be fine,' Lacey reassured her. 'It's just a coupla stitches that've come loose. Once my heart stops beating a mile a minute the bleeding will stop.'

Tess moved his hands again. 'Let me see.'

'You're a doctor or somethin'? No, you said you were a PI. Leave me be, and I'll be OK.' He jammed his hands on the wound again, applying pressure. Fresh beads of sweat broke out under his hairline and ran down his forehead.

'You look as if you've got a fever. When were you wounded?'

Lacey shrugged her question off.

'It was up in Boston, right? Before you escaped Elite the first time.'

'Uh, so you know about those A-holes, then?'

'We know everything,' she lied. She still had misgivings about more than her parentage: could they be harboring a murderer? Fleetingly, she checked for his pistol, but he must have dropped it when scrambling aboard. By pretending to know everything already, he'd be more inclined to elicit the answers she wanted rather than if interrogated. She changed the subject. 'If you were shot more than a week ago, you could be incredibly sick by now. How long have you been feverish like this?' His odour was sickly sweet. 'Is your wound infected?'

'I just saw a doctor yesterday, and everything was fine. I think I've just overexerted myself since then . . . against his advice.' He offered a faint grin of self-admonishment, then laughed, and aimed his next comment at Po. 'Us guys, we never are very good at taking instruction, right? Especially if it means admitting we aren't as young and fit as we used to be.'

'That ain't a conversation I want to be part of, bra,' Po replied sardonically.

Tess rested the back of her hand on Lacey's forehead, forcing him to shy away before relenting again.

'You're on fire.'

'I was just surrounded by four bad guys with guns, and barely escaped with my life. Stands to reason I might be a little hot.' Again he tried to fend her off gently, but Tess was persistent. She tugged at his collar and found another wound, this one a slice in the flesh that had already been sutured, and scabbed over without any apparent complications.

'Have you any other wounds I've missed?' she asked.

He touched his side. 'This is a through and through. Exit wound's in my back, but far as I can tell it's OK.'

'We need to check. But we can't do it here, we'll have to find somewhere I can have a look without attracting any attention.'

'I've told you I'm fine. Look, thanks for saving my ass back there, but if you just let me off at the next corner, I'll take care of things from there.'

His instruction didn't deserve an answer.

Tess glanced at the passing street signs, but couldn't immediately get her bearings, and then it struck her. Po had taken them across Midtown and then north. She recognized the trees and raised flowerbeds of Park Avenue: they were approaching the bridge over 42nd Street on the approach to Grand Central Station. It was a location she knew more these days from movies and TV programs than from any childhood memory. The elevated road swung to the right, towards the towering ebony glass structure of the Grand Hyatt Hotel, before turning left and following the contours of the world famous train station to an underpass, before they exited onto a continuation of Park Avenue. Long before that, she understood Po's destination.

'We can't return to Stella's yet,' she reminded him.

'Not going to.' It was feasible her apartment was under surveillance and showing up there with Lacey might encourage an all-out siege. After what had recently happened at 56th Street the Elite team might not be as keen to hold fire, especially as it was only Lacey they needed alive. 'But I want to get us close. Call Pinky, will ya, and tell him to get ready to move Stella outta there.'

Lacey bolted upright. 'My daughter has nothing to do with this!'

'That was before,' Tess replied, understanding Po's concern. 'Now they know for sure that you're in New York, and you're with us, they'll be looking everywhere connected with us too, and they know we're working on Stella's behalf.'

'Those sons of bitches better not harm my daughter . . . dammit! Why'd Stella have to stick her nose in my business and involve you guys? I tried to keep her out of this—'

'By not letting her know you were even alive?' Tess set her jaw. 'Don't be so damned selfish! What kind of daughter would she be if she didn't look for you?'

Her reproach was double-edged, but it was only Po who caught it. He shot her a glance in the rear-view mirror that asked: *Do you really want to go there?* She seethed for a second longer, then gave a subtle shake of her head. Now was not the time. Lacey didn't want to broach the subject either.

He felt under his shirt, moaning at what he found. His fingers came away scarlet to the knuckles. Tess cast around, seeking something to use as a bandage: their overnight bags were in the trunk, there was a towel in hers. But while they were moving, she didn't want Po to stop so she could fish it out. She struggled out of her jacket, and then yanked off her shirt. Down to her bra, she wadded up her shirt, and forced it under Lacey's hands. 'Keep pressure on that.'

Lacey ogled her. Not in any lascivious manner. She was baring more flesh than she'd have liked, but Lacey's gaze didn't stray inappropriately: he'd centred his attention on her face. He continued appraising her as she worked back into her jacket, and zipped it up. She returned his stare, her mouth pinched.

'You're Mikey Grey's grandkid,' he said. 'Young Michael's your dad.'

'Yes,' Tess confirmed. It was strange hearing her father referred to as 'young', when her brother was known as Michael junior, but she guessed it was a generational thing to Lacey who'd worked alongside 'old' Mikey. 'I'm his daughter.'

'Jeez, that explains everything.' He nodded his head in satisfaction. 'Why I thought you looked so familiar.'

Tess waited, dreading what might come next.

'You know something, Tess . . . or is it Teresa?'

'Tess.'

He smiled. 'Not into all that formal stuff, eh? I'm surprised, 'cause right down to your mannerisms you're the spitting double of your mom.'

She exhaled sharply.

'Barbara was a beautiful woman,' he offered, unaware that it wasn't what she wanted to hear, quite the opposite. 'You look very much like she did when I knew her.'

'How well did you know her?'

She sensed the tensing of Po's shoulders. It didn't affect his driving. He'd slowed as he negotiated the traffic towards the Upper East Side: the last he wanted was to attract the attention of a passing patrol car. The bullet hole in the windscreen was small, and could be explained away as the result of a flying stone, but coupled with the hole in the trunk, and the buckled hood, a nosey cop might deem the car unroadworthy, inviting a closer inspection. The bloody hole in Aaron Lacey wouldn't be as easily explained. He kept quiet, keeping a lookout as he drove, but Tess was aware he was listening keenly.

'You probably don't remember much. You were a little girl when I worked with Mikey, but I was a friend of the entire family. I was more of an age with your parents, so we hit it off. Your grandfather was like my mentor; he had twenty years on me so I'd more in common with Young Mike. We used to party, y'know, your dad and mom, me and Stella's mom.'

She didn't want to acknowledge his words, certainly didn't want to imagine what he meant by 'party together'.

'It was a real shame what happened to your dad. Sheesh! Bowel cancer, what a horrible way to go.' Lacey shook his head in genuine remorse. 'Must've been really hard for your mom to watch him go through that.'

'It was difficult on all of us.'

'I'd say.'

'Keep the pressure on that wound,' she instructed, 'and tell us instead what the hell we're dealing with here.'

'I thought you knew everything . . .'

'We know you stole something from your employers, and they're very determined to get it back. We know one guy already paid with his life, and the way things are going there could be more people hurt. We just risked our lives for you back there, and I want to know it was worth it.'

'You're wondering if I'm really the bad guy?' He wheezed in laughter, the action painful. 'Depends on your perspective, I guess.'

Po was growing restless. 'As much as I'd like to hear yours, bra, there's somethin' *you* gotta do first, Tess. Call Pinky.'

He was right. The operation to capture Lacey had gone wrong for them, and the Elite team would've been forced to make their escape before the police arrived on the scene, but it was odd's on they were already reorganizing for another attempt at bringing him in. Po's driving had put them ahead of the game, but they wouldn't be far behind. If this were her op – and she had the same lack of scruples – she'd go after someone important to him next. Up until now Stella had largely been left alone, but she was a pawn to be shifted. To Lacey she said, 'If ever your daughter's going to be safe again, you're going to have to tell us the truth.' She left it at that, and took out her phone from her jacket pocket.

Pinky's phone rang out. So did Stella's when she rang hers.

Before she'd done trying Pinky a second time, she scrambled into the front passenger seat and Po's foot jammed down heavily on the gas. Any intention of steering clear of Stella's apartment vanished.

THIRTY-SIX

'**S**tand down, pal,' said Hayden James.

Apart from averting his face from the CCTV camera he hadn't bothered with a stealthy approach, he'd gone direct to the door of Stella Dewildt's apartment and kicked his way inside, only to find his passage to the woman barred by some weird-looking black man who appeared to be the product of two magician's apprentices sawn in half, their component parts mixed up, and then sewn wrongly together again at the lower chest.

'You want her, you'll have to go through me.' The man had backed Stella into the kitchen, and swept a large knife from a chopping block. He didn't look fearful of Hayden's suppressed pistol.

'I don't want to shoot you.'

'I don't want shot either, me,' the man replied, his speech pattern as weird as his appearance, 'so put down your gun and walk away.'

'Can't do that. I said I don't want to, but I *will* shoot.'

'Then you'd better hope you kill me first time, or you're goin' to have a real problem, you.'

Hayden wagged his pistol. 'You're a brave man, I'll give you that, but you're misguided if you think you can get to me before I empty this clip in you.'

Opposite him, the black guy cocked his head, as if considering his words. He seemed to come to a conclusion: perhaps Hayden's reticence to shoot gave him false hope. He raised the kitchen knife above the breakfast counter that separated them. 'Well, I'm up for tryin', me, but you don't look so keen on finding out.'

Stella Dewildt cowered beyond her protector, barely visible because of his bulk. She kept glancing at the cell phone ringing on the counter a few feet out of reach, tempted to lunge for it and scream for help. A minute ago, another phone had rung incessantly from the black man's hip pocket, but he hadn't allowed it to distract him: his attention was fully on Hayden since he'd smashed inside the apartment.

'That's probably your friend Villere calling to warn you about me,' Hayden said. 'It's too late for him to help.'

'If you do kill me and take the girl,' the guy replied, 'Nicolas will hunt you down and cut out your heart.'

Hayden shrugged. 'Or I'll cut out his.'

'You don't realize the kind of enemies you're courting, you.'

'Or I don't care.'

The black man shook his head, and a feral smile displayed large white teeth. 'You care, otherwise you'd have pulled that trigger by now.'

Hayden lowered his gun.

His opponent kept the knife up.

'You misunderstand my reluctance,' said Hayden. He wanted to take Stella alive. The big guy's body might not absorb all of his bullets. Besides, he was only stalling, though time was against him and he couldn't keep up the act forever. 'Stand aside, and I promise neither of you will be harmed.'

The man snorted. 'You think I just fell out of a coconut tree? I'm just some kinda dumb nigga man to you?'

'Buddy, I wouldn't insult you like that. Some of my best friends are niggers.' He offered a snarky grin.

'Kiss my black ass.'

The phone on the counter fell silent, and the one in the man's hip pocket burst to life instead. The guy adjusted his weight, but only to press Stella further behind him as she groped for his phone. In that split second, his attention drifted, and his body turned fractionally away. He was returning to front and centre when Hayden's hand snatched up, and he fired.

'Down!' The man spun incredibly fast, engulfing the smaller woman: he seemed not to have noticed the bullet that had cut a chunk of skin from his right thigh. Hayden had purposefully shot wide to avoid hitting Stella behind him. The kitchen counter was briefly between them, and Hayden had to crab around it, never lowering his aim. He could have stitched a pattern in the broad back presented to him, but held fire, waiting for a clean shot where there was no risk of collateral damage.

Stella scrambled to the right, now hidden beyond the far end of the counter, but she'd placed her friend at Hayden's mercy. He paused: his sentiment still held; he didn't want to shoot Stella's protector but he would. He aimed directly between the heaving shoulder blades. But then Stella rose up, her empty hands imploring him to hold fire. Hayden flicked a glance at her, considered her plea, then ignored it: Holbrook's order to clean shop should be obeyed.

Without warning his target unfolded, whipping up and back from a crouch, and the flash of steel yanked Hayden's gun up as he dodged the hurled knife. The blade embedded in the wall behind him, even as his shot struck a cupboard door and broke crockery within. He steadied his feet, and his aim, but a fraction of a second too late. The big man launched up, sweeping the gun high with his forearm, and tackled Hayden with the brutal impact of a Sumo wrestler. Hayden was borne backwards, until they slammed the wall. His assailant – how the dynamic had changed in an instant – heaved up with his shoulders, picking up Hayden and grinding him against the wall. Hayden's gun hand was gripped at the wrist. He strove to bring around the barrel and shoot his attacker, but the extra length of the suppressor made it difficult to place a bullet in the man's back. Another stray shot caromed off the floor and shattered glass somewhere. For fear another ricochet would strike Stella, Hayden held fire, and instead smashed his opposite palm repeatedly against the man's ribs. Ineffectively it turned out. Hayden was dragged along the wall, and slammed sideways into a table and chairs. The racket of scraping chair legs joined the clatter of their feet as they wrestled for control of the gun.

The black man's arms were oddly thin compared to his large thighs and midriff, but there was nothing weak about them. A scarlet flash filled his vision as a clubbing left hook landed on Hayden's jaw. Blackness wavered at its edges. Instinct kicked in without conscious thought, and Hayden drove a knee into his opponent's body. He heard a gasp as the air was forced out of the man's lungs. Briefly there was space between them, and Hayden optimized on the moment, kneeing again at the same spot. Wheezing, the man ducked, protecting his solar plexus, and scooped up Hayden's knee, to mobilize it. He was thrown backwards over the table, his opponent never letting go of his wrist or knee. They rolled, scattering plates and coffee mugs yet to be cleared away after breakfast, and crashed to the floor. Hayden hissed as a shard of ceramic pierced his thigh: karma was a bitch, which demanded immediate recompense for shooting his opponent there. He kicked free of the man's hold around his knee, then slammed a heel into his left kidney. They both scuffled for dominance as they rose to their knees: his gun was practically useless but under no circumstance would he willingly discard it to free up his hand.

His arm was slammed repeatedly against the table, but he held on to his gun, and instead chopped at the man's head with the blade of his left hand. Immediately a headbutt smacked into his face, and Hayden was only saved from a crushed nose as he managed to dip his chin down at the last instant and they went forehead to forehead. Nevertheless, the impact sent another cloud of scarlet and swirling black dots exploding across his vision. The strange notion struck that it was always easier defending another person, than it was one's self when fighting a determined opponent. Distracted he missed the next blow, this time the web between the man's index finger and thumb jammed into his windpipe. Hayden gagged, and couldn't defend against a punch that almost loosened his teeth. *Fuck not shooting for fear of hitting Stella*; he forced the gun around and finally got a bead on the fat bastard.

Something slammed into his head, and Hayden buckled, the gun falling from his fingers and sliding away under the table. Bleary eyed, he blinked up at Stella who stood over him, threatening to smash his skull in with a heavy skillet. He was jostled again by his opponent, and thought he was done.

'Drop it, bitch, or I'll blow your head off!'

Beyond Stella, Megan materialized from the adjoining hallway, a suppressed pistol extended in both hands. Stella remained defiant for a second, the skillet poised to strike again, but there was a different level of threat in the scarred woman's glaring eyes: she'd happily blast holes into Stella's pretty face. Stella dropped the pan and it clanged at Hayden's side. His opponent had also relented beating on him, and had gotten to his knees a few feet away, hands up. Hayden shook lucidity into his brain, watching as Megan stalked all the way to Stella's side and buried the tip of the suppressor in the hair above her left ear. In the next moment, Megan yanked Stella into her grasp, wrapping an arm around her throat and dragged her backwards off balance.

'You took your damned time,' Hayden snarled at his partner as he pushed up from the floor.

'Took longer getting in through the back than I thought. Don't know what you're complaining about, everything turned out well in the end.' Megan sneered down at Hayden's kneeling opponent. 'Didn't think you'd have much trouble with an unarmed slob.'

Hayden felt as if a football team had used his head for practice. The black guy looked soft and weak, he was the epitome of contradiction. If Hayden wasn't in such pain – not to mention shameful that a cooking pot had almost taken him out – he might respect the guy's fighting ability. Instead, he sneered at him with as much bile as Megan did. 'Would've been a different story if I hadn't tried *not* to kill you,' he said.

The guy cocked his head. 'I didn't have the same qualms, me.'

'Who the fuck is this joker?' Megan demanded.

'He's unimportant. Get Stella to the car . . .' Somewhere a phone was still ringing. 'I'll be with you in a minute.'

'Let me kill the fat ass for you,' Megan offered. 'I won't hold back.'

The black man laughed in scorn and Megan's features screwed in rage.

'D'you want to try me?' she spat. 'I'll kick you so hard you'll spray shit all over this place, and then when I'm done killing you, I'll rub this bitch's face in it.'

'Hmm, you've such a ladylike way of speaking,' the man replied. 'I've never willingly hurt a lady before, but for you I'll make the exception. If you hurt as much as a hair on Stella's head—'

'Shut up!' Hayden swung the skillet. It rang dully off the man's skull and he sprawled face down, arms outstretched, blood pulsing from the broken skin above his left eyebrow. Stella yelped in alarm, shouted a name: 'Pinky!'

'Fucking "Pinky", what kind of name's that for a brother?' Megan snarled at her. When Stella opened her mouth to respond, she was rewarded with a slap to her face, and Megan began jostling her for the exit. Hayden retrieved his pistol, and unscrewed the silencer, all the while staring down at the recumbent man. Maybe, he thought wryly, in future he shouldn't be so contemptuous of anyone using a cast-iron pot as a weapon. Blood pooled on the floor around Pinky's skull and he didn't as much as twitch. Hayden crouched alongside him, dug in his hip pocket and pulled out his cell phone. The screen flashed, announcing the caller: *Tess*.

He would speak with her in his own time. Hayden declined the call, but slipped the phone into his jacket pocket for safe-keeping. He paused and regarded his fallen opponent a final time. If he hadn't unscrewed his suppressor he would put a bullet into Pinky's heart, making certain he was dead as per Holbrook's orders. It would be a matter of seconds to refit the silencer but why bother? Pinky's brains were nigh on leaking on the floor as it were. He turned away and followed Megan out with their hostage.

THIRTY-SEVEN

D espite the threat to his welfare, Lacey wouldn't stay hidden in the Mustang, and neither Tess nor Po had the time or inclination to waste trying to keep him there. In fact, if she wasn't so worried about Pinky and Stella, his determination to get to his daughter might have won an iota of respect from Tess. As it were, she rushed for the door, only a step behind Po, barely aware of Lacey's stumbling progress up the short flight of stairs behind her.

Po paused ahead of her, dipped down, and came up with a knife from his boot sheath. She could sense his reticence to entering unarmed. The lock was broken, and the door wide open. There was no other hint of a break-in within the entrance vestibule or the adjoining sitting room, but the evidence was plain to see strewn across the kitchen floor. Broken crockery was scattered on the tiles, a heavy skillet pan among it, and a chair had been upended. Po quickly held up a hand to stall the others. He gestured at Tess to check the sitting room before they all got bunched in the kitchen where they could be cornered. Tess made a brief check, not going further inside than the threshold, and then Lacey roughly pushed past her and followed Po into the kitchen. She entered, scanned left where the men had gone, and felt her heart squeeze. Pinky was face down and unmoving beyond more overturned chairs and a table shoved off-kilter, the obvious wreckage of a fight. Glass and broken dishes littered the floor around him, and a knife was buried almost to its hilt in the wall. Po rushed to his friend, and touched fingers to his throat. Po was still, concern waging with rage for control of his emotions. He looked up at Tess, and she'd never seen him look as desperate before. 'He's got a pulse . . .'

She rushed to Po's side, dreading the full story of Pinky's injuries. An awful amount of blood had poured from the wound on the side of his head; his right eye was swollen to the size of a baseball. They were indications of blunt trauma, and bad enough, but she was more concerned by any wounds they couldn't see because of the way he was lying. Almost unnoticed by her, Aaron Lacey limped from room to room seeking his daughter, though Tess had already concluded she was gone. By the state of the kitchen, and Pinky's face, he'd fought determinedly to protect her but failed.

Pinky's breathing was ragged and noisy.

'Help me get him on his side,' Po said.

She wasn't sure that they should move him, for fear he had a major brain injury, or broken neck, but first and foremost his airway should be opened. She knelt to protect his spine alignment, while Po dragged around one of his knees to help manoeuvre their large friend to a safer position. Pinky bucked and kicked, his left arm pawing at the air to shove them away.

'Whoa!' Tess held onto his head, without a care for the blood getting on her. 'Hold still, Pinky, you're going to hurt yourself.'

His response was an animalistic growl, the sound of ill-contained disappointment. He shrugged out of her hands, even as he pulled free of Po and rolled onto his back. Under him broken crockery scraped and shattered. His one good eye rolled, unfocused, and his lips worked as he cursed under his breath. Tess made reassuring noises, while Po moved in tighter, to help support Pinky, who tried to sit.

'Wait,' he advised, his left palm on Pinky's chest. 'Get your wits together before you try to get up.'

Pinky's tongue lolled between his teeth a moment, and he dribbled a string of bloody saliva down his chin. Unconsciously he swiped it away with the back of his wrist. The glint of lucidity in his eye wasn't as dim. He darted a look from Po to Tess, and settled on her. 'Am I in heaven, because you're a vision, you?' he said, then squinting up at Po, he added, 'Damn, I can't be. There isn't any angel as ugly as you, Nicolas.'

'Right now you ain't gonna win any beauty pageants either, bra.'

Pinky forced a smile, then hissed in pain and touched his fingers to the side of his head. The cut was wide, but

the bone beneath seemed intact. 'Son of a bitch downed me
with a cooking pot.'

Po glanced at the heavy cast-iron skillet. Pinky was fortunate: it was apparent the flat base, and not the sharper edge
had struck him, otherwise it would have been a different
story altogether.

Pinky inspected the blood on his fingers. 'Looks worse than
it is; scalp wounds bleed like a bitch. Here, help me up.'

They both helped him sit up, and then jostled him so that
the kitchen wall supported his back. Overhead, the knife jutted
from the plaster. 'Someone throw that at you?'

Pinky rolled his eye upward, grinned abashedly. 'That was
on me: missed by a damn mile. Never was that good with
sharp implements, me.'

'You could've been killed,' Tess said pointlessly. She could
have wept in relief, but was too busy checking him for other
injuries. There was no sign of bullet or knife wounds, but
for one bloody patch on his right thigh. She knelt to inspect
it closer.

'It's nothing,' Pinky reassured her. 'Just lost a little skin,
is all.'

His head still bled. He touched it again, then transferred his
fingers to the swelling round his eye. 'Man, I bet I look like
Quasimodo's uglier brother, me.'

Tess found a clean tea towel, ran it under the cold faucet
and returned. She wadded it and handed it to Pinky who
daubed it on the cut. 'Try to keep pressure on it,' she advised,
and the words reminded her she'd a second bleeding patient.
As if summoned by thought, Lacey appeared from a second
entrance to the kitchen, one that gave access to an adjoining
utility room and back door. Pinky tensed as he stumbled in
and had to catch his balance against a counter.

'It's OK,' Tess told him, 'that's Stella's father.'

Pinky studied him for a beat, then looked conspiratorially
at his friends. 'He looks in worse shape than I am, him.'

'Back door was forced too,' Lacey announced, 'and there's
no sign of Stella.' He was so pale his skin was almost translucent, but for deep smudges under both eyes. His greying hair
was dark with sweat, which also dripped from his jawline. He

lacked the strength to stand unaided for long. Tess was torn between Pinky and going to assist the older man. He returned her concerned look. 'Forget about me. Where's my daughter?'

'They took her,' Pinky said needlessly. 'I fought for her best I could, but a bitch with a bad attitude and the face to match got the drop on me.'

'Fucking Megan Stein,' Lacey growled. He touched his cheek. 'Scarred here?'

Pinky nodded. 'She was with the tall dude you warned me about, Nicolas. But tell the truth, I think the bitch was the more dangerous. She was all for kicking me to death before her pal brained me with that pot.'

'She's twisted, but Hayden James is the most psychotic fuck I ever met. If he took Stella . . .' Lacey wobbled towards them, but his attention was on the door.

Po stood and grabbed him by an elbow. 'Slow down, partner.'

'I have to get my daughter back.'

'We all do,' Po reassured him. 'But we can't do much with two walking wounded to contend with. We need to get you both to a hospital.'

'No way!' Both Lacey and Pinky spoke simultaneously, and with equal force.

Lacey peered down at Pinky. Took in his swollen face, the blood, and the wreckage of the fight around him. 'What did they do to her?'

'Just some manhandling,' Pinky told him. 'Don't know what happened after I was knocked cold, but I doubt she was harmed. They wanted her alive, and I'm betting she'll stay that way till they get their hands on you.'

There was no other reason for taking Stella other than to force a trade. Tess eyed the man; whatever his response was might forever determine her opinion of him. He held up his hands in surrender. 'They can have me.'

Tess shook her head. 'No, they can't.'

'You can't stop me,' said Lacey.

'Bra, you want me to get you in a headlock?' Po warned, still gripping Lacey's elbow to support him to stand. Lacey curled a lip at him, but thought better of getting in a tussle he couldn't win.

'I don't have anythin' else to offer them,' he groaned, 'so if it's a case of Stella or me, they can have me.'

Again Tess shook her head. 'You've already seen what lengths they'll go to. These guys aren't playing around anymore. If you hand yourself over to them they'll kill you, and what are the chances they'll let Stella go, huh? They're trying to cover something up, right? They won't want anyone left behind who knows their secret.'

'Stella can't tell anyone anything . . . *she doesn't know anything.*'

'She can tell the police she was kidnapped and what they've done to you. They won't let her do that.'

'Bastards, if they—'

'What you need to do is tell us why the hell they took her. What is it you have on Elite they want back so badly?'

Po interjected. 'Listen guys, as much as I want to hear it too, we should get outta here. Somebody's bound to have heard the ruckus and called the cops.'

Stella's street was residential, and while most of the inhabitants probably held jobs in the city, there might be stay-at-home parents, or retirees, in earshot. Ordinarily the area would be quiet this early in the day, and the sound of a door getting kicked in – even if the subsequent fight inside escaped them – wouldn't have gone unnoticed. They were fortunate a patrol car hadn't already arrived to check things out. Calling the cops themselves would be the sensible course, but doing so might sign Stella's death warrant. They all knew they had to leave, and as quickly as possible.

Lacey shrugged free of Po, energized by his need to free Stella, and it allowed Po to assist Pinky to stand. They trooped out of the apartment and down the steps to where Po had abandoned the Mustang. There were neighbours on the street, watching, some with their heads together in conversation as they noted the bloodied aspect of two of them. There was little they could do to dissuade the witnesses from speaking to the police, so they didn't bother. Once they'd squeezed Pinky and Lacey into the back seat, and Tess was once more ensconced in the passenger seat, Po set the muscle car rolling.

'Mr Lacey,' Tess said. 'So we know exactly what we're dealing with, tell us why Elite want you so badly they'll resort to violence and kidnapping.'

'They're covering up a murder,' he stated.

'Who's murder? Ethan Prescott's?'

Lacey grunted in scorn. 'Prescott was collateral damage, Jacob Mathers too.'

'Who was Mathers?'

'He was the son of a bitch that shot me. I killed him in self-defense, and had to do the same with Prescott when he tried to slit my throat. No, they died as a consequence of the cover up of a previous murder that I learned about and decided to—'

'Make some money from,' Tess finished for him snarkily.

Lacey thought about it, and shrugged. 'Yeah. It's pointless lying. I intended blackmailing Elite.'

'It's the only reason you've sat on the evidence as long as you have.'

Lacey nodded. 'I planned on throwing my employers to the wolves, but I had to be practical about it. I mean, I'd be effectively putting myself out of a well-paid job, right? I was gonna demand cash for my silence, but, well, fuck 'em, once they paid up I was gonna send copies of the evidence to the cops and the papers. It's why I went to Si Turpin, who made the copies for me, before betraying me and setting the trap back there at his workshop. He said he'd added some kinda self-destruct virus to the copies if anyone tried opening them, and told me to come back so he could put things right. It's a good job he ran away, if his nose wasn't already broken, I'd flatten it again for the lard-assed bastard!'

Po perked up at the description. 'He's a fat guy with a flattened nose? He didn't happen to be wearing a New York Jets football jersey?'

'Huh? Yeah. You know him?'

'Nah, bra, but I did run into him in the street.'

Po chuckled at the private joke that only Tess would appreciate, except she was too distracted by the import of Lacey's confession. He'd killed in self-defense – twice – and was a would-be blackmailer, but he'd also planned on putting things right by ensuring justice was done: he wasn't all bad, she decided, especially when it appeared that his daughter's welfare was most important to him. All things considered, she couldn't think too badly of him, albeit he wasn't the kind of person she wanted as a potential father. She shook off that final thought. She thought back to when Stella told her about whose protection detail Lacey had worked, and immediately discarded Beyoncé as a suspect. 'This is to do with Jon Cutter, isn't it?'

'How'd you figure that out?'

'When you first ran away, it was from Cutter's home in West Roxbury. You were chased by his protection detail – Mathers and Prescott among them – and that's how Prescott ended up in the river at Mattapan. Why did you go to his house, to get the evidence?'

'No, with some inside help I'd already pulled the evidence from Ben Holbrook's server. I went to see Cutter 'cause . . .' He faltered, unprepared, or unable, to go on.

'You initially thought you could bribe him directly?' Tess suggested.

Lacey sighed. 'No, *initially* I only wanted to kill the sick bastard who'd molested and murdered his little sister.'

THIRTY-EIGHT

Tess was silent as she struggled to absorb Lacey's shocking admission. It wasn't that he'd gone looking to exact swift justice that troubled her but what he'd accused the movie star of.

'Yep, you heard right,' Lacey explained. 'High on drugs and drunk as a skunk Jon Cutter sexually molested his own sister, and when he came down and realized what he'd done, and how it'd affect his career, he drowned her in his swimming pool to shut her up. You asked if I'd planned blackmailing him, I only wanted to put a bullet in his head. Besides, Elite had already beaten me to him with their demands. In a panic he reached out to Holbrook to save him, which he did at a high price.'

'And all this time you had evidence of the sexual assault and murder on the USB stick?' Tess asked.

'CCTV footage of the murder, the molestation occurred behind closed doors. I also had recordings of various telephone conversations between Cutter and Holbrook, plus details of the regular fund transfers made to Elite disguised as retainer fees. There was also a second piece of CCTV footage showing Hayden James' involvement: he was the guy who removed Carly Cutter's body from the swimming pool, and who must have been responsible for getting rid of it. Carly's remains have never been discovered, and to date Cutter's secret has stayed safe. Shit, and now the evidence is gone, it will stay that way.'

'Maybe,' Tess said, 'maybe not. Perhaps there's a way to circumvent Turpin's malware program so the files can be opened safely.'

'He tried to spring his trap on the promise of removing the virus; whether or not it can actually be done is questionable. I think he was only blowing smoke up my ass till I got to his workshop.'

'I'm no expert,' Tess admitted, 'but I'm confident it can be done. It's a pity Turpin is in the wind, or we could have gone back to him and made him remove it.'

'We don't need the evidence,' Po announced. 'We only need to get Stella back safe and sound, then our combined testimony will be enough to bury Holbrook and Cutter, right? Once the FBI's involved, you can bet your asses their tech specialists will be able to retrieve the evidence, either from your data sticks or from Elite's servers, or through confessions. I'll happily beat a confession outta Hayden for what he did to you, Pinky.'

'I'll hold him while you do it, Nicolas,' Pinky said, 'plus that sour-faced witch.'

Tess pondered Po's rescue suggestion, if not his proposal for violence. 'You're right, Po. I'm sure if I ask nicely Emma will advise us on the correct course of action, and hopefully how we can keep our butts out of prison for being accessories after the fact. The difficult and most important part's getting Stella back alive, and not getting ourselves killed in the process. We are outgunned, outnumbered, and – I hate to admit it – also outmatched.' She shrugged apologetically at Po, but she was stating facts. Elite's assets were trained close protection operators, with backgrounds in the military and law enforcement, and they were still alive only because, until the events at 56th Street, there clearly hadn't been a shoot-to-kill policy in place. That had invariably changed. One look at Pinky was enough to convince her that his life had only been spared through oversight: his head wound should've killed him, and only the slightest miscalculation in the angle of the blow had saved him from a fatal skull fracture. Hayden James hadn't struck him to spare his life, but to permanently shut him up.

Pinky removed the wet towel from his head, inspected the blood on it and was satisfied he'd finally gotten his bleeding under control. 'We're maybe outmatched, us,' he said, 'but there's no need to be outnumbered or, heaven forbid, be outgunned. I got my ass kicked back there, but I'm not done yet. I might still be able to help even things in our favour, me.'

'Before you do anything, we need to get your head looked at,' Tess said.

'I've been tellin' him that for years,' Po quipped.

'I'm fine. The bleeding's almost stopped now.' In evidence, Pinky waved the tea towel at her, and she grimaced.

'You could have a concussion for all we know. You need checking over, Pinky, and I'm not taking no for an answer.'

A quick glance at Aaron Lacey showed her wadded shirt was equally stained red but he'd pushed it aside on the bench seat. She should have borrowed a shirt from Stella's wardrobe, but her semi-nakedness beneath her jacket was her least concern back at the apartment. She could rectify that later, and grab a shirt from her overnight bag in the trunk next time they stopped. Which should be soon.

'We need you checked out again, too,' she said to Lacey. 'I think your wound could be infected.'

Lacey and Pinky exchanged frowns. Tess frowned equally

as hard. Lacey sighed. 'OK. I know just the place to go. Hey, Po, is it?'

'That's me.'

'Yeah, well take a left and go five blocks, and I'll point out a doctor's place I've used before. He's off the radar and I trust him to keep his mouth shut.'

Po nodded affirmative. If the cops had circulated a description of the Mustang they were risking things by staying on the island but it was a case of needs must. Witness testimony was unreliable at best; perhaps nobody had given a clear description of the make and model of his car, but the dinged hood and bullet-scarred windshield and trunk wouldn't stand up to close inspection. Plus, his back seat passengers were bleeding all over his upholstery. It wouldn't make any difference that they had either been victims of violent assault or rescuers of those under attack, they would be all whisked to the nearest precinct for questioning, and that'd mean Stella wouldn't be freed.

Minutes later, Lacey indicated an unassuming doorway on the lower level of a six-storey brownstone, whose nearest neighbours were a family deli and a beauty salon. The Harlem River was less than two blocks east, and the whistle of moving vehicles on the adjacent Harlem River Drive was a constant background noise. On the doctor's street there was little traffic, and pedestrians were few. Po pulled the Mustang into a free spot outside a red brick housing authority building. 'I'll stay with the car,' he said as he stepped out and lit a cigarette.

'Those things will kill ya,' Lacey told him as he squeezed painfully out of the car.

'Not as quickly as an infected bullet wound,' Po replied. 'Go and get yoursel' fixed up, bra, and I'll worry about myself.'

'Hold on, I'm coming with you.' Tess wasn't prepared to let Lacey out of her sight: she wouldn't put it past him to try to give them the slip and head off to a confrontation with Elite alone. Lacey chewed his bottom lip, but waited until she had helped Pinky from the back seat, and they joined him on the sidewalk.

'Doesn't look much like a clinic to me,' Pinky observed as

they approached the scratched front door: windblown trash
had piled up either side of it, and a broken bottle kicked into
a corner of the doorstep, 'more like a rat's nest.'

'Wait till you meet the doc, he's a vision of insanitary too.'

'And you expect me to let him stitch me up?'

'He's good with a needle, just don't let him hack any phlegm
in your cut.'

Pinky gagged.

Lacey grinned at his expense, then aimed a wink at Tess
for her approval.

Tess ignored the nonsense, contemplating instead the man
who could be her biological father. She had mixed feelings.
His love of Stella was admirable to a point, but it was still
his greed that had placed her in danger to begin with. Why
hadn't he immediately gone to the police with the evidence
instead of trying to extort cash? His assertion that he was
effectively severing his employment and needed to secure his
revenue was weak; it wasn't as if he was unemployable by
another more reputable company. In fact, after being hailed a
hero for revealing the identity of a murderer, the offers of
work would probably flood in. No, for all he had a sense for
justice, she didn't think it was as widely felt as the streak of
avarice that afflicted him. What was it Stella had said about
her father: it was all about him? Tess had to concur with the
assessment. If it turned out that he was her progenitor . . . no!
She didn't want to think of him as her parent.

Lacey rang the doctor's doorbell.

The two men stood on the sidewalk, mouths open,
splashed with blood, looking at the door like extras from
a zombie movie sensing warm flesh inside. There was no
sound from within. Lacey rapped his knuckles on the door,
and felt it shift in its frame. He glanced over his shoulder
at Tess. Then his natural ex-cop's inquisitiveness kicked in
and he placed his hand flat and gave the door a gentle shove.
'Yo! You there, Grover?' he called as the unlocked door
swung inward.

Again there was no answer. Both men sought guidance
from Tess: she was as an ex-cop too and as inquisitive as
they were. She nodded at Lacey to go in. He entered, but

with a touch of trepidation. It was as if everywhere was a potential trap to him these days. Pinky stepped inside behind him, while Tess brought up the rear. She detected the smell before any of them saw Grover's body. The apartment was grimy, and hadn't been redecorated in years, and it was imbued with the odours of lingering illness, but over and above there was a scent of blood and voided bowels. Tess had visited enough scenes of sudden and violent death to recognize it. She clutched Pinky's arm, holding him back from entering the sitting room. It was too late to halt Lacey. He'd gone in, alerted also by the smell, and they heard his guttural oath as he made the discovery. Tess and Pinky both took a peek inside, then exchanged sickened expressions.

Herbert Grover was lying alongside an easy chair, its fabric faded and worn thin: the man was almost as insubstantial. His clothing was bags of formless material piled around a skeletal frame. His skull also lacked recognizable shape; it had been crushed so severely. His blood and brain matter had leaked into the threadbare carpet under him, as had his urine when death released his control over his bodily functions. Tess pressed the back of her hand to her mouth.

'Those sons of bitches . . .' Lacey crouched over the old man, shaking his head in dismay. 'They didn't have to hurt him, he was dying anyway. He deserved a more dignified ending than *this*.'

'We don't know that Elite are responsible,' Tess cautioned.

'Who else could it be?' Lacey snapped.

Grover was running a backstreet surgery; his clients were often desperate people. Perhaps one of those, eager for a fix, had beaten the man to death in a burglary gone wrong. But what were the odds that the timing should be so coincidental? Lacey was probably correct, and one or other of Holbrook's hired guns had beaten the doctor, for clues where to find Lacey.

'We have to call the cops now,' Lacey said, as he stood again. 'I'm not leaving him to lie here and rot.'

'We will,' Tess assured him, 'but not until we're out of here.'

'Those bastards need to be stopped,' Lacey said, more forcefully.

Pinky stared down at Grover's crushed skull, then fingered

the wound on his head: he could have suffered a similar fate. 'They do,' he agreed.

'And we will stop them,' Tess went on. 'But we won't get Stella back unharmed if we alert the police to their involvement. Mr Lacey, as horrible as this is, it only confirms how much danger Stella's in, and we have to think about her first.'

'I'm thinking about nothing else now.'

'Good. Now, before we go back to the car, we need to have a look around. This doesn't look as if the doctor used it as his consultation room . . .?'

Lacey waved towards the rear of the apartment. 'Back there. Come on, I'll show you where he kept his drugs and stuff.'

While Pinky retreated to inform Po of their discovery, she followed Lacey to a small room decked out with a gurney-style bed, a sink, and a brushed-steel worktop above a series of cupboards and drawers. Lacey had lain on the bed only yesterday morning while Grover tended his wounds: the soiled dressings lay on top of an open waste bin nearby. He'd made note of where the doctor kept his supply of antibiotics. He pulled open a drawer, and collected a handful of containers. 'These are penicillin-based antibiotics,' he told Tess.

'They'll do for now. I need bandages and gauze, maybe some sterile strips because my needlecraft isn't what it should be. Oh, and see if you can find any painkillers . . .'

Between them they gathered what she required to field dress both men's wounds, and they placed them all inside a garbage sack Lacey fetched from the kitchen. They'd taken care only to touch the items they were taking away with them, and Lacey wiped down the handle on the drawers and cupboards they'd opened. 'Remember to wipe down the door-bell and where you touched the front door,' Tess advised, as they moved for the front street. They studiously avoided looking at Grover's corpse again.

'Don't worry,' said Lacey, 'I knew how to cover up my dodgy behaviour long before you were born.'

She clucked her tongue at his inappropriate choice of words, and walked for the car, carrying the bag of medical supplies while he used his sleeve to wipe down the door.

Pinky was already seated in the back. Po allowed Lacey to squeeze in, before putting back the seat and getting in. Tess took a lingering check of the street. Their visit to Doc Grover's had apparently gone unobserved, or his neighbours were used to people skulking in and out and barely took note anymore. She slid inside the car, placing the meds at her feet, and once she was settled, Po drove away. They all sat in sullen silence, contemplating the latest turn of events. They were heading out of Manhattan on the Alexander Hamilton Bridge, aiming for the I-95 when Lacey spoke.

'Someone ought to inform Paul.'

It hadn't crossed Tess's mind that Stella's husband was blissfully unaware of his wife's predicament. It was best that he was kept in the dark, though. 'Hopefully we'll have her safely home again before he finds out. If we tell him she's been kidnapped, there's nothing stopping him from alerting the authorities, and we'll lose any hope we have of saving her.'

'How's your mom?'

His question came out of left field and left Tess momentarily dumbstruck. She shifted in her seat, coughed to clear her throat. 'Why do you ask?'

'Just wondered if she knew what kind of danger you're about to put yourself in, on behalf of my kid. If our roles were reversed, I'm not sure I'd like my daughter risking her life for someone she barely knows.' Again he was wholly unaware of how ironic his choice of words was, but at least his sentiment was genuine.

'My mom worries about me crossing the street,' Tess said, and felt an unexpected flicker of fondness for Barbara's protective ways. 'I must give her a lot of sleepless nights, because I've this tendency to run towards danger.'

Lacey laughed in recognition. 'Boy, you're definitely Young Mike's kid!'

'Yes,' she declared. 'Yes, I am.'

Po squeezed her a smile and a look that said: *Great, let's leave it at that, shall we?*

She was happy to lay the question over her parentage to rest . . . for now. She began delving in the bag of supplies.

'Po, you might want to find somewhere we can lay low while I stitch them up.'

By then, they were passing signs for the Bronx Zoo, and the cloverleaf with the Bronx River Parkway: he took the turn, hoping to find somewhere secluded in the park where they could clean up and plan. Minutes later he parked the muscle car beneath a shady canopy of trees at a far corner of the zoo's parking lot, next to the Bronx River. At that time of day there were few other visitors to the park, and most of those had parked their cars nearer the entrance, so they were secluded for now. They'd taken a chance their wounded passengers would attract attention at the entrance barrier, but the young attendant had delivered her chirpy greeting by rote and didn't as much as glance in the back when Po paid admission for four adults.

He stepped out and folded the front seats down so Tess could climb in and work on her patients. He smoked, brooding over what was destined to follow, as he stood watch, prepared to deter any passing visitors from getting too close. Tess was too absorbed applying sterile strips to Pinky's head wound to notice when her cell phone rang. It was tucked under the folded seat back, on Tess's chair. Po went to the open door and peered in at it, reading the caller ID.

'You might want to answer that, Tess,' he said.

'Who's calling?'

'Well, if my eyes ain't deceiving me,' he said with a sardonic smile, 'it's Pinky.'

THIRTY-NINE

'I bet receiving a call from a dead man gave you a moment's pause?' Hayden James stood on the tarmac of a private airstrip in New Jersey, supervising as Megan Stein and Vera Seung assisted their hostage up the steps onto Elite's corporate jet. It had been moved from La Guardia in anticipation of receiving an unwilling passenger; it would've been difficult getting Stella past security at the major airport, especially in her tranquilized state.

'You stole our friend's cell,' Tess Grey said accusingly.

'He didn't need it anymore, but I needed a way to contact you.'

'My number's in the book.'

'Yeah, but ringing you from your dead buddy's phone ensured I got your attention. Now listen up.'

'No, you son of a bitch! *You* listen up. Things have gone too far. It has to stop!'

'You're emotional,' Hayden said, his voice dripping with mockery, 'and understandably in light of losing *dear, dear Pinky*, not to mention your client. So I expected a little churlishness from you, but I won't allow you to dictate to me. Do you hear me, Miss Grey? I'm the one who says what is and what isn't going to happen.'

She countered him immediately. 'Here's what will happen: more people will die. For what reason? So that a sexual deviant gets away with murdering his own sister, and Ben Holbrook continues growing rich? You know that's not how this is going to end. If you live to see the end of this, it'll be from a prison cell.'

Hayden chuckled. 'You seem very sure of that.'

'I am. What other way is there for this to end up?'

'You give me Aaron Lacey, I will give back Stella, and we all walk away. Cutter's secret doesn't come out, Elite keeps making money off him, and I disappear with a big fat bonus for services rendered. There might be something in it for you too: if you keep your mouth shut, you can go back to chasing philandering husbands in Maine. You don't bother them and Elite leaves you and Stella alone.'

'Once upon a time a deal might've been on the table, but not after people have died.'

'You're upset about your pet homo?'

'Buddy,' Nicolas Villere interjected. 'For that comment alone I'll happily kill you.'

'Was hoping you were listening in. I've nothing personal against your pal, he gave his best and I respect him for that. It's why I ended him without any unnecessary suffering.'

'That won't stop me from killing you.'

'You can try. Pinky tried and you've seen where it got him.'

'Did Herbert Grover, a sick old man with only weeks left to live, also try to kill you?' Tess posed.

'Oh, so you've found the good doctor, have you? Stands to reason, I heard from some of my guys that Lacey wasn't looking too good when you snatched him from them: I genuinely didn't think Lacey would go back to that quack or I'd have waited there for him. But no, to answer your question, Miss Grey, Doc Grover's death wasn't on me.'

'You might not have personally killed him,' Grey said, 'but you gave the order.'

'I followed an order from my superior. It's what good soldiers do.'

'You're not a soldier, you're a murderous son of a bitch,' Villere snarled.

'Takes one to know one,' Hayden replied, then as an addendum, 'if you really intend keeping to the threat you just made.'

'I don't make threats lightly.'

'Good then I can count on you coming to Boston to find me. You too, Miss Grey, and, oh, don't forget the main man. That's the deal: bring Aaron Lacey and any evidence he still has to me, and I'll let his daughter go. As for the rest of us . . . well, we'll have to see how things play out, won't we?'

'We need some time,' said Grey. 'Lacey isn't fit to travel, and seeing as you had his doctor killed I'm going to have to patch him up first.'

'Don't bother. Dead or alive, get him to me. I'm happy either way but I want to see his body and the USB sticks. You have four hours to get to Boston.'

'We need more time than that.'

'I'm not giving it to you. Four hours, y'hear, and the clock starts ticking *now*. And don't lose your phone; I'll be calling you back on it with further instructions. Oh, and need I add—'

'Don't worry,' Villere interjected again. 'I don't want any witnesses to our next meeting, least of all the cops.'

'Good man, I'm happy to hear we're on the same page.'

Hayden pondered a moment. 'I assume you've already left Grover's place, so there's no need to send a team there. You can also be assured that you won't be troubled on the road to Boston. I expect a similar level of cooperation from you. Do not report the deaths of Grover or your friend to the NYPD. If I hear you've involved the cops, the deal's off and Stella will disappear. If that makes you think I'll lose leverage over you, consider again.'

He ended the call.

Megan was watching him from the jet's doorway. Her dark eyes glistened in anticipation.

Her psychotic nature had caused him undue complication. Stamping Grover to death had helped calm her murderous rage, but only slightly. He'd taken the opportunity away from her to kill Pinky when he'd smashed the man's skull in with the skillet, otherwise there could have been another corpse with the tell-tale marks of her boot heels all over it. As it was – as long as Grey and Villere didn't report the deaths and point an accusatory finger at Elite – they should remain unconnected when the police got round to investigating them. He couldn't count on the private eyes staying quiet, particularly since they'd lost one of their own, so it had become imperative that they were silenced as resolutely as he planned for Lacey. Pinky died during a fight to the death, his slaying was unavoidable, but in hindsight allowing the woman to beat the old man to death was a massive mistake: Grover could have been compelled through fear to keep schtum, and allowed to slip quietly into death when his illness took him.

However, in a way, Megan had also helped simplify matters in his mind, as had Tess Grey's recent assertion that this could only end with him dead or behind bars. Despite the pains Ben Holbrook was going to, there was no possible way now that Jon Cutter's secret could be protected, or Elite's, specifically Hayden's, part in the cover-up. Too many people were involved now; too many loose ends. Holbrook's people could hunt down and kill the key players, but who knew how many others had been reached out to in the meantime? Si Turpin was on the run and could finger them all. Stella was married to a businessman who'd demand answers, Grey and Villere had connections to a specialist inquiry firm up in Portland, Maine, and Grey, he'd learned, had siblings who were active law enforcement officers, who would push for an investigation into their sister's disappearance. For all he knew Grey had already confided in one or all of the above and Elite couldn't stop them all. While everything was being blown all out of proportion, Megan's question to him earlier had helped clarify his intention.

She'd asked if he had a contingency, perhaps an escape plan to a country with no extradition treaty with the US. He hadn't answered, only used her concern to help motivate her, but the answer was yes. He'd planned his escape ever since the day Holbrook had him dredge Carly Cutter's body from her brother's swimming pool. He knew as he lifted her dripping from the water that somewhere down the line covering up her murder would come back to destroy them all. A secret was never safe when more than one person knew about it. Since that day, he had been preparing for when Cutter's sin would explode in their faces, and sure as shit that fuse had been lit the second Mathers failed to take out Aaron Lacey with his first bullet. In the past few days things had gotten more out of control, and he was under no illusion, the situation was going to grow worse. He'd gladly commandeer the jet and force the pilot to fly him somewhere south of the border and put the whole damn mess behind him, but for two reasons. First, he hadn't been kidding when he told Grey and Villere he had a fat bonus coming. Though he'd stashed money away in offshore accounts, when he disappeared he wanted enough money to maintain a lifestyle worth running away to, and his bonus promised him that. To earn it though, he had to kill Lacey and get back the evidence. Second, ever since they'd met gazes across Copley Square, he knew a final confrontation with Nicolas Villere was in his stars, and who was he to deny fate? He'd purposefully goaded a reaction from Villere by his comments about Pinky, because he wanted to end things with him before he ran: the lack of extradition treaties meant fuck all to a vengeful man, and Hayden had no intention of constantly watching over his shoulder for when Villere inevitably came to even the score. During their confrontation Pinky warned him against the type of enemies he was courting, but Hayden knew. He'd already decided that Villere wasn't a cold-blooded murderer, but he was vengeful, and Hayden had bought his sincerity when Villere said he didn't make threats lightly.

Megan continued to stare.

He walked towards her, and she stirred at the top of the steps, tempted to go inside but also expectant. Maybe she wanted him to tell her she was right, maybe he should tell her to get the hell away as quickly as possible, maybe she would refuse until Lacey was dead: she too was a vengeful thing. So he didn't bother with a warning.

'Everything ready?' he asked.

She thumbed towards the cabin. 'Everyone's onboard, and Vera's guarding the bitch. We're just waiting on you, Hayden.'

'Then let's get moving.'

She didn't clear the doorway. 'I should warn you, boss; some of the team are uneasy about being kept in the dark.'

'They have their instructions; they know what happens next. They growing squeamish all of a sudden?'

'It isn't that they're afraid of the situation, Hayden: I think they've shown that already. It's more about the pay-off.'

'They want more money? Yeah, well they'd better form a queue . . . behind me.'

'It's not about their fee. It's how far they should risk their lives when they aren't trusted.'

'They wouldn't be on my team if I didn't trust them.'

Megan shook her head, eyes tilted down. 'You know what I'm talking about, Hayden.'

'You're having second thoughts, too?'

She raised her head, shook it emphatically. 'I told you already, I'm with you till the end.'

Hayden sneered. 'Till Lace's end, you mean.'

'Yeah, I want to see him dead, and I'd like to be the one to pull the trigger. My reason is personal, but the others want to know what they're fighting for, considering Lace was once one of us.'

'And I've told you before, none of you need to know. In fact, you should be relieved you've no idea what's on those files. Otherwise it'd be you guys going to your executions instead of Lace.'

'So it's that old cliché?' She smiled conspiratorially. 'You'd tell us, but then you'd have to kill us, huh?'

'Do I look as if I'm kidding?'

Megan checked out the cold promise in his eyes.

'No, boss, I can see you're deadly serious.'

'Good. Now let's go.' He waved her ahead of him, and this time she obeyed. He entered the cabin, watching the others raise quizzical eyebrows at Megan, only for her to shake her head. She found a seat and slumped into it. Hayden briefly met each of their gazes. Nobody pushed him for an answer, and he knew they wouldn't because he'd pitched his voice to Megan so all onboard had heard. Each of his team had picked window seats where they could stretch out and grab some sleep on the short flight home, except for Vera Seung who had taken an aisle seat. Next to her, Stella Dewildt was crammed against the window – the blind down – her chin resting on her chest. The sedatives given to her would ensure she slept through the flight to Boston, and probably for a few hours after. Hayden studied her for a moment. She was a good-looking woman, and from what he'd observed of her to date, a good person who didn't deserve this. It was a shame she had to die, but her death wasn't on him. He took a second look around the cabin. *All of you*, he thought, *could die because Lace couldn't keep his fucking nose out of Elite's business*. He mentally shrugged off any concern, because that wasn't on him either.

FORTY

'He's keeping us moving so we can't think straight,' Po said, smiling at the thought. They had left the parking lot at the Bronx Zoo shortly after Hayden James ended the call, Po driving just a shade beneath the posted speed limit though he was severely tempted to put his foot down. Still, having only made one brief stop at a Fed-Ex office in Eastchester, they'd picked up I-95 and the Wilbur Cross Parkway and were now two hours closer to Boston and still on schedule to meet Hayden's timescale. 'He knows we've barely slept, have an injured man onboard and are unarmed, and doesn't want us rectifying our situation. He's gonna be pissed when he finds out he underestimated us.'

Pinky chortled from the back seat. His head was bulked out on one side by a gauze pad held in place with porous tape: Tess had knitted his wound with sticky sterile sutures. He'd downed enough painkillers to tranquilize a horse, but was surprisingly perky, galvanized by the promise of payback. 'I can't wait to see his face when a dead man gives him pause, me.'

They'd elected to keep Pinky's survival from Hayden: he was their acc up their sleeve in more ways than Hayden could know. Pinky had borrowed Po's cell phone, and had put it to good use over the past couple of hours on the road. Tess's cell phone was restricted to one purpose only: waiting for Hayden's next instructions.

Aaron Lacey was drowsy, though he constantly fought sleep. Tess had gotten him started on a course of strong antibiotics, but it would be a while until they had any effect on his infected wound. In a bout of fatalism, he'd first refused the medicine. What good was it wasting them on him when he was going to die in exchange for his daughter's safety? Tess had made two promises: he wasn't going to die at Hayden James's hands, but she'd kill him if he didn't damn well take his meds.

Once Pinky had made his calls, Tess used Po's phone to contact Emma Clancy in Portland, Maine, but didn't tell her future sister-in-law any details regarding Stella Dewildt's abduction, only to expect an important delivery of a malware-infected USB drive that required specialist attention to protect its integrity. On it, she promised, was evidence of a murder and its subsequent cover-up, and that she trusted Emma to ensure justice was served.

'If I don't make it home, make sure the bastards responsible are all sent to prison,' she said morosely.

'You'll have to give me more than that, Tess!'

'I can't, Emma, otherwise I'd be putting you in an untenable position with the police and FBI. You'd be duty bound to immediately inform them, and I can't have you do that before I try to save another life.'

'Tess, what the hell is going on?'

'Sorry, Emma, I can't say. I trust you to keep quiet for now too. Please don't mention this to Alex . . . or my mom. Just watch out for the package, I've sent it priority delivery, but it'll still be a few hours until it arrives. And remember, don't open it without having a tech specialist negate the malware first.'

'Tess, you need to tell me right now—'

Tess ended the call before Emma could press for more detail. She hated leaving her employer, not to mention her brother's partner, in a state of worry over her, but it was unavoidable. Had she admitted to being on the way to a dangerous encounter with Stella's kidnappers, nothing would stop Emma raising the alarm: she'd call in the police, FBI and even the National Guard if necessary. Which, of course, was the sensible course to follow, except here it had become too personal for any of them to stand aside and hope the authorities could save Stella.

They caught the I-84 at East Hartford, and the going was faster. Po burned rubber through Connecticut, and crossed the state line in record time. As the Mustang roared through Massachusetts towards Boston on the coast, Emma tried to ring back half a dozen times but Tess declined each attempt. Her personal phone rang, and she had to decline that call too: it was from her mother, and there was still much to be said between them, but she couldn't risk missing Hayden James's next set of instructions. .

She checked Po out, and he sensed her appraisal. When he glanced from the road, she aimed a flickering smile at him. He must have known the kind of mixed feelings she was enduring, because he offered a smile of his own, reached across and gently squeezed her knee. 'One way or another,' he told her, 'this will end tonight.'

She averted her face, staring out the passenger window at

the Massachusetts countryside flashing by and grew lulled by its hypnotic regularity. At some point she must have zoned out, because next when she checked the road signs they were only thirty miles outside of Boston.

Lacey had been silent for some time. A delirious cackle had Tess twisting quickly to check on him. His features had the hue of bones bleached under a desert sun, and instead of being awash with sweat his skin was set to crack. His lips flaked skin. He was seriously dehydrated. In contrast his eyes were alert, shining with his sudden burst of humour. He must have noted the manic edge to his laughter, because he held up a hand, signaling he was OK.

'I used to joke about knowing where I was going to die,' he explained, 'and staying the fuck away. Damned if I ever thought I'd rush towards it.'

'You're not going to die, Mr Lacey,' she said.

'Look, for starters, I don't want to die, but if that's what it takes, I'll gladly trade places with my daughter.'

'You're not going to die,' Tess repeated.

He rolled his neck. 'I brought this on myself. I should've gone directly to the police and it would be all over by now, but I let greed take over, and now look what's happened. If I die, it's my own damn fault, and I accept that, but nobody else needs get hurt. When we get there, just do what Hayden says and hand me over, then get the hell outta there with Stella.'

'Handing you over's no guarantee he'll release Stella. In fact, he won't because he can't allow her to go to the police. We've already gone over this, Mr Lacey.'

'I know, but I've been thinking, and I don't want any of you risking your lives for mine.'

'We ain't doing this for you,' Po said, forthright.

Lacey was lost for words.

Tess said, 'What Po means is we're doing it for Stella, for you, and for the rest of us. We have a personal stake in the outcome too. Also, we're doing this for Carly Cutter, she deserves justice too.'

He lowered his head. Probed his side.

'How does your wound feel?' Tess asked.

'Better. The bleeding's stopped.'

'You don't look too strong. When was the last time you ate anything?'

'I don't recall. Yesterday morning maybe?'

'Then you need food and something to drink.' She aimed an unspoken question at Po.

'I'll pull in at the next stop,' he said.

'You don't need to on my behalf,' Lacey argued.

'We do. The last thing we want is you fainting on us when we're in the thick of things. You have to keep your strength up to play your part, Mr Lacey.'

'What does that entail, apart from you marching me out to meet Hayden?'

'Trust me, there's more you're going to help with than being a sacrificial goat. Something you mentioned earlier . . .'

Lacey met her eye again, his mouth open in miscomprehension.

'When you first stole the data from Holbrook's server, you said you had some inside help.'

'That's right,' he said. 'I don't know one end of a thumb drive to the other, so I needed someone to do the technical stuff for me. It's why I also had to trust that fat-ass, Si Turpin back in New York, and we all know where that got me.'

'Maybe you shouldn't be so down on Turpin,' Po put in, 'without his involvement you wouldn't have been in the right place at the right time for us to help you. In the long run, maybe he did you a favour.'

'Don't expect me to thank him.'

'I don't. Can't say as I'll thank him for buckling my hood either, but if the dude hadn't run out in front of me when he did, we might've driven straight on past you.'

'So now he's my fuckin' guardian angel?' Lacey laughed, and Po joined in.

'Can we get back to your "inside help"?' Tess asked.

'Sure. It was him that first came to me, after eavesdropping a conversation between Holbrook and Clarissa Glenn, and being shocked by what he heard. Apparently Holbrook said somethin' like, "He'd better not quibble about the price, or I'll have Hayden dig up his sister and dump it back in Cutter's fucking swimming pool and see how much it costs him then!" At the time, he didn't know the extent of what was happening, but knew it was bad, and not something he could sit on. He sought me out, 'cause he knew I was an ex-cop, and thought I'd pay more attention than any of the jarheads on Elite's payroll. At first he only wanted advice, or maybe somebody to share his load, but we both knew that without evidence, we couldn't prove a damn thing. Between us we came up with a plan to dig through Holbrook's computer and see what we could find: I'll be fucked if either of us expected what turned up!'

'Your insider got you into Holbrook's office undetected then?'

'Yeah. We waited until he was on night shift, and the building was quiet, and then he snuck me back in. The kid was almost crapping his pants, but if not for his help, none of this would've come to light.'

'The kid?' Po mused, and Tess knew why as she'd had a similar flash of inspiration.

'Are we talking about the new guy . . . Harris?' she asked.

Taken aback, Lacey only stared.

'We met him,' Tess said, 'when we went to Elite's HQ. He denied ever hearing your name, or about Ethan Prescott's death, but I can understand why now. What surprises me – after what happened with Mathers and Prescott, and then you going missing – is that he stuck around. I'd've thought he'd have run away too.'

'No. I told him to stay put, and keep up the naïve, new boy act. If he'd gone missing too, they'd've figured out who helped me get to the files and he'd have a target on his back. I told him to hang on until I could blow the lid on them, and then it'd be safe for him to come clean with the cops. Of course, we were only expecting that to last a day or two, but then I let my anger get the better of me, and I fucked things up. Sounds as if Harris's still hanging tough, poor kid. We should warn him to get out—'

'No,' Tess jumped in, and she glanced pointedly at Pinky so he got the message too. 'We need him exactly where he is.'

'You want him to try to get more evidence? By now Holbrook will've made sure that every trace of it has been wiped from his server.'

'It's not evidence we want,' Tess assured him, 'it's something far more important to Ben Holbrook we can barter for Stella's life.'

'There's a gas station coming up,' Po announced as they crossed the Charles River into the village of Auburndale, part of the city of Newton and the larger conurbation of Boston. 'You still want me to pull over, Tess, time's growin' short.'

'Yeah. We're close enough now. Hayden didn't specify where in Boston he wanted us, so this's as good as anywhere else. If he doesn't like it, tough!' She directed her words at all three of her companions, feeling much better about what lay ahead. 'You guys go and get something to eat and drink, and maybe grab me something too. Po, can I use your phone again, I need to make another call?'

'F'sure,' he said as he took the off-ramp to the gas station. 'Do what you gotta do, Tess.'

FORTY-ONE

Hayden James had taken the time to organize, and get his most dedicated people in place. He stood on a raised dais at the head of an echoing space, from where his voice would carry with the surety of a hellfire preacher at the pulpit. It was an ideal location for issuing instructions to the most distant of his team, but not great for conducting a conversation that required more privacy. He pushed through the gap between two large stud boards and into a short corridor that gave access to a stairwell, and also to a series of smaller antechambers. He chose one of the latter and rang Tess Grey's phone four hours to the minute as promised. 'You're in Boston?'

'Yes,' replied Tess. 'It wasn't easy getting here in that time.'

'I don't care. You're here and that's all that matters.'

'All that matters is that you come to your senses and end this the right way.'

'When you give me Lacey and the files, I'll uphold my end of the bargain. Stella will be released.'

'You know as well as I do that things can't end that way. People have been killed.' She rhymed off the list. 'Two of your people: Mathers and Prescott. Herbert Grover. Carly Cutter and . . . our friend Pinky.' She sniffled, speaking the latter name hurt her. 'Even if you get your hands on Lacey, and destroy the files he took, it can't end there. The murders can't stay buried; everyone affected has friends, family, people who will demand answers about their disappearances. Surely you see this, Hayden? Whatever happens today, you'll be a hunted man for the rest of your life.'

'I'm not an idiot. I know the consequences, but I've a job to do, and I'm going to do it.'

'However much you're being paid for this isn't enough. Are you prepared to live the rest of your life as a fugitive for whatever payment you've been promised?'

'Miss Grey,' he said as sanctimonious as the preacher he'd felt a moment ago, 'whatever the outcome I'll be a fugitive. Whether I spare Lacey or not, you know by now that I became implicated in Carly Cutter's murder when I disposed of her body. There's no coming out of this clean for me, so I may as well do my job and take the payment. It will make life on the run more manageable than if I leave now without the cash. So, don't waste any more time. You must decide whether or not you want Stella back, or if you're prepared to risk her safety and hope for the best.'

'I've no control over her father. Ultimately it's his final decision. I won't force him to do the trade.'

'You should help convince him. I know Lace cares for Stella. Remind him of his parental responsibility . . . because Stella will be killed if he refuses to come.'

'You seem confident he's going to come. But what guarantees have we that you'll free Stella once he's in your hands?'

'It's like you said yourself, Miss Grey, whatever the outcome, questions will be asked, and I don't care if Stella's alive to answer them or not . . . by then the cash will be in my account and I'll be gone.'

'Perhaps we can come to another deal . . .'

'You want to pay me off? Tell me, Miss Grey, can you get your hands on a cool half-million in the next two hours?'

She didn't bother answering because it was obvious to both she couldn't. Instead she posed a question: 'Are you genuinely prepared to execute an innocent woman?'

'If I have to.'

'What of Aaron Lacey? You said you had previous conversations with him. You worked together. You were colleagues . . . friends . . .'

'That's right, but he became my enemy when he turned on his own team,' Hayden said. 'He killed two of his *former* colleagues, two of his *former* friends.'

'They were trying to kill him at the time,' she countered. 'You didn't expect him to just stand there and let them kill *him*? You once called yourself a soldier, would you expect any soldier not to defend themselves?'

'Lacey wasn't a soldier. When he betrayed my team he became an enemy combatant, and that's a different thing entirely. I've no qualms about killing an enemy . . . any enemy.'

Again she fell silent, deep in thought. Hayden prepared for her to issue another pointless plea for mercy, but instead she showed more mettle. 'I'm wasting my time trying to get you to see reason. Tell me where and when, and let's not bother with the unpleasantries.'

'Before I do that, did you obey my previous instructions?'

'You know that I did.'

'Good, so there won't be any funny business with the cops showing up. The first sniff of a cop'd force my hand; I'd have to kill you all.'

'Where and when, Hayden?'

'The Anderson Memorial Bridge. You have thirty minutes.'

'You're assuming I know where that is.'

'You're supposed to be a detective. Find it.'

'We are going to do the exchange in a public place?'

'You'd like that, wouldn't you?' He hung up. Striding back to the dais in the main room, he called out. 'Listen up, people!

They're inbound. Eyes, ears and brains switched on. Seung: prepare Stella.' He indicated the dais. 'Bring her here, I want her front and centre so there's no confusion about my intentions. Aiken, Nicholls, you're on the door. Johnson and Seung, you stay on Stella. Megan, you're with me.'

His team moved into their pre-arranged formation smoothly, Vera Seung and Brian Johnson frog-marching their hostage up a creaking flight of steps onto the dais, where a chair had already been placed to receive her. Megan waited at the bottom, checking over her suppressed sidearm. At the far end Grant Aiken and Sean Nicholls flanked the entrance door, each also armed with a suppressed weapon. Seung and Johnson had their handguns holstered, but would draw them soon enough. For now, Hayden left his Beretta out of sight under his jacket, holding the phone instead so he could periodically check the countdown. 'C'mon,' he said to Megan and she marched a few feet behind him towards the exit.

FORTY-TWO

The Anderson Memorial Bridge straddled the Charles River, marking the boundary with Boston and Cambridge, Massachusetts. On the Cambridge side, there was parkland dedicated to John F. Kennedy, and beyond that more of the sprawling campus of Harvard University. Po had drawn the Mustang to a halt before the approach to the southern side of the bridge, parking at roadside opposite the entrance to Harvard sports stadium. The intersection at the bridge was busy with traffic.

'This isn't the place,' Po said.

Tess had come to the same conclusion. She checked the time and saw there was only a minute left on the clock: getting across town hadn't been easy because it was rush hour, workers and students heading home in their thousands. Hayden had purposefully made the timeline difficult, to keep them anxious and frustrated, meaning they'd no time to counterplan.

'It won't be the last place he sends us either,' Lacey offered from the back seat. Tess checked on him. Earlier he'd been corpselike, now he had some colour in his cheeks and his eyes weren't as sunken, but he was far from well.

'How are you holding up? Do you think you'll be able to walk unassisted?'

'I'll crawl if I have to.'

Tess felt a pang in her chest. She couldn't fault his commitment to getting Stella back safely. She wondered if he'd do the same for her if he knew . . . No, she wasn't going there again, because it'd only complicate matters and she must be focused.

Her cell phone rang, and she turned on the speakerphone.

'You're at the bridge?' Hayden asked without any preamble.

'You know we are,' said Tess. 'Where are you?'

'Watching.'

'So you're satisfied we haven't got a police tail?'

He didn't answer except to issue an instruction. 'Cross the bridge and take a right on Memorial Drive. Be at Bunker Hill Monument in fifteen minutes.'

'Why don't you just cut the theatrics? Tell us where you want us and we'll do the exchange.'

'Bunker Hill. Fifteen minutes. Don't make me wait.' He ended the call, and Po set the muscle car rolling.

Tess smiled in satisfaction at her double bluff: Hayden was playing games keeping them moving around; unbeknown to him he was buying them some much needed time. On the dash was Po's cell phone, on an open line so that Pinky could monitor what was going on from his location.

'He was lying about watching us,' Po said loudly for their friend's benefit. 'We don't have a tail. It's doubtful he'll be at Bunker Hill, but we'll have to go there in case I'm wrong. How's things at your end?'

'All good. Just keep those updates coming, you.'

Po negotiated the traffic along Memorial Drive, following a wide curve of the Charles River, and passed under the Northern Expressway into Charlestown. From there he deferred to Lacey's directions, who guided them through the neighbourhood to the site of the historical battlefield. Po drew the car to a halt outside a small museum dedicated to the American Revolution, from where the memorial obelisk loomed over the surrounding park. It was reminiscent of the much taller Washington Monument. They'd made good time and had six minutes to spare. The fact that Hayden allowed them the entire quarter hour confirmed he didn't have spotters in place watching for them.

'We're at the monument,' Tess stated the instant she answered the call.

'Good. Now turn about and cross Charlestown Bridge and then find Copp's Hill Burying Ground. Be at the Hull Street entrance in fifteen minutes.' Before he was done, Po swung the car around in the road and set off for the new rendezvous point, again following hand signals from Lacey.

'We're meeting in a cemetery?' Tess asked aloud, but only so there was no confusion for Pinky on the other open line.

Hayden didn't confirm it was their ultimate destination. 'There'll be another corpse going in a grave if you don't get a move on. Fifteen minutes, starting now.'

'We're on our way.' Tess announced, though Hayden had already hung up. 'Pinky, where are you?'

'I'm not a million miles away, me,' Pinky reassured her. 'That Copp's Hill, you realize it's only a long stone's throw from Elite's headquarters?'

Lacey confirmed Pinky was correct. 'I think this could be our next to last stop.'

'We won't know until we know f'sure,' Po said. By then they were headed for the graveyard, but they'd gotten snarled up in slower moving traffic again as they headed for the crossing over the Charles River. 'How much time have we got?'

'We're still good for twelve minutes,' said Tess.

'He isn't going to leave if we're late, and he isn't going to harm Stella either. He needs her alive to control us.' Lacey didn't sound too sure.

'We should've demanded proof of life before now,' said Tess, 'but I don't think it's the right thing to do now. Telling him to put her on the phone will only aggravate Hayden, and we don't want that. Right now he's confident he's got the

upper hand and is pulling our strings. If we give him any idea
he's answerable to our demands he might up the stakes, or
hurt Stella while we're listening just to prove his point.'

'Yep, let's just stay cool,' Po said, acting anything but as
he swerved aggressively around a slow-moving bus and cut
ahead of it through a red light and took a left onto the bridge.
A minute after they were on Commercial Street in North
Boston, and Lacey again offered directions for the ancient
burial ground. Po slowed on Hull Street, and collectively they
all peered into the cemetery. An iron gate blocked the entrance:
according to an information board the cemetery closed daily
to visitors at four p.m.

Po updated Pinky with their location, then warned him to
stay silent as Tess's phone began ringing. Tess answered.

'All three of you get out of the car,' Hayden instructed.
'You're on foot from here.'

'Where do you want us?' Tess asked.

'Out of the car, and into the graveyard.'

'So we are meeting here?' she stressed.

'Out and walk.'

'The gate's closed.'

'So climb the damn thing.'

'Lacey isn't fit to climb.'

'So get your knuckle-headed boyfriend to throw him the
fuck over it.'

'Why don't you come over here and I'll stick your head on
one of the railings?' Po growled.

'Get moving, Villere, we'll meet soon enough.'

'Lookin' forward to it.'

'Miss Grey, stay on the phone.'

Tess checked on Lacey. He was in the process of sitting
up, tucking in his shirt having bent forward. His blood had
dried on the material but there was no sign of anything
fresher. 'Can you climb the wall?' she asked. Either side of
twin granite gateposts the wall was only a couple of feet
tall, but it was topped off by another two feet or so of metal
spikes.

'I'll need a leg up, but, yeah, I should make it.'

They got out of the car, checked around for observers. The

graveyard was on the historic Freedom Trail, and a destination of tourists flocking to visit and pay homage to the unmarked graves of African American slaves interred there, but with the grounds closed for the evening all the tourists had gone elsewhere. They were unobserved as first Tess clambered over the railings, then assisted Lacey up and over, while Po steadied him from the sidewalk. Lacey – encumbered by his wounds, and the chronic pain in his limbs – struggled with the climb, but finally staggered into Tess's arms on the other side. Po stepped up onto the wall and vaulted the railings with alacrity.

The graveyard wasn't massive. Trees dotted its grounds, and there were rows of ancient headstones, most leaning at angles, but few places to conceal Hayden or another observer. Both Tess and Po made visual sweeps of the entire grounds, and there wasn't a living person in sight. 'Where now?' Tess demanded into the phone, holding it close to where her's was nestled in her inside pocket, still on an open line to Pinky.

'Follow the path,' said Hayden.

'You want us to go to the other side of the graveyard?'

'Isn't that obvious?'

'You made us struggle with Lacey over the damn railings when we could've just walked around?'

'Get moving, you've another gate to climb once you get there.'

There was a reason why he made them walk across the burial grounds. It was a wide-open space across which they could be viewed. They'd made it halfway when Hayden commanded them to stop. 'OK, each of you, lift up your jackets and show me your belts. I want to see skin.'

Po was first to comply, lifting his leather jacket and shirt and performing a slow pirouette. Tess, who'd yet to grab a replacement shirt, opened her jacket and displayed her bra. She too completed a full circle to show she wasn't carrying a weapon.

'Lacey too.'

Lacey also complied.

'What's that shit strapped to your side?' Hayden demanded. It was the first confirmation that he had a visual sighting of them.

Tess replied for Lacey: 'It's gauze dressings and bandages over his wounds. You remember he was shot, right?'

'I remember. Now I want to see each of your ankles. Lift up your pants.'

They each did so, and no ankle-holsters held weapons. Po wore high-topped lace-up boots, but there was no room to shove a gun down them. 'OK, I'm satisfied. Walk on. Do you see the tomb to your right, Miss Grey? That's where you dump the cell phone; you aren't going to need it from here.'

Tess walked a few paces up an adjoining path and placed her phone on the top of a rectangular stone box that barely came up to her waist. If it was somebody's final resting place she couldn't tell, and didn't really care: she surreptitiously searched for where Hayden was hiding, as she rejoined her companions. No sign of him. As they approached the gate out of the grounds the situation changed, though it wasn't Hayden who showed himself. The scarred woman, Megan Stein, emerged from a terraced park across the street, jerking her head in annoyance for them to get a move on. As they began the process of clambering the gate, she backed away, then took a left through what amounted to a shaded rest area: the terrace was surrounded by a wall of roughly hewn stone that looked as if it could have been erected when local hero Paul Revere was still a boy. The woman didn't wait, only marched to the far end and indicated they follow her down a steep, narrow track towards Commercial Street, and the harbor front. Hayden James finally showed his face, walking down some steps at the far end of the terraced park. He nodded at them to follow Megan, and fell in step behind, never gaining on them. Megan Stein jogged across the main street and led them towards the waterfront. Without moving her lips, Tess relayed their position to Pinky.

'I know where we're going,' Lacey announced loud enough for their ears only. 'That construction site up ahead. It's going to be a new multiplex cinema and theatre. Elite supply the uniformed security to the site.'

Tess whispered a touch louder. 'Did you hear that, Pinky? It looks like we're heading for the new build opposite where all the yachts are moored.'

'I see it, and I see you too,' said Pinky's voice from her pocket. Discreetly she fixed her jacket front, feigning modesty, but also switched off the phone. Now Pinky had them in view there was no need to risk blowing their plan if she was searched and the open line to a supposed dead man discovered on her cell. Ideally she should get rid of the phone, but there was no way of dumping it without Hayden seeing. They continued following Megan, who paused only long enough to ensure they were obeying instructions, then she darted into the construction site through a gap in the hoarding. Tess glanced back at Hayden, who fixed her with his gaze. He nodded 'go ahead'.

They entered through the tall wall of hoarding and approached the recently erected building, so new in fact that its façade and roof were unfinished and the windows were all boarded; however, temporary external doors had been fitted to afford an extra layer of security to the site. Inside they'd be out of sight and hearing of any witnesses: it was secluded amid the hubbub of a major city, suitable as a private execution place. Megan Stein waved them forward with a sound suppressed pistol; behind them, as Hayden entered and closed the hoarding gate, he too drew a suppressed handgun from under his jacket.

FORTY-THREE

'Inside *now*.' Megan Stein's order was clipped, and brooked no argument. She aimed her pistol directly at Po's head, having identified him as the greatest threat. Po snorted at the command but did as he was told. Tess assisted Lacey, one arm cupped under his elbow. The older man had struggled to walk the last fifty yards or so. Megan bared her teeth at his plight: there wasn't an iota of pity in her gaze. The extended barrel of her gun trembled as she fought the urge to shoot him immediately.

Behind them, Hayden closed the door to the outside world and they were thrown into twilight in the unfinished foyer of the entertainment complex. If Elite held the contract to supply a uniformed guard presence at the site, Hayden had used his influence with the company to send them away while he conducted his business with Lacey. Without a word he strode past and indicated they follow him. Megan threatened them all with her pistol from behind and they were ushered through a wide set of doors into a broad corridor with bare concrete underfoot and stud-board walls awaiting decoration. Permanent lighting was yet to be installed, but many electrical cables snaked along the edges of the floor. Doorframes awaited doors. The air was redolent with floating motes of dust, enough to catch in their throats.

Hayden's boots sucked at the floor as he marched, and their footsteps made a collective shuffle in his wake. No words were spoken. Hayden rapped his knuckles three times against the wall as he approached the end of the corridor, where doors had been installed. It was a prearranged signal. The doors opened and he stood to one side, ensuring there wasn't a last ditch attempt at overpowering Megan in the corridor.

Megan sneered, 'Like lambs to the fucking slaughter.'

Hayden didn't answer, only met Po's gaze as he passed. Po eyed him coolly, and Hayden's mouth twitched in mockery. 'Don't make me shoot you . . . yet,' he said.

Po disdained the threat as he stepped through the doors and extended his arms by his sides. Tess saw his reason. Two of the operatives they'd snatched Lacey from in Manhattan flanked him; one covering him with a gun while the other frisked him for weapons. The one with the gun, red-haired and freckle-faced growled something about Po hitting him with his car and knocking him flying.

'Yeah, that was my bad,' said Po. 'I was hoping to squash you under the wheels but mistimed my skid.'

'Prick,' Grant Aiken called him.

The second man – Sean Nicholls – finished frisking Po, and nodded the all clear at Hayden. Po was directed forward a few paces and told to kneel and put his hands behind his head: he complied. Tess was next to be searched, and there was no consideration given to her sex. The stocky guy approached her while Megan grabbed Lacey's collar and dragged him aside.

'Unzip your jacket,' Nicholls commanded her.

'I'm not fully dressed,' Tess protested.

'Unzip.' His pale eyes grew as hard as stone.

Exhaling, Tess drew down the zipper, and held open her jacket. Nicholls moved in.

'Touch her and I'll break both your hands,' Po warned him.

'Really?' asked Hayden. 'You're on your knees with a gun to your head and you're making threats.'

'Yup, and I mean what I say. You already checked we're unarmed, there's no need to go through this again. If he touches Tess in an inappropriate way I'm gonna take umbrage.'

'Check her,' Hayden said with a sneer.

Nicholls patted her down, but avoided laying his hands on her bare flesh. He found Po's phone tucked in the inside breast pocket, and showed it to Hayden, who snapped his fingers and accepted it from Nicholls.

Tess tensed: if Hayden checked the call record it would show she'd been in contact with someone up until only a few minutes ago. But Hayden only dropped the cell phone and stamped it underfoot. Tess was inwardly relieved.

'She's clear,' Nicholls announced.

'OK,' Hayden directed at Tess, 'step forward and assume the position.'

'We didn't come here as your prisoners,' Tess replied calmly. 'We came to do an exchange. Where's Stella?'

'You'll see her once I'm satisfied you've no surprises in store for me. Now kneel and put your hands behind your head, or things will get noisy in a few seconds.'

Tess, nor Po, expected to lay eyes on Stella, not if they'd been positioned for a swift execution. It was over to Lacey to buy them some time.

He yanked suddenly out of Megan's grasp, and lurched at Hayden. His face was set in rictus, his eyes feverish. 'Where's my daughter, you son of a bitch? I want to see her *now*!'

Megan was only a pace behind him, and she grabbed angrily at him with a vile curse. Hayden's palm planted squarely on Lacey's chest, stopping him in his tracks.

Surreptitiously, Tess stepped aside, as if clearing space for them but really to avoid complying with Hayden's instruction. Nicholls watched her, his gun wavering between her, Po and Lacey, while Aiken also stepped to the far side so he had a clear shot at them if necessary. Objecting loudly, Lacey pushed against Hayden, squirmed to avoid Megan's grasp, and forced past them both. He strode for the far end of the echoing room, shouting Stella's name.

Their plan relied heavily on using an inherent flaw in Hayden's team's strength. Throughout their previous interactions, Tess and Po had come to realize that though professional in one respect, they mostly lacked killer instinct. Whether that was through poor leadership, a lack of communication or not being satisfactorily rewarded, they didn't know, but it was as if the operatives weren't sure what they were fighting for and it sapped their motivation. Also, they were ex-military or ex-law enforcement, but Hayden's team were intrinsically amateurs when it came to kidnap exchanges. The team was experienced at protecting a 'principal' – their client usually observing their directions – not at controlling a highly emotive group of hostages, and when control was ripped out of their hands they were momentarily in disarray, and looked to Hayden for instruction. He too was briefly thrown by Lacey's actions, and it took him seconds before he snapped an order at Aiken to grab him.

By then, Tess had also walked briskly after Lacey. Hayden's team was forced to play catch-up, and for a few seconds all was chaos. Warnings about being shot held little force when those holding the guns were caught in confused flux.

Making it approximately halfway into the large room, Tess halted in her tracks. Ahead, and above her, seated on the framework of some kind of stage, Stella Dewildt peered back at her, the whites of her eyes almost sparkling through the gloom. Either side of her stood a guard, the Korean woman, Vera Seung, and the tall man Lacey had briefly fought in Manhattan, Brian Johnson. They'd both moved forward a pace or two, in anticipation of helping to stop Lacey's progress, but they were loath to abandon their seated hostage.

Aiken caught up with Lacey, but was elbowed roughly in

the midriff. The man woofed out air, and hissed at the pain: he still wasn't on top form after being on the receiving end of the Mustang's bruising impact. Lacey staggered away, and the man groped to grab him. Megan suddenly broke ranks and ran after him, swearing in vitriol.

'Don't hurt him,' Hayden barked. He swung to and fro, saw how too close for comfort Po was and brought up the suppressed barrel of his pistol. 'Everybody hold it, or I swear to God I'll put a bullet in Villere's head!'

Tess didn't move, only continued staring at Stella, trying to imbue a state of calmness on the woman. She didn't want to look back at her partner, in case it encouraged Hayden to follow through with his warning. After a quick dip towards his ankle, Po also stood, relaxed, arms hanging at his sides as he peered back at the gunman.

Megan caught up to Lacey. Encumbered by her pistol and Hayden's warning, she had little recourse. She practically jumped on his back, wrapping an arm around his neck. She was trawled a few yards, before Lacey's strength gave out and he went down to one knee. Megan stumbled over him, and then swung around, raising her pistol to his face. 'You piece of crap!' she squawked at him. 'I should fucking kill you right here, right now!'

Ignoring her, Lacey dug in his jacket pocket, and came out clutching two identical USB sticks. He craned so that he caught Hayden's attention. 'It's these you want back. Let Stella go, and fucking take them!'

Lacey sent the USB sticks flying and their clatter across the bare concrete floor only hinted at their final destinations somewhere in the shadows of the far wall. Megan grabbed a handful of his hair and yanked his head up, and forced the end of the suppressor against his forehead. 'You just signed your own life away, asshole,' she hissed.

'No, Megan,' Hayden barked. 'We don't know if they're the only copies. I think we're still missing one.'

Megan's lips writhed in poorly contained rage, but Hayden was correct: they had to confirm the USB sticks were the only remaining copies of the files. She relaxed the pressure on the trigger a fraction.

'Nicholls,' Hayden said. 'Go and get them, and bring them here.'

Nicholls was still in a state of confusion. He looked dumbly between Po, Tess and then Lacey.

'The fucking USB sticks!' Hayden snapped.

Nodding in embarrassment, Nicholls chased after the USB sticks like a dog after a thrown ball.

Lacey attempted to rise.

'Stay down,' Megan snarled. Aiken joined her, but just stood, unsure what to do.

'Let Stella go,' Lacey responded.

They were strung out through the large room. Not how Hayden had planned things working out.

'You,' he said to Po, and he jerked the gun a couple of times so his message was clear. 'Get moving.'

Po turned aside and began strolling nonchalantly to where Tess waited. Presently she was unguarded while Megan and Aiken were crowding Lacey, and Nicholls scrambled around trying to locate the thumb drives among the detritus of the construction site. Hayden commanded Po to stop when he was alongside his partner.

Tess mouthed words at Stella, then turned and eyed Hayden steadily. She sneered at the threat of his gun. 'You haven't done anything like this before, have you?' she said.

He didn't rise to her scorn. 'I'm a fast learner,' he said instead.

'No, buddy,' Po drawled. 'You learn by making mistakes and not repeating them. You ain't gonna get the opportunity at a second go.'

Behind Hayden the doors creaked open, and there was an instant shift in the light bleeding in from the outer corridor. It was enough to note the grin of satisfaction on Po's face. Hayden snapped around, aiming his gun at the new arrivals, but didn't pull the trigger. Instead he wheezed out a curse.

'Surprised, you? You shouldn't be. I'm the proverbial bent penny,' Pinky Leclerc announced. 'I keep turning up.'

Alone, even armed as he was, Pinky's inclusion in the dynamic wouldn't have made much difference, but Pinky was not alone. A trio of armed men accompanied him, and between them they ushered hostages of their own. Gagged with duct tape and their hands cuffed behind them, Ben Holbrook and Clarissa Glenn glared at Hayden for allowing their capture.

Hayden didn't lower his weapon.

'Are you still confident of earning that bonus now?' Tess asked from behind him.

FORTY-FOUR

'You tried killing me once and failed. Care for a second try, you?' Pinky aimed his pistol directly at Hayden James.

Hayden didn't reply, but neither did he lower his weapon. He flicked another glance over his bosses and knew the second he pulled the trigger would be their last, and quite probably his too. The trio of men surrounding his bosses had protected their identities with scarfs wrapped around their faces. They looked ready to spray everyone in sight with their submachine guns.

Hayden aimed his gun at the ceiling, then unfurled his grip so the Beretta hung on his index finger by its trigger guard.

'Didn't think so,' said Pinky. 'Now . . . the rest of you asshats, drop your damn weapons or you'll see what your beloved leaders look like in matching crimson.'

Holbrook and Glenn were forced to their knees, and one of his mysterious companions held the stock of his weapon tight to his shoulder, its barrel a hand's breadth from their heads. The other two spread apart, one training his weapon on Nicholls who had taken to a knee in the shadows, hoping he'd been missed. The third man took a position where he had Megan and Aiken in his sights.

'Did I not make myself clear, goddammit?' Pinky barked.

Nicholls threw aside his pistol and held up his hands. Aiken wasn't stupid either. He set down his weapon and kicked it away and raised his hands in surrender. Up on the stage, Seung and Johnson didn't move, but neither did they dispose of their guns. However, they didn't try to stop Stella either when Tess mouthed another instruction, and then hurried to the side of the stage to meet her friend coming down. Stella had shed the after effects of sedation, but was still weak with fear, and also trepidation for her father. She almost fell into Tess's arms, and Tess moved her aside, so she was out of the line of fire.

'You on the stage,' Pinky went on. 'I'll give you the benefit of not hearing me the first two times, but the third will be the last. DROP YOUR FUCKING WEAPONS NOW!'

Seung and Johnson dropped their weapons.

Pinky smiled in faux gratitude, then aimed a wink at Po.

'Good work, brother,' said Po, because his friend deserved the praise, having achieved so much in short order.

Pinky's smile was genuine this time. He was having serious misgivings about his chosen career path, and was in the process of formulating the best way to leave it behind, but it had its advantages too. In short order, during the drive up from Boston, he'd pulled in favours and secured the assistance of a trio of criminals who hadn't balked at the notion of his plan. Their price was a large chunk of Pinky's current empire, but it was worth it to him and not to be missed once he walked away from the rest of it. Based in Providence, Rhode Island, the outfit had no connection with Po Villere's enemies in Boston, but was close enough to travel up and meet with Pinky within the time frame given to them by Hayden James, and to carry out the swift and daring counter-snatch of Holbrook and Glenn. Their task was sped up by the assistance of Harris Collins; the guard who'd first raised the cover-up of a murder to Aaron Lacey and who'd helped him download the incriminating files. Tess had made contact with the guard, and he'd not only agreed to spirit Pinky's outfit inside Elite's HQ, but to also ensure they went unchallenged as they abducted the company heads. As it were, there were few on site involved to any degree with what their bosses and the troubleshooting team were involved in, and Pinky's group were in and out in minutes, and Holbrook and Glenn confined inside a van until the appropriate time came to walk them inside. Unlike Hayden James's people, Pinky's were hardened criminals who wouldn't think twice about ending any resistance to their plan. To prove a point they'd come armed with military-issue Heckler & Koch MP5K submachine guns and supplied Pinky with a tactical semi-automatic SIG Sauer P226R pistol, and a secondary weapon, a more compact P228 originally destined for Tess's hand. At the moment, she had her hands filled with Stella Dewildt, so Pinky offered it to Po instead.

Po shook his head.

He moved on Hayden James.

He met his stare, then almost disdainfully stripped the man's gun from his hand and shoved it into his belt at the back.

'So what happens now, Villere?' Hayden asked.

Po ignored the question. He sought Tess in the gloom. 'Get Stella outta here,' he called.

'What are you going to do?' Hayden pressed.

'I should give *you* something to remember *me* by,' said Pinky, and tapped the muzzle of his SIG below the scar on his head: without the gauze padding the full extent of his injury was vivid and looked the more permanent due to the sterile sutures holding together his skin. 'Leave you with a head like a split gourde.'

'You should be grateful that I spared your life,' Hayden rasped. 'I hit you with that skillet so's Megan didn't put a bullet in your brains.'

'No, bra,' said Pinky. 'Saving my life was never your intention.'

Po had walked away during their brief exchange. His attention was on Megan Stein. She still controlled Lacey with one hand furled in his hair.

'It's over,' Po told her. 'Put down your weapon and you won't be hurt.'

Megan shook her head vehemently. She hauled on Lacey's hair, drawing him up so that she could use him as a shield. She stuck her gun in the side of his neck. 'I'm walking out of here and this piece of shit's coming with me. Now back the fuck up, all of you!'

'Po,' said Lacey, 'if you let her take me, I'm done for the second she's in the clear.'

'You were done for the second you killed my Ethan!' Megan screeched. Her gun went from his neck, to Po, then back again. 'I'm not fucking kidding! Get out of my way, or you'll be wearing his brains.'

'You're not leaving this place with him,' Po warned.

'Then he's not leaving this place at all!'

'No, Megan, don't—' Hayden's warning was lost in the immediate aftermath.

Chaos erupted as a gunshot rang out.

Lacey collapsed to the floor, even as Megan backed away, freeing her weapon to shoot at Po.

Po's hand whipped up, and he released the blade he'd cupped in his palm and concealed under his sleeve since secretly removing it from its boot sheath earlier. The knife sank to its hilt in Megan's shoulder, but she still held onto her weapon, and she let off a shot at Po. But he'd moved instantly, ducking and lunging to one side, so the shot went wide. Megan tracked him.

From the floor, Lacey aimed his revolver. Unbeknown to all, Tess and Po included, he'd discovered it lying under the passenger seat of the Mustang, dropped there when he'd dived inside on 56th Street in Manhattan, and had concealed it under the bulky dressings and bandages on his wounds before exiting the car at the old burying grounds. While Megan had prepared to murder him in cold blood, he'd dug out the gun, and fired under his armpit into her gut. She was on her feet, but dying, only not as fast as he'd hoped. He shot her again. This time his bullet found her chest, and she staggered back on wooden legs, her face a picture of dismay. Again she proved more resilient than he'd hoped, and she lowered her gun and returned fire. Lacey got off a final shot before they both collapsed wearing fresh bloody wounds. The scar on Megan's face bore a new hole, and it was barely discernible among the puckered flesh: not so the hole at the back, as it had taken a large chunk of bone and scalp with it.

'Dad!' Stella's scream rang out from the wings of the stage where Tess had moved her out of harm's way. Her footsteps thundered as she raced back onto the stage, and Vera Seung, nearest her, also grasped at a chance of a hostage. She lunged for Stella, even as Johnson leapt for where his gun lay on the stage. Their actions added fuel to an already incendiary situation.

A submachine gun roared, and Nicholls died under a blistering hail of bullets, his hand still inches from where he'd earlier tossed his gun aside. The sound was startlingly loud in the large room, and in reaction, it scattered those able to run. At a gallop Grant Aiken snatched up his fallen gun, and he loosed three suppressed shots in quick succession before he too was torn apart by one of Pinky's men.

Po vaulted over Lacey, even as he plucked Hayden's gun from his belt and fired at Johnson. Johnson was saved by his elevated position, and the angle of the stage, and returned fire. A bullet nicked leather from Po's jacket before he ducked and his counterfire went high and wide.

Seung grappled Stella around her waist and yanked her off her feet. She braced her hostage against her, moving sideways as she sought her dropped gun. From nowhere, Tess powered into her and all three women went down on the stage in a bundle of furiously struggling limbs. Johnson turned to get a bead on his partner's attacker, and Po bobbed up over the stage and placed a better-aimed bullet in his prone body. Johnson gasped, readjusted his aim, but before another shot could be fired by either of them, Pinky blasted the man with a short burst of three 9mm Parabellums from his SIG.

Holbrook and Glenn had nowhere to go. They were forced flat by their guard, but he didn't kill them. They weren't to know his intentions, and both emitted muffled pleas through their gags. In the meantime, Hayden James abandoned them to their fate, racing for where he knew there was a gap between the loose boards on the far side of the room. Gunfire chased him every step, and he felt the tug of one bullet as it exited the flesh of his right thigh. Fortunately for him, his leg didn't collapse beneath him, and he made it through the gap in the wall. Bullets punched through the drywall, showering dust and shrapnel, but to his right when he had lunged left. By the time his would-be killer adjusted his aim, Hayden was hurtling away along a service corridor, and the sounds of battle fell behind him.

Within what was destined to become the destination of theatregoers, a drama continued to be acted out on its stage. Stella proved a hindrance in the fight, only attempting to escape the melee to reach her father's side, while Tess strove to protect her from Vera Seung's determined attack. Immediately after they'd spilled apart, the woman had gone on the offensive, kicking and punching, and it was unclear if she intended killing them both or forcing a path through them. Tess inserted herself in harm's way, and took a couple of heavy blows to her body before she landed a punch in retaliation. Seung had unarmed combat skills Tess couldn't ordinarily match, but she was more ferocious in her defense. As Seung powered a roundhouse kick at her face, Tess ducked under the streaking foot and clasped both hands around the woman's upper thigh, then charged her off her supporting leg. They went down again, and this time the barely constructed stage gave way under their combined weight, and they crashed together through loose planks into the void beneath.

Tess blinked in the almost complete darkness, trying to get her bearings, before realizing she had found her way on top of the woman. Blindly, she threw aside the pinioned leg, and crawled up Seung's chest, throwing punches down into Seung's body and head. Her previously injured wrist threatened to come apart again with each blow she landed, but she didn't let up. Not until she was dragged off the unconscious woman by Pinky, who offered her a roll of his eyes. 'Damn, Pretty Tess, remind me to never get on your wrong side.'

'Where's Stella? Where's Po?' she asked in a rush.

'Stella's with her dad, Po's gone after that Hayden James dude.'

'What?' Tess croaked, still partially in a daze from her short but brutal battle.

'He saw you had that bitch there in hand, him, then went after Hayden.'

'That boneheaded man!' Everything was under control, with all of the Elite people either dead, unconscious, or under armed guard. Hayden could run for all she cared, because without his promised reward he wouldn't get far before the police caught up with him, but damn it if Po didn't have a point to prove! He had nothing to prove except how stupidity could get him killed! She was about to race after him, when Stella's keening wails reminded her there was somebody in need of more urgent assistance. Leaving Pinky to dig Seung out of the wreckage under the stage, Tess rushed to Lacey's side and knelt down opposite Stella, who was futilely attempting to staunch too many wounds with too few hands. Remarkably, Lacey was not yet dead, but it would only be a matter of minutes if they didn't get him to hospital.

FORTY-FIVE

He felt like a rat in a maze, every corner he took, every passageway he ran down was a dead end or sent him deeper into the labyrinth. With the benefit of previously reconnoitring the site Hayden James should've been able to escape, but he kept getting turned about. There were footfalls close behind, his pursuer dogged, and he'd be swiftly caught unless he found a way out. He couldn't return to the front of the building, not while Pinky's crew were still in attendance armed with submachine guns, as he'd be torn to pieces the instant he showed his face. Instead he chose to keep running and try to find access to the building site at the rear, and from there use the mounds of dirt and heavy equipment as cover until he could find a way out and onto the harbor. When he'd planned the exchange and subsequent executions, figuring out where his team was going to dispose of the bodies had taken precedence over an escape route. He'd earmarked the area towards the rear where an annexe building would eventually complement the larger entertainment complex. The construction crew had only recently broken ground, and dug deep foundations, and Hayden had judged the deep pits ideal graves. Ironic that it might be him filling one of those graves . . .

No! He wasn't going to die today, no way, no how. Running

away wasn't an act of cowardice, only about self-preservation, because it was an intrinsic trait to wish to live to fight another day. Right then he was at a supreme disadvantage having lost all of his people, his weapons, and even his damn sense of direction! He had to turn things around, and quick, but couldn't do that while running blind. He slowed, stopped and took stock.

Nearby the footfalls also fell silent.

More distantly he could make out the voices of those still in the auditorium, although he couldn't discern actual words. A woman was crying, and he supposed it was Stella Dewildt: he'd watched Megan die, and he suspected that Vera Seung hadn't gotten out alive either. He felt no pity for either, especially not for Megan who'd given into rage and gotten the others killed. His small sense of gratitude towards her was only because she'd also given him the opportunity to flee, and to fight again. Had she not shot things out with Lacey and Villere, they would all have been taken prisoner and handed over to the cops. As it were, while he was at liberty, he could possibly get Holbrook and Glenn away from their captors, and salvage what was left of his get-out plan. How he was going to do that was the issue, but it was apparent he was going to have to re-arm and reposition, and to do that he must kill the one stalking him through the twilit gloom of the building. He was under no illusion about his hunter. It wasn't Pinky's man who'd unloaded a clip at him as he'd first ran from the auditorium, his sole hunter must be Nicolas Villere, because they'd been destined to fight since first laying eyes on each other. Hayden was fine with that, just not while he was at the disadvantage of being unarmed.

Behind him, spots of his blood marked his route. The wound to his thigh wasn't serious, but it bled like a bitch and Villere didn't have to be a bloodhound to follow it. He set off, walking this time, and Villere moved after him. Partition walls separated them, some already cladded with drywall boards, others temporarily sheathed in semi-opaque plastic sheets to keep down the dust. Other dust sheets hung at regular intervals down the passageways he'd followed, sometimes forming separate mazes to further confuse his route. Of course they equally impeded

Villere, and offered Hayden concealment, so he shouldn't complain. As he progressed he sought a weapon, but soon he considered a different strategy.

Villere had Hayden's pistol, and most likely that damn knife he'd spirited as if from thin air, except through previous observation Hayden had concluded that Villere wasn't prone to using either in cold blood. Perhaps he could use Villere's reluctance against him, to control their confrontation.

He ducked under a hanging plastic sheet and found a space more familiar to him. During his earlier recce he'd visited the large room assigned as a bar/diner area. The fitters had dressed the walls here, and the windows were in place albeit concealed from without by secure boards to protect the glass. The diner's permanent fixtures and bar area was still under construction, and tables had been stacked in serried ranks at the far end of the room. Beyond the bar area, a door led to a kitchen he'd earlier checked out and found almost ready to go, but for the necessary utensils: there was no chance of finding a conventional weapon in there, or even a heavy skillet like he'd once used to good effect, but plenty other objects adaptable to use should he have misread Villere's reticence to murder.

He headed inside the kitchen, knowing he was entering a bottleneck, but it was also an arena where he could meet Villere that was difficult for the others to find if they came to his assistance. His plan required a swift death for Villere, where he could re-arm and then launch an ambush to liberate his bosses. The brushed-steel countertops were devoid of sharp implements, but stacked against one wall was some metal shelving waiting for assembly. He selected one of the upright supports, a steel bar as thick as a broom handle and two feet long. It wouldn't level the field against a gun, but would give him reach on what was obviously Villere's weapon of choice. It hadn't escaped his notice when Villere refused to take the gun offered to him by Pinky, or when he'd shoved away Hayden's gun in his belt after taking it off him: Villere was a knife man.

He took a couple of practice swings with his impromptu club, and was satisfied with its weight and manoeuvrability.

Then he deliberately knocked the tubular steel against a countertop to lure in his prey. Nicolas Villere didn't dally, he filled the doorway within seconds, and after one cursory check of Hayden's position he entered the room. Initially he held the Beretta loosely by his side but brought it to bear and aimed it directly at Hayden's heart.

'So many people have died already,' Villere said, 'I guess one more won't matter.'

'That depends on who walks out of this room alive,' Hayden countered.

'Buddy, who gets to live isn't even in question.'

Villere squeezed the trigger and the suppressor did little to muffle the retort in the enclosed space.

FORTY-SIX

Another man was seconds from death. Stella cradled her father's head in her lap, one hand stroking his cheek as he gasped for breath. Blood flecked his lips, and made vivid streaks on his unshaven chin where Stella's fingers touched. She wept for him, and didn't know what to say except she loved him and didn't want him to die: sadly she had no influence over the latter. Pinky had used his replacement cell phone to call an ambulance, and the police, before joining his friends who were in the act of leaving, as now they'd played their part in the rescue they'd no intention of sticking around. Tess feared that the emergency services would be too late to help Lacey, and all she could do for him was to help keep him comfortable in his last moments alive. Megan Stein had only temporarily lost in the exchange of gunfire, as she'd fulfilled her promise to slay him. Her bullets had taken one lung, and scrambled more of his internal organs; his wounds were catastrophic, and it surprised Tess that he'd clung on this long. His eyelids fluttered, slid shut.

'Dad . . . Dad, stay with me! Help's coming, but you have

to stay with me.' Stella's tears dripped on his face. 'Don't you dare die, I won't let you!'

'Don't cry for me,' Lacey whispered as he roused, and he aimed a pained smile up at her. 'I never expected . . . to get out of here alive, but I came anyway.' He wheezed out a laugh at the irony. 'But that's OK. I created . . . the diversion I promised, and saved you. I love you so . . . so much, Stella, and I'm happy that you're safe. That's what's really important.' He flicked his gaze from Stella to Tess, as if she was included in the sentiment too. Tess squeezed his hand gently, but it was cold and clammy, and it was doubtful he could feel her. Again he slipped towards eternal darkness.

'No, Dad,' Stella cried. She shook him, and once more his eyelids fluttered.

'I . . . I have to go . . .' he said, his voice barely audible, 'but first I need to tell you . . .' His focus swam in and out, and both Stella and Tess crowded a little closer, and it was unclear for whom he directed his final words: 'I love you, and my only regret is that I wasn't always the father I should've been . . .'

He died, and Stella folded over him, wrapping him in her arms as she sobbed uncontrollably. Tess hugged her, her hands smoothing Stella's hair as she whispered condolences, but her friend was inconsolable. Tess finally withdrew to allow her friend to grieve. It was as if a pillow had been stuffed in her chest and her eyes were hot, but she fought back the tears. She looked to where Pinky stood guard over Holbrook, Glenn and Seung. He met her gaze, and though he'd only recently shot dead Johnson in heated battle, he'd reverted to the man of good heart she knew him as. He directed a look of shared sorrow at her, and then Stella beyond. Shaking his head, he looked down at his prisoners and muttered something harsh. Holbrook hung his head in shame, but it wasn't enough.

Tess strode towards the prisoners, a finger pointed back at where Lacey lay in his daughter's arms.

'Was his death worth it, you?' She threw out her arms in an all-encompassing gesture of the other corpses in the room. 'All of this death, to feed your damn greed?'

The Elite heads remained gagged, and she couldn't bear to listen to their excuses anyway, but she still wanted to vent. 'This is your fault, because you chose to line your pockets. You protected a murderous pig over good, decent people, and look where it has gotten you. All of these people died . . . and you are going to prison. Well? *Was it fucking worth it?'*

Clarissa Glenn scowled up at her, and made a grunt of scorn behind her gag. Tess stepped forward sharply, balling her fists. She was tempted to strike the hawk-faced bitch, but once she began she might not stop until she'd beaten her to a pulp. She aimed a finger of warning down at Glenn, and Holbrook both. 'You're going to prison, and I'm going to see to it that it's for a very long time.'

Tess returned to Stella's side, and again tried to soothe her friend. Stella looked at her in disconsolation. 'Why did my dad have to die, Tess?'

'He died so that you didn't, Stella. He sacrificed himself so that you could be saved, because that's the kind of man he was. He was a good man, a good cop, who wanted to ensure justice was done, and we're going to make sure it happens.'

Stella had never been party to any of their discussions about the horrendous crime her father had uncovered, but now wasn't the time to tell her the details. It was enough that she understood her dad had died for something nobler than cashing in on a blackmail scam. It was better too that she remained ignorant to the full facts until after she was questioned by the police, so she was deemed a victim; the same might not be extended to the rest of them, specifically Pinky who would have to lie his way through a police inter-rogation to protect his allies, and Po who had gone off in single pursuit to exact vigilante justice.

Even as she thought about him, she caught the distant sound of suppressed gunfire – a series of soft thuds to her ear – and feared it was too late to dissuade him from killing Hayden James, and securing himself a place in prison. But that fear was only fleeting, because Po might not be the one doling out an execution. She ran to Pinky, held out her hand

and after a moment's pause, where he considered he should be the one going to Po's assistance but decided he served best by watching their prisoners, he handed over the SIG P228.

'Be careful,' he said as she raced off to where the gunfire had fallen silent. Once she was out of earshot, he leaned towards Holbrook and Glenn. 'You'd best hope she gets there in time, you. If your boy has hurt Nicolas, I don't care about the consequences, me: I'll shoot you both like the sick mutts you are.'

FORTY-SEVEN

P o cast aside the empty gun.
'There,' he said, with a note of satisfaction, 'it can't be used if you do happen to get past me.'
Hayden had weathered the bullets skimming so close to his head and shoulders he'd felt the heat of their passing. Behind him broken wall tiles clattered to the countertops and the floor, making almost as much racket as the pistol had a moment before: suppressed pistols were still noisy in close confines. With each pull on the trigger, Po watched the reflexive jerk of anticipation from Hayden as he steeled for the killing shot. Only after Po threw away the gun did he relax again, and offer a sneer at the dramatics.

'I didn't take you for a cold-blooded murderer,' he said.

'I'm not. But that doesn't mean you're getting outta here intact.'

'You've been anticipating this fight as long as I have, huh?'

Po danced his eyebrows. Nodded at the steel bar. 'You don't want to go hand to hand?'

'There's the matter of that knife of yours . . .'

Po shrugged. 'Ask your girlfriend where it is when next you see her.'

'You telling me you left it sticking in Megan's shoulder?' Hayden shook his head. 'Sorry, Villere, but I don't believe you.'

Po held up his empty hands. 'Aah, to hell with it. You can keep the bar if you think you'll need it.'

'Sure of yourself, huh?'

'Yup. We doing this?'

Hayden watched him for a long beat. Then he tossed aside the bar on a countertop. Waited.

'The cops will be coming,' Po reminded him.

'They won't get here in time to save you.'

'That ain't my concern, bra; I don't want them stopping me from kickin' your ass.'

'So come ahead.'

Po walked to the centre of the kitchen. Underfoot was non-slip flooring. The walls were tiled. The steel counters, discounting the gaps where the cooking ranges were still to be fitted, formed a neat oblong thirty by twenty feet in dimension. It was as good an arena as any to fight in. He slipped out of his jacket and set it on top of one brushed-steel counter, allowed Hayden the opportunity to disrobe too, but the man didn't bother. Hayden settled his stance, left leg forward and bent at the knee, his right extended slightly behind him. He formed a guard, again with his left arm and shoulder forward. Po knew a karate practitioner when he saw one, most likely from one of the modern rather than more traditional styles judging by the loose guard.

'You're not the only one with a few tricks,' said Hayden, noting how Po had scrutinized his stance.

'Tricks are for play fighting,' Po responded, 'you ready for the real thing?'

They moved forward, circled left, then switched and moved right. Po threw a lazy left jab, and Hayden didn't bother pawing it away, only swayed out of reach. Po's second jab was faster, and delivered at a tighter angle. His knuckles crunched into Hayden's shoulder: this time he batted at Po's forearm, then switched stance fluidly and his right fist flailed at Po's head, then his open left slashed at his throat. Now Po had to sway and bob to avoid the bruising impacts. They eased apart, and both men smiled slyly.

'Kempo, huh?' asked Po.

'You know your fighting styles.'

Po nodded. Kempo practitioners were prone to blitzing their opponents with blindingly fast combinations of strikes from all angles and all the body's natural weapons, dominating and destroying them in short order. Po respected their skill set, but not always their commitment, because in launching so many strikes in quick succession, some – not all – failed to deliver any with intent before the next was on its way.

'If I knew we were going to have a catfight I'd have left you to the girls,' said Po.

'Not impressed, huh?'

'Nope.'

Again they met, and their punches and blocks were a blur. All had been directed towards the head and body; Hayden switched to a low line, and kicked at Po's shin. Po retreated, the skin barked, but then snapped off a kick that skimmed Hayden's knee. Hayden pivoted and raked Po's forehead with an elbow. The impact set of a flurry of black spots through his vision.

'How's about now?' Hayden crowed.

Po shook his head, his smile set, but he was fooling nobody: he was also shaking lucidity back into his brain.

Hayden tried to capitalize on Po's injury, stepping in and kicking again, this time spearing the toe of his boot at Po's groin. Po knocked the foot aside with a swipe of his left knee, and it overbalanced Hayden. Po slashed in with his elbow, ramming the tip in the man's exposed ribs. Hayden staggered away, and fetched up against the metal counter holding Po's jacket. Po followed, kicking at the wound on his opponent's leg.

'Son of a bitch!' Hayden wheezed, barely able to catch his breath. He turned quickly, and used the counter to catapult him towards Po, throwing a rapid combination of knife-hand slashes. One blow slammed Po's cheek, and it immediately puffed up the size and colour of a ripe plumb. His right eye watered. But he weathered the blow and threw one of his own, his knuckles raking Hayden's eye socket. When Hayden reared back, blood trickled from a split eyelid. He shook the blood away to clear his vision.

Already Po was on him. He swept apart Hayden's arms,

caught his neck in both hands and dragged him forward onto his knee. The first blow was to his chest, but Po wasn't finished, he rammed the knee up again, this time to Hayden's jaw. Hayden's knees wobbled, but he jammed a forearm over Po's knee to avoid a third soul-destroying impact, then wrapped both arms around Po's slim waist and hauled up and back. He flung Po down on the counter. Po scrambled, his heels squeaking on the brushed steel, but Hayden followed, peppering him with hammering blows of his fists and elbows. Hayden overreached.

Swinging around on his butt, Po shot his right leg past Hayden's neck, then immediately bent it at the knee. His other leg forced under Hayden's extended right arm, and his right foot hooked under the knee. Po grabbed the back of Hayden's head and it was almost as if he hugged the man to his own chest: it was an innocuous-looking hold, but Hayden was in immediate danger of suffocation. He panicked.

As he tried to prise off Po's legs, Po caught his flailing arm and hyperextended it at the elbow, without ever releasing the choke hold with his legs. Hayden had little recourse: he tried biting, but that only filled his mouth with denim, and added to the overwhelming sense of suffocation, so instead he hauled backwards, holding Po elevated for a second or two, then arched forward at the floor.

Po's spine took the impact, and he lost his hold on Hayden's arm, but his legs were cinched in too tight. He wriggled his butt backwards a few inches, stretching out Hayden, who'd dropped to both knees, and the crown of the man's head became a target. Po dropped the tip of his elbow repeatedly, like a volley of bombs on Hayden's skull. He felt the strength go out of the man, and kicked him away without rancour: Hayden had given his best, but it was not good enough. Po stood, peered down at the semi-conscious man. He could kill him if he wished, with a stamp to the nape of his neck, but Po wasn't a psychotic scumbag, the likes of the scarred woman Hayden had held near. He took another couple of steps backward, wiping at the swollen lump on his cheek with the back of his wrist, but never taking his gaze off his opponent.

Hayden groaned, and with little strength to his fingers, he touched the sore spots on his skull. He swore and moaned again, and finally lifted his head high enough to peer up at his vanquisher. 'Y'know,' he said, his voice desultory, 'I once told Megan I'd hire you in an instant. You've got skills, Villere, better than any of my team. I could use you, man, if—'

'Don't say it,' Po warned. 'You were set to execute us all back there, and it's not somethin' I'll ever forget. There's no amount of money buys me after you threatened my girl. Get it into your soft head; you're not gettin' away with any of this.'

Hayden wasn't surprised. 'You can't blame me for trying.'

He scooped broken shards of tiles from the floor and flung them in Po's face.

Po reeled away, shielding his eyes with his arms, feeling the bite of razor-sharp porcelain slicing into his forearms. Before he could swat away the stinging shrapnel, Hayden dragged himself up with the aid of the counter, and he snapped up the bar he'd thrown aside earlier. Without pause, he charged across the kitchen, clubbing Po. Po's arms took the impacts, and after the first he knew that his left ulnar was broken. He kicked blindly at Hayden, but the man was remorseless in his need to finish Po off. The bar struck at him repeatedly, and Po sacrificed his arms for his skull, but he was weakened and in agony, and fell back against the opposite counter. Po clutched at any lifeline, found his leather jacket and whipped it around the bar. He yanked down, and Hayden fell against him. They grappled close, Po's teeth set in rictus, his turquoise eyes blazing.

'You sumbitch,' he snarled, 'I'd'a let things go at that. But you just made a false move, pal, and that changes the rules.'

Po smashed his forehead into Hayden's face, flattening his nose. The ex-soldier was tough and resilient though, and was hard-wired to keep on fighting even when a lesser man would have folded. He tried to spear the butt end of the bar in Po's eyes, despite it being encumbered by the leather jacket. Po jerked aside, but his ear was slashed, and he felt blood pour down his neck. He broke away to one side, hanging on to the jacket with his weakened left hand, but Hayden yanked the other direction and freed the bar. He flung back his arm, ready to hurl it directly through Po's chest.

From the doorway, Tess shot Hayden three times in rapid succession. The bar fell from his nerveless fingers, and Hayden James keeled over dead.

Po blinked tears and blood from his eyes, looked down at the corpse, then up at Tess. He was a mass of bruises and cuts and he cupped his broken arm in his other hand. He still managed a sheepish smile through his pain.

'I coulda taken him,' he said.

'I know,' she reassured him, 'but I wanted payback too.'

'How's Lacey doing?'

She shook her head, and he watched the workings of her throat as she struggled against emotion.

'Come here,' he said, an offer not an instruction.

She moved into his one-armed embrace and held on to him.

'Can I ask you to do somethin' for me, Tess?'

She blinked tears away as she peered up at him.

'My arm's broken, and maybe that's not all; I'm gonna need some help around the house . . .'

'Yes,' she said without pause.

'You will move in?'

She held his gaze. 'Yes. But not as your housekeeper. There's something I need from you too.'

'D'you want to ride pillion on my new Harley Davidson?' His eyes twinkled in humour, and she reached up and kissed him, because it was as good as a marriage proposal from him.

FORTY-EIGHT

Without exception, everyone found alive at the construction site was taken into police custody until some sense could be made of the mess, where immediately Ben Holbrook attempted to pull on favors from certain senior officers he kept in his back pocket. For a worrying period of time, it looked as if both he and Clarissa

Glenn were going to be released on their own reconnaissance until Emma Clancy, with the weight of the Portland District Attorney's Office behind her, interceded, and their opportunity to flee proper justice was snatched from them. As soon as the package sent as a priority delivery from Tess arrived in her office, she got her best technical analysts on the case, and they circumvented the malware program installed by Si Turpin, and found the horrifying truth in the files. Tess used her telephone call to contact Emma and informed her that she, along with Po, Pinky and Stella Dewildt, had been arrested, and immediately Emma got the ball rolling with the local FBI office. Because the crimes perpetrated by Hayden James's team, under the direction of Holbrook and Glenn, had occurred across various state borders, the FBI took jurisdiction over the case, and those police officers beholden to Holbrook were ostracized from the proceedings, some of them pending further investigation, and it was then that the genuine victims of the case were shown leniency and a hefty amount of professional courtesy. Po, who'd previously been under armed guard in hospital while his injuries were tended to, walked free on bail, shackled now only by a cast on his broken arm.

Her husband, Paul, summoned to Boston in the aftermath of her rescue, collected Stella Dewildt. He was accompanied by a flock of journalists and TV cameras, and he strongly objected to the treatment his grieving wife had endured by unsympathetic law enforcement officers who'd taken the word of liars, blackmailers and would-be executioners over an innocent victim. Public opinion was initially divided over the rights and wrongs of the gunfight, because on balance a number of lawfully licensed close-protection operatives had died under the guns of people with obvious ties to the criminal underworld, whereas only Aaron Lacey had perished among the 'supposed' good guys. Briefly the identification of Pinky's allies had been a sticking point in the matter, and his reticence to say other than that they were 'anonymous but concerned members of the public' didn't help his case. However, when it came to light that he'd almost been murdered in defense of Stella Dewildt during her abduction from New York, not too many people objected to his subsequent actions in attempting to free her. He too was bailed pending further investigation, but Emma Clancy was confident that once the full details of the case were released he'd avoid prosecution, as would Tess, who'd shot and killed Hayden James, who was in the act of trying to kill her unarmed partner at the time.

The news of Jon Cutter's arrest for the murder of his sister Carly sent a seismic shockwave throughout the world, and it took most of the attention off Tess and her friends' shoulders, and they were given some space to grieve and to heal. With the shocking revelation that Hollywood's brightest star was in fact a murderous rapist, and that he'd been assisted in covering up his terrible crime by his security detail, the sudden shift in public opinion became a landslide of support for Stella Dewildt, who'd almost become his next proxy victim. Her deceased father's attempts at first blowing the lid off the cover up, and then giving his own life in defense of his child, became the stuff of heroism. Harris Collins and even Si Turpin – whose actions were somewhat questionable in reality – were subsequently lauded as supporting players in Lacey's heroic endeavours. So was – albeit posthumously – the retired Doctor Herbert Grover, who'd striven to keep Lacey healthy enough to continue his quest and who was brutally murdered by the psychotic Megan Stein, whose murderous nature had also initiated the gun battle at the construction site, leading to the deaths of all but one of her team. Vera Seung, sole survivor of the troubleshooters was in holding pending trial, and would go to prison for her part in the abduction of Stella Dewildt, but compared to her bosses, she'd probably get off lightly. Holbrook and Glenn were facing life imprisonment alongside Jon Cutter, whose shining star was totally eclipsed by the awful truth.

Barbara Grey attended Aaron Lacey's funeral alongside her daughter. It was a show of respect to an old family friend, and an attempt at sealing the widening rift in their mother–daughter relationship. Po originally offered to drive them, but Tess argued that he was in no fit shape for the more than six hundred and fifty miles round trip, and he'd acquiesced to her better sense, albeit because he wasn't too comfortable about taking the flights: he was as brave as a lion when it came to a fight, but suffered crippling nerves when flying. However, he tamped down the anxiety, and spent the flight seated next to Pinky, his mind kept off crashing and burning by his effervescent friend's good humor. It allowed Tess and her mother to sit together, and talk things over in private, and for Tess to make her humble apologies for ever doubting her mom's commitment to her dad after she explained how she knew the location of Aaron Lacey's second home.

'I told you once before that I disapproved of Aaron and Rachel's open marriage, but that didn't mean I held them in contempt. They were our friends, and if they were in trouble they turned to us. Sometimes you can get caught up in matters you'd prefer not to, but you get involved any way, right?'

'Definitely.' Tess nodded at the irony. 'It's the story of my life.'

'Well, the thing was,' Barbara went on, 'Rachel wasn't as open to the idea of extramarital sex as perhaps her husband was, and she was regularly tormented by jealousy. Her rules about their relationship included not knowing anything about his mistresses, and Aaron upheld his side of the bargain, but unfortunately Rachel couldn't stick to it. There were times when she would allow envy to get a hold of her, and she'd dwell on where Aaron was and whom he was with. Your father received a call from Aaron asking us to go and collect Rachel from his apartment in Hell's Kitchen after she turned up blind drunk and made a hell of a scene. She wasn't happy, no way, no how, and tried to break down his door when he refused to open it. Being NYPD the last he wanted was for a patrol to turn up, so he asked your dad to come and take her away before she embarrassed them both. We collected Rachel, and had a time of it trying to calm her down before she sobered up. It was a horrible, uncomfortable situation to get caught up in, but we couldn't refuse to help our mutual friends, could we?' Barbara turned and fixed her with an earnest stare. 'I swear to you, Teresa, that was the one and only time I ever visited Aaron's second home, and I had no wish to return. In fact, I'd forgotten about the incident until you mentioned where you were looking for him in Manhattan.'

Tess accepted her mom's word on the matter, whereas before she might still have questioned it as she'd already done some further sleuthing. After they were released from custody in Boston, and Po collected his abandoned Mustang from the burying ground on Hull Street, she'd discovered on the back seat her shirt used by Lacey to stem his blood, and she couldn't resist the urge to clear things up. Using her genealogical connections she'd sent the shirt, along with a sample of her own DNA to a lab for testing. Aaron Lacey's DNA had not been a paternal match. On reading the test results, she'd experienced a moment of disappointment, because Aaron Lacey hadn't proven to be the worst father ever when it came to his love of Stella. The sensation was fleeting, swiftly replaced by relief, then joy. She'd only shared the results with Po, the only person other than her mom who knew about her misgivings about her parentage. Typically Po, he'd merely shrugged and said, 'Told ya that you'd nothin' to worry about.'

But Tess didn't like loose ends.

There was still the matter of the photograph of Barbara and Tess that Lacey had kept on display in his motel room, but Tess hadn't broached it on the flight down: she could only assume that Lacey had been fond of her mom, though his feelings were never reciprocated, or perhaps he'd held on to the old photo as a reminder of Tess herself. She'd been the apple of her granddad's eye, and maybe Lacey had kept her image close, as a reminder of how he'd failed to save Mikey Grey's life when they'd walked in on the convenience store robbery. Whatever the meaning of the photo, it would have to remain a mystery, because when others scattered rose petals and consecrated dust on Aaron Lacey's coffin, she deposited the photograph in the grave, and never mentioned it again.

During the flight home to Portland, mother and daughter sat comfortably together, and it was some time until Barbara noticed the sparkling new band on Tess's third finger. To Tess's pleasant surprise, Barbara was overjoyed that, for once at least, Tess had done something her mom agreed with. They laughed, and then wept together with a sense of sad maudlin, at how proud her father, Michael, would have been to walk her down the aisle. Spotting their tears, Pinky lightened their mood by lamenting: 'You're marrying this brute! Is there no hope for me now, Pretty Tess?'

'There's always space for you in my affections, Pinky,' she assured him.

'And at my side, brother,' Po added. 'Oh, by the way, did I ask you to be my best man yet?'

Pinky shrieked in delight, and the other passengers on the airplane broke into impromptu cheers and a round of applause.

They waited until the visible bruising on Po's face subsided before making their engagement official – in truth allowing some respectful time to pass between Lacey's internment and their cause for celebration – at a gathering of close friends and family at Bar-Lesque, Po's retro bar-diner. Barbara attended. Pinky too. Stella and her husband, Paul, made the trip up, as did Po's sister Emilia, who'd come all the way from Louisiana for the festivities. Tess's brother Alex accompanied Emma Clancy, and her eldest brother, Michael Jnr, and his wife, Penny, had flown in from Ohio, to complete the family reunion. Charley, the head mechanic from Po's auto shop was there. Jasmine Reed and Chris Mitchell, Bar-Lesque's management team, had been given the night off, as they were more than employees to Po and Tess, both of them now their firm friends. Before joining the guest list they'd gotten the place ready for the private party, except for one item on the agenda: Po had personally organized the live entertainment, and it was to Tess's satisfaction. Neither of them had felt good about their last skip-tracing job, so Po made reparation for their lost gig by hiring the Moondog Trio to liven the party.

'Can I have this dance?' Po asked her.

'Can you manage with a broken arm?'

'I've still got two good feet for jiving, and the stamina of a guy half my age, Tess.' With a wink at their private joke, Po pulled her on to the dance floor, just as Thomas Becker launched into the song Po had requested to open the show, a raucous version of the classic road trip song 'Route 66'.

THANKS

Writing can be a lonely business, but the end result is never the product of a single person. There are others who help me along the way, and without their invaluable support and guidance this book wouldn't now be in your hands. I'd like to extend my gratitude and thanks to my agent Luigi Bonomi and the team at LBA; to all the team at Severn House Publishers; to my wife Denise; to my family, friends and peers; to the booksellers, librarians, bloggers and reviewers; and lastly, but most importantly, to you, the reader. I write the words, but it is all of you that make this a book.

Lightning Source UK Ltd.
Milton Keynes UK
UKHW011951171019
351785UK00003B/65/P

9 781847 519887